P9-DFZ-185

"Snappy dialogue, well-developed characters, and the details of the three women's hard work to build their ...sion between Paige

S.S.F. PUBLIC LIBRARY
West Orange
840 West Orange Avenue
South San Francisco, CA 94080

DEC 1 6

...eepless in Manhattan

...-lit romance—
...y with a tech flair."
—*RT Book Reviews* on *Sleepless in Manhattan*, Top Pick!

"Morgan's breezy dialogue will keep readers turning the red-hot pages and wishing they could sit down with this trio of women and the men who capture their hearts."
—*Booklist* on *Sleepless in Manhattan*

"Uplifting, sexy and warm, Sarah Morgan's O'Neil Brothers series is perfection."
—Jill Shalvis, *New York Times* bestselling author

"Morgan's romantic page-turner will thrill readers. The well-paced narrative is humorous [and] poignant... the chemistry between the misunderstood hero and the victimized heroine is combustible [and] her storytelling rocks. Brava!"
—*RT Book Reviews* on *Suddenly Last Summer*, Top Pick!

"*Sleigh Bells in the Snow* [is] a great wintery romance with plenty of chemistry and heart... You will be swept away by the winter wonderland and steamy romance... Morgan has really shown her talent and infused so much love, both romantic and familial, into her characters that I am anxiously looking forward to what she writes in the future."
—*All About Romance*

"This touching Christmas tale will draw tears of sorrow and joy, remaining a reader favorite for years to come."
—*Publishers Weekly*, starred review, on *Sleigh Bells in the Snow*

"Morgan's brilliant talent never ceases to amaze."
—*RT Book Reviews*

**Also available from
Sarah Morgan
and HQN Books**

The O'Neil Brothers

Maybe This Christmas
Suddenly Last Summer
Sleigh Bells in the Snow

Puffin Island

First Time in Forever
Some Kind of Wonderful
One Enchanted Moment

From Manhattan With Love

Midnight at Tiffany's (ebook novella)
Sleepless in Manhattan
Sunset in Central Park

SARAH MORGAN

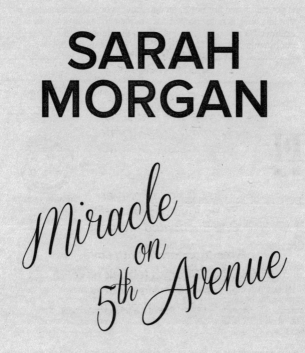

Miracle on 5th Avenue

HQN™

If you purchased this book without a cover you should be aware that this book is stolen property. It was reported as "unsold and destroyed" to the publisher, and neither the author nor the publisher has received any payment for this "stripped book."

HQN™

ISBN-13: 978-0-373-78934-4

Recycling programs for this product may not exist in your area.

Miracle on 5th Avenue

Copyright © 2016 by Sarah Morgan

All rights reserved. Except for use in any review, the reproduction or utilization of this work in whole or in part in any form by any electronic, mechanical or other means, now known or hereinafter invented, including xerography, photocopying and recording, or in any information storage or retrieval system, is forbidden without the written permission of the publisher, HQN Books, 225 Duncan Mill Road, Don Mills, Ontario M3B 3K9, Canada.

This is a work of fiction. Names, characters, places and incidents are either the product of the author's imagination or are used fictitiously, and any resemblance to actual persons, living or dead, business establishments, events or locales is entirely coincidental.

This edition published by arrangement with Harlequin Books S.A.

For questions and comments about the quality of this book, please contact us at CustomerService@Harlequin.com.

® and TM are trademarks of Harlequin Enterprises Limited or its corporate affiliates. Trademarks indicated with ® are registered in the United States Patent and Trademark Office, the Canadian Intellectual Property Office and in other countries.

www.HQNBooks.com

Printed in U.S.A.

Dear Reader,

If you've picked up one of my books before, it will come as no surprise to you to learn that I love happy endings. I'm a pretty optimistic person and generally like my cup to be half-full (preferably with strong coffee). I read widely, but rarely what might be classed as "horror" fiction. I'm not good with scary suspense, serial killers or things that go bump in the night, which makes me similar in some ways to the heroine of this book.

Eva is a romantic who always looks on the bright side, so when a work assignment requires her to spend some time with Lucas, a crime writer who explores the darkest side of human nature, she is going to do her best to make it work, even though it's clear to her right away that they are opposites. She might be looking for romance, but Lucas is definitely not her type. Or is he?

Lucas doesn't just write about other people's demons, he has a few of his own, but kindhearted Eva is determined to shine a light into the dark corners of his life.

This is a book about second chances, but it's also about hope and the power of love. I hope you enjoy *Miracle on 5th Avenue*! If you haven't already, don't forget to look out for Paige's and Frankie's stories, *Sleepless in Manhattan* and *Sunset in Central Park*, and I hope you'll join me on Facebook to chat at Facebook.com/authorsarahmorgan.

Love,

Sarah

Xx

www.sarahmorgan.com

For Sue. I write about fictional friendships, but ours is the real thing. Lucky me.

Give a girl the right shoes and she can conquer the world.

—Marilyn Monroe

CHAPTER ONE

There are plenty of fish in the sea, but that's no use if you live in New York City.

—Eva

"WE CANNOT SEND two turtledoves! I know he's proposing at Christmas and he thinks it's romantic, but it won't be romantic when the room is covered in bird droppings. The venue will blacklist us and the love of his life will say no to his question, which will not give us the happy-ever-after we're all hoping for." Moving her phone to a more comfortable position against her ear, Eva Jordan snuggled deeper into her coat. Beyond the windows of the cab the snow was still falling steadily, defying attempts of those who tried to clear it. The more they shoveled the more fell, or so it seemed. In a contest between man and the elements, man was most definitely losing. The snowstorm almost obliterated her view of Fifth Avenue, the glittering shop windows muted and veiled by the falling flakes. "I'll help him reframe his idea of 'romantic,' and it won't include calling birds, hens of any nationality, nor geese, laying or otherwise. And while we're on the subject, one gold ring is more than enough. Who needs five? He wants exceptional, not excessive, and the two are not the same."

As always, Paige was practical. "Laura has been dreaming about this moment since she was a little girl. He's under pressure to make this perfect."

"I'm pretty sure her dream didn't include a menagerie of wildlife. I'll come up with a plan, and it will be spectacular. No one does romance better than I do."

"Except when it's for yourself."

"Thanks for reminding me my love life is extinct."

"You're welcome. And having agreed on the facts, perhaps you'd like to tell me what you intend to do about it."

"Nothing at all. And we are not having this conversation again." Eva delved into her bag and pulled out her notebook. "Can we get back to business? We have a month until Christmas."

"We don't have enough time to create anything elaborate."

"It doesn't need to be elaborate. It needs to be emotional. She needs to be overwhelmed by his words and the meaning behind them. Wait—" Eva tapped her pen on the page. "They met in Central Park, didn't they? Dog-walking?"

"Yes but, Ev, the park is buried under two feet of snow and it's still falling. A proposal there could end in a trip to the emergency room. That could be memorable for all the wrong reasons."

"Leave it with me. I'll have plenty of time to think

about it over the next two days because I'll be on my own in this guy's apartment decorating and filling his freezer ready for his return from the wilds." She made a note to herself and then slid the notebook back into her bag.

"You're working too hard, Ev."

"I cannot believe I'm hearing that from you."

"Even I take time off to chill occasionally."

"I must have missed that. And in case you hadn't noticed, our business is growing fast."

"You taking an evening off to go on a hot date isn't going to stop it growing."

"Thank you, but there is one teeny tiny drawback to your plan. I don't have a hot date. I don't even have a lukewarm date."

"Do you think you should try online dating again?"

"I hate online dating. I prefer meeting people in other ways."

"But you're not meeting people at all! You work. You go to bed with your teddy bear."

"It's a stuffed kangaroo. Grams gave it to me when I was four."

"That explains why it looks exhausted. It's time you replaced it with a flesh-and-blood man, Eva."

"I love that kangaroo. He never lets me down."

"Honey, you need to get out. How about that banker guy? You liked him."

"He never called when he said he was going to call. Life is stressful enough without waiting around wondering if a guy you're not even sure you like is going to call you and invite you on a date you're not even sure you want to go on."

"You could have called him."

"I did. He screened my calls." Eva stared out of the window. "I don't mind chasing after a dream when it's about building our business and our future, but I'm not chasing after a man. And anyway, everyone knows you never find love when you go looking for it. You have to wait for it to find you."

"What if it can't find you because you never leave your apartment?"

"I've left my apartment! I'm here, on Fifth Avenue."

"Alone. To stay in another apartment. Alone. Think of all the great sex you're missing. At this rate you'll meet Mr. Right when you're eighty and have no teeth and dodgy hips."

"Plenty of people have good sex when they're eighty. You just have to be creative." Ignoring the hollow feeling in the pit of her stomach, Eva leaned forward to talk to the cabdriver. "Can you make a stop at Dean & DeLuca? If this storm is as bad as they're predicting, I need to pick up a few extra things."

Paige was still talking. "I've barely seen you over the past two weeks. It's been crazy busy. I know this is a tough time of year for you. I know you miss your grandmother." Her voice softened. "Do you want me to come by after work and keep you company?"

She was so tempted to say yes.

They'd open a bottle of wine, curl up in their pajamas and talk. She'd confess how bad she felt a lot of the time, and then—

And then what?

Eva looked down at her lap. She didn't want to be that friend. The one who constantly whined and moaned. The burden. And anyway, telling her friends how bad she felt wasn't going to change anything, was it?

Her grandmother would be ashamed.

"You have meetings downtown and then that dinner thing with Jake."

"I know, but I could easily—"

"You're not canceling." She said it quickly, before she could be tempted to change her mind. "I'll be fine."

"If the weather wasn't so bad you could come home and stay here tonight and then go back tomorrow, but they're saying the storm is going to be a big one. Much as I hate to think of you all alone there, I think it's better that you don't travel."

Eva chewed her lip. It didn't matter where she was, her feelings stayed the same. She had no idea if it was normal to feel this way. She'd never lost anyone close to her before, and she and her grandmother had been more than close. She'd been gone a little over a year and the wound was as fresh and painful as if the loss had happened only the day before.

It was because of her that Eva had grown up feeling safe and secure. She owed her grandmother everything, although she knew that there was no way of attaching a value to something so priceless. Her payment, although she knew none had ever been asked for, wanted or expected, was to get out of bed every day and live the life her grandmother had wanted her to live. Make her proud.

If she was here right now, her grandmother wouldn't be proud.

She'd tell her that she was spending far too many nights alone in her apartment with only Netflix and hot chocolate for company.

Her grandmother had loved hearing about Eva's romantic adventures. She would have wanted her to go out and meet people even if she felt sad. To begin with she'd tried to do just that, but lately her social life revolved round her friends and business partners, Paige and Frankie. It was easy and comfortable, even though both of them were now crazily in love.

It was ironic that she, the romantic one, led the least romantic life.

She stared out of the window through the white swirl of flakes to the darkening sky. She felt disconnected. Lost. She wished she didn't feel everything so deeply.

Still, at least she was busy. This was their first holiday season since the three of them had set up Urban Genie, their event and concierge business, and they were busy.

Her grandmother would have been proud of what she'd achieved in her work.

Celebrate every small thing, Eva, and live in the moment.

Eva blinked to clear her misted vision.

She hadn't been doing that, had she? She lived her life looking forward, planning, juggling. She rarely paused for breath or to appreciate the moment. She'd been running for a year, through a freezing winter, a balmy spring, a sweltering summer and, here now, full circle, to another winter. She'd muscled through, pushing the seasons behind her, moving forward step by step. She hadn't lived in the moment because she hadn't liked the moment she was living in.

She'd done her best to be strong and keep smiling, but it had been the toughest year of her life.

Grief, she thought, was a horrible companion.

"Ev?" Paige's voice echoed down the phone. "Are you still there? I'm worried about you."

Eva closed her eyes and pulled herself together. She didn't want her friends to worry about her. What had her grandmother taught her?

Be the sunshine, Eva, not the rain.

She never, ever, wanted to be the black cloud in anyone's day.

Opening her eyes, she smiled. "Why are you worried about me? It's snowing. If this blizzard eases I'll go across to the park and build a snowman. If I can't find a guy in real life, at least I can build a decent one out of snow."

"You are going to build yourself a sexy guy?"

"I am. With broad shoulders and great abs."

"And no doubt you won't be using the carrot for his nose."

Eva grinned. "I was thinking maybe a cucumber for that part of his anatomy."

Paige was laughing, too. "You're so demanding it's no wonder you're single. And, by the way, you have the sense of humor of a five-year-old."

"It's the reason we've been friends forever."

"It's good to hear you laugh. Christmas used to be your favorite time of year."

It was true. She'd always loved it. Every smiling Santa, every happy note of music that played in the stores and every sparkly snowflake. She especially loved the snowflakes. They made her think of sleigh rides and snowmen.

To Eva, snow had always seemed magical.

Enough, she thought. *Enough.*

"It still is my favorite time of year." She didn't need to wait until New Year's Eve to make a resolution.

She was going to get out there and live every day the way her grandmother would have wanted her to live it. Starting right now.

CHRISTMAS.

He hated it. Every smiling Santa, every discordant note of music that blared in the stores and every freezing snowflake. He especially hated the snowflakes. They swirled with deceptive innocence, coating trees and cars and landing on the palms of enchanted children who saw falling snow and thought of sleigh rides and snowmen.

Lucas thought of something different.

He sat in darkness in his Fifth Avenue apartment, staring out across the wintry expanse of Central Park.

It had been snowing steadily for days, and more was on the way. It was predicted to be the worst blizzard in New York's recent history. As a result, the streets far below him were unusually empty. Everyone who wasn't already home was hurrying there as fast as possible, taking advantage of public transportation while it was still running. No one looked up. No one knew he was there. Not even his well-meaning but interfering family, who thought he was on a writing retreat in Vermont.

If they'd known he was home they would have been fussing over him, checking on him, forcing him to participate in plans for Christmas celebrations.

It was time, they said. *It had been long enough.*

How long was long enough? The answer to that eluded him. All he knew was that he hadn't reached that point.

He had no intention of celebrating the festive season. The best he could hope for was to get through it, as he did every year, and he saw no point in inflicting his misery on others. He hurt. Outside and inside, he hurt. He'd been crushed and mangled in the wreckage of his loss, and crawled away with his life but very little else.

He could have traveled to Vermont, buried himself in a cabin in a snowy forest like he'd told his family, or he could have gone somewhere hot, somewhere untouched by a single flake of snow, but he knew there was no point because he would still be hurting. It didn't matter what he did, the pain traveled with him. It infected him like a virus that nothing could cure.

And so he stayed home while the temperature swooped low and the world around him turned white, transforming his building into a frozen fortress.

It suited him perfectly.

The only sound that intruded was his phone. It had rung fourteen times in the past few days and he'd ignored each and every one of the calls. Some of those calls had been his grandmother, some had been his brother, most his agent.

Reflecting on what his life would look like if he didn't have his career, Lucas reached for the phone and finally returned the call to his agent.

"Lucas!" Jason's voice came down the phone, jovial and energetic. There were sounds of revelry in the background, laughter and Christmas music. "I was starting to think you were buried under a snowdrift. How are the snowy wastelands of Vermont?"

Lucas stared out across the Manhattan skyline, the sharp edges of the city muted by falling snow. "Vermont is beautiful."

It was the truth. Assuming it hadn't altered since his last visit, which had been a year ago.

"*TIME* magazine has just named you the most exciting crime writer of the decade. Did you see the piece?"

Lucas glanced at the towering pile of unopened mail. "Haven't gotten around to reading it yet."

"That's why you're at the top of your game. No distractions. With you, it's all about the book. Your fans are excited about this one, Lucas."

The book.

Dread stirred inside him. Dark thoughts were eclipsed by sweaty panic. He hadn't written a word. His mind was empty, but that was something he hadn't confessed to his agent or his publisher. He was still hoping for a miracle, some spark of inspiration that would allow him to wriggle free from the poisonous tentacles of Christmas and lose himself in a fictional world. It was ironic that the twisted, sick minds of his complex characters provided a preferable alternative to the dark reality of his own.

He eyed the knife that lay on the table close by. The blade glinted, taunting him.

He'd been staring at it for the best part of a week, even though he knew it wasn't the answer. He was better than that.

"That's why you've been calling? To ask about the book?"

"I know you hate to be disturbed when you're writing, but production is hounding me. Sales of your last book exceeded even our expectations," Jason said gleefully. "Your publisher is tripling the print run for the next. Are you going to give me any clues about the story?"

"I can't." If he knew what the book was about, he'd be writing it.

Instead, his mind was terrifyingly blank.

He didn't have a crime. Worse, he didn't have a murderer.

For him, every book started with the character. He was known for his unpredictable twists, for being able to deliver a shock that even the most perceptive reader failed to anticipate.

Right now the shock would be the blank page.

It was worse this year than it had been the year before. Then, the process had been long and painful, but he'd managed to somehow drag each word from inside him by November, before memories had paralyzed him. It was like trying to get to the top of Everest before the winds hit. Timing was everything. This year he hadn't managed it and he was beginning to think he'd left it too late. He was going to need an extension on his deadline, something he'd never had to ask for before. That was bad enough, but worse were the questions that would follow. The sympathetic looks and the nods of understanding.

"I'd love to see a few pages. First chapter?"

"I'll let you know," Lucas said, before proffering the season's greetings that were expected of him and ending the call.

Lucas rubbed his hand over the back of his neck. He didn't have a first chapter. He didn't have a first line. So far the only thing that had been murdered was his inspiration. It was lying inert, the life squeezed out of it. Could it be resurrected? He wasn't sure.

He'd sat at his open laptop hour after hour and not a single word had emerged. The only thing in his head was Sallyanne. She filled his head, his thoughts and his heart. *His bruised, damaged heart.*

It was on this day, three years ago, that he'd had the phone call that had derailed his seemingly charmed life. It had been like a scene from one of his books, except this time it had been fact not fiction. He'd been the one identifying the body in the morgue, not one of his characters. He no longer had to put himself in their shoes and imagine what they were feeling because he was feeling it himself.

Since then he'd struggled through every day, dragging himself from minute to minute, while outwardly doing what was needed to make people believe that he was doing fine. He'd learned early on that people needed to see that. They didn't want to witness his grief. They wanted to believe he'd handled it and "moved on." Mostly, he managed to meet their expectations, except for this time of year, when the anniversary of her death came around.

Eventually he was going to have to confess to his agent and his publisher that he hadn't written a single word of the book his fans so eagerly awaited.

This book wasn't going to make his publisher a fortune. It didn't exist.

He had no idea how to conjure the magic that had sent him soaring to the top of the bestseller charts in more than fifty countries.

All he could do was carry on doing what he'd been doing for the past month. He'd sit in front of the blank screen and hope that somewhere in the depths of his tortured brain an idea might emerge.

He kept hoping for a miracle.

It was the season for it, wasn't it?

"This is it?" Eva peered out of the window of the cab. "It's incredible. He has a view of Central Park. What I wouldn't give to live this close to Tiffany's."

The cabdriver glanced in his mirror. "Do you need help with all those bags?"

"I'll manage, thanks," Eva said as she handed over her fare.

It was bitterly cold and the snow was falling heavily, thick swirling flakes that reduced visibility and settled on her coat. A few flakes found the small, unprotected section of her neck and slid like icy fingers under her coat. Within moments the bags were covered and so was she. Worse was the sidewalk. Her feet slithered on the deep carpet of ice and snow, and finally lost traction.

"Agh—" Her arms windmilled and the doorman stepped forward and caught her before she hit the ground.

"Steady. It's lethal underfoot."

"You're not kidding." She clutched his arm, waiting for her heart rate to slow. "Thank you. I wouldn't have wanted to spend Christmas in the hospital. I hear the food is terrible."

"We'll help you with those bags." He lifted a hand and two uniformed guys appeared and loaded her bags and boxes onto a luggage cart.

"Thank you. I'm taking it all to the top floor. The penthouse. You should be expecting me. I'm staying a few days to decorate an apartment for a client who is out of town. Lucas Blade."

He was a crime writer with a dozen global bestsellers to his name.

Eva had never read a single one of them.

She hated crime, both real and fictional. She preferred to focus on the positive side of people and life. And she preferred to sleep at night.

The warmth of the apartment building wrapped itself around her as she stepped inside, comforting after the chill of the blizzard swirling on Fifth Avenue. Her cheeks stung and despite wearing gloves her fingertips were numb with cold. Even the wool hat she'd pulled over her ears had done nothing to keep out the savage bite of a New York winter.

"I'm going to need to see ID." The doorman was brisk and businesslike. "We've had a spate of break-ins in this area. What's the company name?"

"Urban Genie." It was still new enough that saying it brought a rush of pride. It was *her* company. She'd set it up with her friends. She handed over her ID. "We've not been around long, but we're taking New York by storm." She shook snow off her gloves and smiled. "Well, it's maybe more of a light wind than a storm, given what's happening outside the window, but we're hopeful for the future. I have Mr. Blade's key." She waved it as evidence and his gaze warmed as he looked first at it and then at the ID she'd handed him.

"You're on my list. All I need is for you to sign in."

"Could you do me a favor?" Eva signed with a flourish. "When Lucas Blade shows up, don't tell him I was here. It's supposed to be a surprise. He's going to open his front door and find his apartment all ready for the holidays. It'll be like walking in on a surprise birthday party."

It occurred to her that not everyone liked surprise

birthday parties, but who was she to argue with his family? His grandmother, who had been one of their first clients and was now a good friend, had given her a clear brief. Prepare the apartment and make it ready for Christmas. Apparently Lucas Blade was in Vermont, deep in a book and on a deadline; the world around him had ceased to exist. As well as decorating, her job was to cook and fill his freezer and she had the whole weekend to do it because he wasn't due home until the following week.

"Sure, we can do that for you." The doorman smiled.

"Thank you." She peered at his name badge, and continued, "Albert. You saved my life. In some cultures that would mean you now own me. Fortunately for you, we're in New York City. You'll never know what a lucky escape you had."

He laughed. "Mr. Blade's grandmother called earlier and said she was sending over his Christmas present. I wasn't expecting a woman."

"I'm not the gift. Just my skills. Saying I'm his Christmas present makes it sound as if I should be standing here wrapped in silver paper and a big red bow."

"So you're going to be staying in the apartment for a couple of nights? Alone?"

"That's right." And there was nothing new in that. Apart from the occasional night Paige slept over in her apartment, she spent every night alone. She couldn't remember the last time she'd been horizontal with a man, but she was determined that was going to change. Changing it was right at the top of her Christmas wish list. "Lucas isn't back until next week, and with the weather this bad there's no sense in traveling backward and forward." She glanced at the snow falling thickly beyond the tinted glass. "I'm guessing no one is going to be traveling anywhere far tonight."

"It's a bad one. They're saying snow accumulation could hit eighteen inches, with winds gusting fifty miles an hour. Time to stock up on food, check the batteries in the flashlight and get out those snow shovels." Albert glanced at her bags, brimming with Christmas decorations. "Looks like you're not going to be too worried about the weather. Plenty of Christmas cheer right there. I'm guessing you're one of those people who loves the holidays."

"I am." Or she used to be. And she was determined to be that person again. Reminding herself of that, she tried to ignore the hollow ache in her chest. "How about you, Albert?"

"I'll be working. Lost my wife of forty years two summers ago. Never had kids, so Christmas was always the two of us. And now it's just me. Working here will be better for me than eating a frozen dinner for one on my own in my apartment. I like being around people."

Eva felt a rush of empathy. She understood needing to be around people. She was the same. It wasn't that she couldn't be on her own. She could. But given the choice she would always rather be with other people.

On impulse, she dug her hand into her pocket and gave him a card. "Take this—"

"Romano's Sicilian Restaurant, Brooklyn?"

"Best pizza anywhere in New York City. It's owned by my friend's mother and on Christmas Day Maria cooks for everyone who shows up. I help her in the kitchen. I'm a cook, although most of the time now we're running big events and I'm outsourcing to external companies and vendors." *Too much information*, she thought, and gestured toward the card. "If you're free on Christmas Day, you should join us, Albert."

He stared at the card in his hand. "You just met me five minutes ago. Why would you invite me?"

"Because you saved me from landing on my butt, and because it's Christmas. No one should be alone at Christmas." Alone. There it was again. That word. It seemed to creep in everywhere. "I'm not going to hole myself away totally either. As soon as the snow eases enough for me to see my hand in front of my face, I'm going to pop across to Central Park and build a snowman the size of the Empire State Building. The Empire State Snowman. And speaking of giant structures, I have a tree being delivered later. Hopefully it will arrive before the blizzard stops everything. You're going to think I stole the one from outside Rockefeller Center, but I assure you I didn't."

"It's big?"

"The guy lives in the penthouse. The penthouse needs a big tree. I just hope we'll be able to get it up there."

"Leave it to me." He frowned. "You're sure you

shouldn't be getting home to your family while you can?"

His words poked at the bruise she'd been trying to ignore.

"I'll be fine right here, safe and warm. Thanks, Albert. You're my hero."

She walked toward the elevator, trying not to think about everyone in New York going home to their families. Home to warmth, laughter, conversation, *hugs*…

Everyone except her.

She had no one.

Not a single living relative. She had friends, of course, great friends, but for some reason that didn't ease the ache.

Alone.

Why was the feeling always magnified at Christmas?

The elevator rose through the building in smooth silence and the doors slid open.

Lucas Blade's apartment was straight ahead and she let herself in, thanked the two men who'd delivered all her bags and packages and carefully locked the door behind her.

She turned, and was instantly mesmerized by the spectacular view visible through the floor-to-ceiling glass that made up one entire wall of the apartment.

She didn't bother putting on lights. Instead, she toed off her boots to avoid trailing snow through the apartment and walked in her socks to the window.

Whatever else he had, Lucas Blade had taste and style.

He also had underfloor heating, and she felt the luxurious warmth steal through the thick wool of her socks and slowly thaw her numbed feet.

She stared at the soaring skyline, letting the cold and the last of the snowflakes melt away.

Far beneath her she could see the trail of lights on Fifth Avenue as a few bold cabs made what was probably their final journey through Manhattan. Soon the roads would be closed. Travel would be impossible, or at least unwise. New York, the city that never slept, would finally be forced to take a rest.

The snow fell past the window, big fat flakes that drifted and swirled, before settling lazily on the already deep layer that blanketed the city.

Eva hugged herself, staring out across the silvery-white expanse of Central Park.

It was New York at its dreamy, wintry best. Why Lucas Blade felt the need to go on retreat to write, she had no idea. If she owned this place she'd never leave it.

But maybe he needed to leave it.

He was grieving, wasn't he? He'd lost his beloved wife three years ago at Christmas. His grandmother had told her how much it had changed him. And why wouldn't it? He'd lost the love of his life. His soul mate.

Eva leaned her head against the glass. Her chest ached for him.

Her friends told her she was too sensitive, but she'd come to accept that it was just the way she was. Other people watched the news and managed to stay detached. Eva felt everything deeply, and she felt Lucas's pain even though she'd never even met him.

How cruel was it to meet the love of your life and then lose her?

How did you pick up the pieces and move on?

She had no idea how long she stood there or when, exactly, she sensed she wasn't alone. It started with a faint warning prickle at the back of her neck, which rapidly turned to the cold chill of fear when she heard a nearby clunk.

She was imagining things, surely? Of *course* she was alone. This apartment block had some of the best security in the city and she'd been careful to lock the door behind her.

No one could have followed her in so there couldn't be anyone else in there, unless—

She swallowed as a different explanation occurred to her.

—*unless someone had already been in the apartment.*

She turned her head slowly, wishing now that she'd taken the time to find the lights and switch them on. The storm had darkened the sky and the apartment was full of cavernous shadows and mysterious corners. Her imagination burst to life and she tried to reason with herself. The sound could have been anything. Maybe it had come from outside the building.

She held her breath, and then heard another noise, this one definitely inside the apartment. It sounded like a footstep. A stealthy footstep, as if the owner didn't want to reveal himself.

She glanced up and saw something move in the shadows up above her.

Fear was sharp and paralyzing.

She'd interrupted a break-in. The hows and whys didn't matter. All that mattered was getting out of here.

The door seemed a long way in the distance.

Could she make it?

Her heart was racing and her palms turned sweaty.

She wished now that she hadn't removed her shoes.

She made for the door and at the same time grabbed her phone from her pocket. Her hand was shaking so much she almost dropped it.

She hit the emergency button, heard a woman say "911 Emergency—" and tried to whisper into the phone.

"Help. There's someone in the apartment."

"You'll have to speak up, ma'am."

The door was there. Right there.

"There's someone in the apartment." She needed to get downstairs to Albert. He'd—

A hand clamped over her mouth and before Eva could utter a squeak she'd landed on her back on the floor, crushed by the hard weight of a powerful male body.

The man pinned her. One of his hands was across her mouth and the other gripped her wrists with brutal strength.

Holy crap.

If she could have screamed, she would have, but she couldn't open her mouth.

She couldn't move. She couldn't breathe, although bizarrely her senses were still sufficiently alert for her to realize her attacker smelled *really* good.

It was an irony that finally, after almost two years of dreaming and hoping, she was finally horizontal with a man. It was a shame he was trying to kill her.

A shame and a tragic waste.

Here lies Eva, whose Christmas wish was to find herself up close and personal with a man, but didn't specify the circumstances.

Was that really going to be her last thought? Clearly the mind was capable of strange thoughts in the last moment before it was robbed of oxygen. And having written her eulogy, she was going to die, right here in the dark in this empty apartment mere weeks before Christmas, flattened by this gloriously smelling hunk of solid muscle. If Lucas Blade decided to postpone his return, her body might not be found for weeks. They were in the middle of a snowstorm, or a "winter weather emergency" as it was officially called.

The thought rallied her.

No! She didn't want to die without saying goodbye to her friends. She'd found Paige and Frankie perfect Christmas gifts and she hadn't told anyone where they were hidden. And her apartment was a total mess. She'd been meaning to tidy up for ages, but hadn't quite found the time. What if the police wanted to look through her things for clues? Most of her possessions were strewed across the floor. It would be horribly embarrassing. But most of all she didn't want to miss enjoying New York City at Christmas, and she didn't want to die without having amazing, mind-blowing sex at least once in her life.

She didn't want this to be her last experience of having a man on top of her.

She wanted to *live*.

With a huge effort she tried to head-butt him, but he took evasive action. She heard the rasp of his breath, caught a glimpse of jet-black hair and fierce, smoldering eyes, and then there was a hammering on the door, and shouts from the police.

Relief weakened her limbs.

They must have traced the call.

She sent silent thanks and heard her attacker curse softly moments before the police burst into the apartment, followed by Albert.

There were no words for how much Eva loved Albert at that moment.

"NYPD, freeze!"

The apartment was flooded with lights and the man crushing her finally relieved her of his weight.

Sucking air into her starving lungs, Eva screwed up her eyes against the lights and felt the man wrench the hat off her head. Her hair, released from the confines of wool and warmth, unraveled itself and tumbled over her shoulders.

For a brief moment her gaze collided with his and she saw shock and disbelief.

"You're a woman."

He had a deep, sexy voice. Sexy voice, sexy body—shame about his criminal lifestyle.

"I am. Or at least, I was. Right now I'm not sure I'm alive." Eva lay there, stunned, gingerly testing the various parts of her body to check they were still attached. The man sprang to his feet in a lithe, fluid movement and she saw the expression on the police officer's face change.

"Lucas?" There was shock on his face. "We had no idea you were here. We had a call from an unknown female, reporting an intruder."

Lucas? Her attacker was Lucas Blade? He wasn't a criminal, he was the owner of the apartment!

She took her first good look at him and realized that he did look familiar. She'd seen his face on book covers. And it was a memorable face. She studied the slash of his cheekbones and the bold sweep of his nose. His hair and his eyes were dark. He looked as good as he smelled, and as for his body—she didn't need to study the width of his shoulders or the power of those muscles to know how strong he was. She'd been pinned to the ground under the solid weight of him, so she already knew all there was to know about *that*. Remembering triggered a fluttery feeling in her tummy.

What was *wrong* with her?

This man had half killed her and she was having sexy thoughts.

Which was yet more evidence that she'd gone far too long without sex. She was *definitely* going to fix that this Christmas.

In the meantime, she dragged her gaze away from the magnetic pull of his and tried to be practical.

What was he doing in the apartment? He wasn't supposed to be home.

"*She's* the intruder." Lucas's expression was grim and Eva realized that everyone was glaring at her. Everyone except Albert, who looked as confused as she felt.

"I'm not an intruder. I was told the apartment was empty." The injustice of it stung. "You're not supposed to be here."

"And how would you know that? You research which apartments are empty at Christmas?" He might be sexy, but he didn't give away smiles lightly.

Eva wondered how she'd suddenly turned into the bad guy. "Of course not. I was asked to do this."

"You had an accomplice?"

"If I was an intruder, would I have dialed 911?"

"Why not? Once you realized there was someone home, it would have been the perfect way of appearing innocent."

"I *am* innocent." Eva looked at him in disbelief. "Your mind is a strange, twisted thing." She glanced at the police officer for support, but found none.

"On your feet." The officer's tone was cold and brusque and Eva eased her bruised, crushed body into a sitting position.

"That's easier said than done. I have at least four hundred broken bones."

Lucas reached down and hauled her upright. "The human body does not have four hundred bones."

"It does when most of them have snapped in half." His strength shouldn't have surprised her given that he'd already crushed her to the ground under his body. "Why is everyone glaring at *me*? Instead of interrogating me about breaking and entering, they should be arresting you for assault. What are you doing here, anyway? You're supposed to be in Vermont, not skulking here."

"I own the apartment. A person can't 'skulk' in their own apartment." His brows came together in a fierce frown. "How did you know I was supposed to be in Vermont?"

"Your grandmother told me." Eva tested her ankle gingerly. "And you were definitely skulking. Creeping around in the dark."

"You were the one creeping around in the dark."

"I was admiring the snow. I'm a romantic. As far as I know, that isn't a crime."

"We'll be the judge of that." The officer stepped forward. "We'll take her down to the precinct, Lucas."

"Wait—" Lucas barely moved his hand but it was enough to stop the man in his tracks. "Did you say my *grandmother* told you I was in Vermont?"

"That's right, Mr. Blade," Albert intervened. "This is Eva, and she's here at the request of your grandmother. I verified it myself. None of us knew you were in residence." There was a faint hint of reproach in his voice. Lucas ignored it.

"You know my grandmother?" he asked Eva.

"I do. She employed me."

"To do what, exactly?" His eyes darkened. It was like looking at a threatening sky before a very, very bad storm.

His grandmother had told her many things about her grandson Lucas. She'd mentioned that he was an expert skier, that he had once spent a year living in a cabin in the Arctic, that he was fluent in French, Italian and Russian, was skilled in at least four different forms of martial arts and that he never showed anyone his books until they were finished.

She'd failed to mention that he could be intimidating.

"She employed me to prepare your apartment for Christmas."

"And?"

"And what? That's it. What other reason could there have been?" She saw the sardonic gleam in his eyes. "Are you suggesting I broke in here so that I could meet you?"

"It wouldn't be the first time."

"Women do that?" Outrage mingled with fascination. Even she couldn't imagine ever going to those lengths to find a man. "How exactly does that work? Once they get inside they leap on you and pin you down?"

"You tell me." He folded his arms and looked at her expectantly. "What plan did you cook up with my grandmother?"

She laughed and then realized he wasn't joking.

"I'm good in the kitchen, but even I've never managed to 'cook up' a romance. I wonder what the recipe would be? One cup of hope mixed with a pinch of delusion?" She tilted her head to one side. "Not that I'm not one of those women who thinks a guy has to make the first move or anything, but I've never gone as far as breaking into a man's apartment to get their attention. Do I look desperate, Mr. Blade?" In fact she *was* pretty desperate, but he had no way of knowing that unless he searched her purse and found her single lonely condom. She had hoped to give it a spectacular end to its so far uneventful life, but that was looking increasingly unlikely.

"Desperate wears many faces."

"If I *were* to break into a man's apartment with the intention of seducing him, do you really think I'd do it while wearing snow boots and a chunky sweater? I'm starting to understand why you need such a large apartment even though there's only one of you. Your ego must take up a lot of space *and* need its own bathroom, but I forgive you for your arrogance because you're rich and good-looking so you're probably telling the truth about your past experience. However, the flaw in your reasoning is that you were supposed to be in Vermont."

His gaze held hers. "I'm not in Vermont."

"I know that *now*. I have bruises to prove it."

The police officer didn't smile. "Do you believe that story, Lucas?"

"Unfortunately, yes. It sounds exactly the sort of thing my grandmother would arrange." He swore softly, his fluency earning him a look of respect from the hardened New York cop.

"How do you want us to handle this?"

"I don't. I'm grateful for your speedy response, but I'll take it from here. And if you could forget you ever saw me here, I'd be grateful for that, too." He spoke with the quiet authority of someone who was rarely questioned and Eva watched in fascination as they all melted away.

All except Albert, who stood as solid as a tree trunk in the doorway.

Lucas looked at him expectantly. "Thank you for your concern, but I've got this."

"My concern is for Miss Eva." Albert stood his ground and looked at Eva. "Perhaps you'd better come with me."

She was touched. "I'll be fine, Albert, but thank you. I may be a little vertically challenged, but I'm deadly when I'm cornered. You don't need to worry about me."

"If you change your mind, I'm on until midnight." He glared at Lucas, his expression suggesting that he'd be keeping an eye on the situation. "I'll check in with you before I leave."

"You're really kind."

The door to the apartment closed.

"You're deadly when you're cornered?" His dark drawl held a hint of humor. "Forgive me if I find that hard to believe."

"Don't underestimate me, Mr. Blade. When I attack, you won't see it coming. One minute you'll be minding your own business, the next you'll be on your back, helpless."

"Like I was a few moments ago?"

She ignored his sarcasm. "That was different. I

wasn't expecting anyone to be here. I wasn't ready. Next time I'll be ready."

"Next time?"

"Next time you leap on me and try to imprint me into your floor. It was like the Hollywood Walk of Fame only you were using my whole body, not just my hand. Your floor probably looks like a crime scene with the outline of my body right there."

Lucas studied her for a moment. "You seem to have a close relationship with the doorman of my building. Have you known him long?"

"About ten minutes."

"Ten minutes and the guy is willing to defend you to the death? Do you have that effect on all men?"

"Never the right men. Never the young, hot, eligible ones." She changed the subject. "Why did the police not make an arrest?"

"According to you, you weren't committing a crime."

"I was talking about you. They should have cautioned you. You flattened me and scared the life out of me." She remembered the way his body had felt against hers. She could still feel the hard pressure of his thigh, the warmth of his breath on her cheek and the heaviness.

Her gaze met his. The way he was looking at her made her think he was remembering that moment, too.

"You were creeping around my apartment. And if I'd wanted to kill you, you'd be dead by now."

"Is that supposed to be a comfort?" She rubbed

her bruised ribs, reminding herself that however her imagination played with the facts, it hadn't been a romantic encounter. Lucas Blade was looking at her with a hint of steel in his gaze. There was something about him that didn't seem quite *safe*. "Do you assault everyone who enters you're apartment?"

"Only those who enter uninvited."

"I was invited! As you would have found out if you'd bothered to ask. And I would have thought a man with your expertise in crime would have been able to tell the difference between an innocent woman and a criminal."

He gave her a speculative look. "Criminals aren't always so easy to identify. They don't come with a twirling moustache and a label. You think you can recognize a bad guy just by looking at them?"

"I'm pretty good at identifying 'loser guy,' and I definitely know 'hot guy,' so I'm confident 'bad guy' wouldn't slide under my radar."

"No?" He stepped closer to her. "The 'bad guys' live among us, blending in. Often it's the person you'd least suspect. The cabdriver, the lawyer," he paused before saying, "the doorman."

Was he intentionally trying to scare her? "Your doorman, Albert, happens to be one of the nicest people I've ever met so if you're trying to persuade me he has a criminal past I'm not going to believe you. In my experience most people are pretty decent."

"You don't watch the news?"

"The news presents only the bad side of humanity, Mr. Blade, and it does it on a global scale. It doesn't report the millions of small, unreported acts of kindness that take place on a daily basis in communities. People help old ladies across the street, they bring their neighbors tea when they're sick. You don't hear about it because good news isn't entertainment, even though it's those deeds that hold society together. Bad news is a commodity and the media trade in that."

"You really believe that?"

"Yes, and I don't intend to apologize for preferring to focus on the positive. I'm a glass half-full sort of person. That's not a crime. You see the bad in people, but I see the good. And I do believe there is good in most people."

"We only ever see what a person chooses to show. You don't know what they might be hiding under the surface." His voice was deep, his dark eyes mesmerizing. "Maybe when that kind man has helped the little old lady across the street he goes home and searches indecent images on a laptop he keeps hidden under his bed. And the kind person who takes their neighbor tea might be an arsonist or a dangerous psychopath and his, or her, intention is to get a closer look at how and where their neighbor lives to assess access points and vulnerabilities. You never know, just by looking, what a person is hiding."

Eva stared at him, unsettled by the image of the world he'd painted. It was as if someone had sprayed ugly graffiti over her clean vision of life. "You may look good on the outside, Mr. Blade, but inside you need a makeover. You have a dark, cynical, twisted mind."

"Thank you." The faintest of smiles touched the corners of his mouth. "The *New York Times* said the same thing when they reviewed my last book."

"I didn't intend it as a compliment, but I can see that maybe you need to be like that to be successful. Your job is to explore the dark side of humanity and that has twisted your thinking. Most people are simply what they seem," she said firmly. "Take me as an example. Take a good, hard look at me. And now tell me, do I *look* like a murderer?"

CHAPTER TWO

A frog is always a frog, never a prince in disguise.

—Frankie

Do I LOOK like a murderer?

Lucas scanned her sweet, heart-shaped face. Her eyes were a dark blue and with those bouncing golden curls and the dimple in her cheek, she looked as harmless as a fluffy kitten.

Nothing like a murderer.

She'd be the warm, kindly nurse no one would ever imagine to be capable of killing her patients, or the sweet-natured kindergarten teacher whom people assumed would nurture the children in her care. She looked like the poster girl for health and vitality—she could advertise the juiciest orange juice, or the crunchiest salad.

A woman with a face and body like hers could evade suspicion for months or years.

His heart pounded and he felt the spark of creative energy that had eluded him for months flicker to life.

She eyed him cautiously. "Why are you staring? What have I said? I can assure you I'm *not* a murderer and frankly I can't imagine why you'd think it for a moment. I don't even kill spiders. I carry them to the nearest safe place, although if I'm honest I do usually use a glass and a piece of cardboard because I don't like the way their legs feel on my skin."

I don't even kill spiders.

And neither would his murderer.

Just humans.

"That's it." He didn't even realize he'd spoken. Without thinking, he walked up to her and slid his fingers into her hair. Blond, silky, it flowed through his fingers and framed her face with lustrous gold. Her hair alone would be enough to dazzle any man. Dazzle and distract him. He'd be dead before he knew what had happened.

"That's *what*?" She sounded exasperated. "Mr. Blade?"

"You're the one."

His mind, roused from its soporific state, was racing ahead so fast it took him a moment to realize he still had his fingers in her hair.

How would it happen? How would she commit murder?

Could her hair be a weapon? Or a motif? Something she left at the crime scene?

No. She'd be caught within a week.

Maybe she changed her hair each time she committed murder.

Maybe she wore a wig.

"Mr. Blade!" Huge blue eyes were fixed on his face. "What do you mean, 'I'm the one'? I've never committed a crime in my life if that's what you're implying."

But she would. *She would.* "You're perfect."

Her cheeks turned from whipped cream to fondant pink. "P-perfect?"

She even blushed. A woman who could blush like that wouldn't hurt a fly. *Or would she?* "Can you do that at will or is it just something that happens?"

"What?"

"Blushing." He stroked his fingers across her smooth skin, exploring the silky texture. He wanted to know everything about her. He wanted to deconstruct her so that he could decide which traits to give to his character.

"I tend to blush when a man I've only known for a few minutes tells me I'm perfect. You're right that first impressions can be wrong. If you'd asked me ten minutes ago I wouldn't have said you were the friendliest person I'd ever met, but now I can see you were just being defensive. And that's understandable if women break into your apartment to meet you."

"What?" Her words finally penetrated his subconscious and his fantasy world melted away.

He'd been thinking aloud and she'd misinterpreted his words.

She thought he was interested in her.

And why wouldn't she? She was most men's idea of a fantasy woman, all soft curves and blond hair with a mouth as pink and tempting as sugar icing. There had been a time when he would have been interested himself, but that time seemed like an age away.

His wife had tamed that side of him. The wild, restless side that had driven him to rip through life taking what he wanted. But now she was gone and he had no one to please but himself, and invariably he didn't even manage that.

Denied any sort of internal peace or personal satisfaction, he channeled all his emotions into his work. His writing came first. At his lowest point, it had saved him, which had made the fear that he might have lost it forever all the more acute.

But he hadn't lost it. His gift had simply been lying dormant, waiting to be reawakened and this woman had done that.

The relief was profound.

It was like a drowning man discovering the life preserver he'd thought he'd lost bobbing in the water right next to him. He grabbed it and hung on, determined not to sink back down beneath the murky water.

His mind wouldn't stop racing. Was that his murderer's motivation? Had she lost someone and was intent on revenge? Or was she a psychopath with no conscience or emotion, someone incapable of empathy who used her looks as a trap?

If there had been a notebook and pen in hand he would have started scribbling right there. For the first time in months he felt an almost overwhelming urge and impatience to open his laptop. He wanted to sit down and write. He wanted to write and write until the book was finished. He could feel the idea growing inside him. His mind was like a dry riverbed after a flood, replenished, drenched with ideas.

Finally, finally, after months of waiting for inspiration, he'd found his murderer.

HE THOUGHT SHE was perfect? His reaction was unexpected given everything she knew about his life. Over the many slices of cake she'd shared with his grandmother, she'd discovered that Lucas Blade had shown no interest in dating since he'd lost his wife three years ago, despite the repeated attempts by various women to engage his attention. His life was a shadowy mystery, a private wasteland of grief and hard work. He wrote, he participated in whatever international book tours were required of him, he spoke, he signed books. In between the forced public appearances, he shut himself away.

He displayed all the signs of a man who was going through the motions.

He'd deflected his grandmother's less than subtle attempts to introduce him to suitable women, all of which made it all the more surprising that he was looking at her as if she was the answer to his dreams.

She wasn't convinced he was the answer to hers, although there was no arguing that he was outrageously good-looking, in a rough, buyer-beware type of way.

Was it insane to be attracted to someone who had just proved he could crush her like a bug? Having already discovered his strength, it surprised her that he was capable of the gentleness he was showing now as he slowly stroked her face with skilled fingers. But it wasn't his touch that turned her knees to water, it was the raw hunger she saw in his eyes.

"You really think I'm perfect?"

The hunger was replaced by caution. "You have perfect bone structure."

Perfect *bone structure*?

She'd been told she had nice hair. She knew her figure was good. She would have added a few inches to her height if she'd had a choice, but apart from that there wasn't much about herself she'd change. No one had ever mentioned her bones before.

He stared at her from every angle until Eva grew more and more uncomfortable.

Lucas Blade was a mega successful writer with an international reputation and a global audience of fans, but that didn't change the fact that he was basically a stranger. A stranger surrounded by an aura of dangerous tension. He prowled, rather than walked. Glowered, rather than smiled. And right now he was studying her as if he was a predator and she was his next victim.

His words rang in her head. *You never know, just by looking, what a person is hiding.*

Despite her tendency to trust most people, if she'd seen him coming toward her on the street at night she would have leaped straight into a cab.

"Do you always stare at people?" She glanced toward the door, judging the distance, and he followed her gaze with a frown.

"I've made you uncomfortable. I apologize." He

stepped back, giving her space, and she forced herself to breathe deeply, reminding herself that he wasn't really a stranger. She knew his grandmother well.

"This is the most unusual first meeting I've ever had. First you try to kill me—"

"I did *not* try to kill you. I was trying to incapacitate you."

"Given the differences in our height and weight, that pretty much amounted to the same thing."

She couldn't stop thinking about the way his body had felt pressed against hers. When was the last time she'd been held like that? Felt the delicious hardness, the masculine strength, the feeling of safety—safety? He'd been attacking her! Holy crap, her mind was warped. It hadn't been romantic. It had been self-defense. "I think you might have damaged me mentally. All that talk about people's hidden dark sides has freaked me out a little. You've made me nervous. I'm going to be passing people in the street wondering what secrets they're hiding." And she wondered what secrets he was hiding behind that wickedly handsome face.

The gleam of mockery was back. "I thought you saw good in everyone."

"I do, but now you've put doubt in my mind. Thanks to you I'm going to be looking over my shoulder all the way home."

"A healthy dose of caution is a useful thing."

"Maybe, but you've scared me."

"Scaring people is my job."

"No, your job is to write books that scare people,

not scare them in person!" She rubbed her palm over the small of her back and saw the expression in his eyes change.

"Did I hurt you?"

"I landed awkwardly and your floor is hard." She rolled her shoulders experimentally. "I'll live."

"Turn around and I'll take a look at you."

"Are you suggesting I remove my clothes and turn my back on you? I don't think so. You're not the sort of man a sensible woman would turn her back on, Mr. Blade. I'm trying not to imagine what might have happened if the police hadn't arrived when they did. You would have shattered all my bones with one of your judo throws."

"It was jujitsu."

"Good to know. Your grandmother told me you're an expert at several martial arts. She'll be thrilled to know you're putting that expertise to good use. I'll be sure to mention it when I call her."

His expression froze. "You won't be calling my grandmother."

"But—"

"If I'd wanted my grandmother to know I was here, I would have told her."

"Why didn't you?" It puzzled her. "She adores you. Why would you hide from her?"

"It's more that I'm hiding from her uncontrollable urge to interfere and fix my life."

"She does that because she loves you." Eva felt a pang of envy. "She cares *so* much."

"Maybe, but it doesn't make it less exasperating."

He dismissed family with the ease of someone who took it for granted. What wouldn't she give to have someone interfere and try to fix her life? To call and check she was all right. To worry that she was working too hard and not eating properly.

She blinked rapidly.

She should probably leave. He didn't want her here, did he? It was obvious that this wasn't a man remotely interested in decorating for Christmas.

Now that the lights had been switched on, she was able to take a proper look around her. The apartment was beautiful, but the decor was impersonal. It felt more like an exclusive hotel than a home, as if someone had moved in and forgotten to add any personal touches.

The space was incredible but it had no soul. No character. There were no clues about the person who lived there. It was hard to believe anyone had ever sat on the sofas, or put glasses or cups down on the smooth glass table. The place seemed almost abandoned, as if Lucas had forgotten it existed.

She wanted to add flowers and cushions. She wanted to drop a few items of clothing around the place to soften it and make it seemed lived in.

Where had he been when she'd entered the apartment? Upstairs in one of the bedrooms? In his study?

For the first time since she'd been flattened underneath him, she took a serious look at his face and saw things she'd failed to notice the first time. She saw the shadows under his eyes that suggested he hadn't slept for weeks. The lines of tension that bracketed his firm mouth.

She looked away and something else caught her eye. A sharp knife, the long blade gleaming under the lights. Had they been standing in the kitchen its presence wouldn't have drawn a second glance, but they weren't in the kitchen.

She stared at it uneasily.

There was something unsettling, almost menacing, about that knife.

She contemplated all the possible reasons he might have for leaving it lying on the table. Maybe he used it for opening the mail. Except that she'd already noticed a towering stack of unopened letters.

No matter how much she racked her brain, alternative suggestions eluded her.

The blade taunted her and unease turned to alarm. She wasn't experienced at solving mysteries, but she could read clues as well as the next person. He had a knife in the living room and he was here alone, cut off from the outside world.

Christmas made some people desperate, didn't it?

She glanced at the bare floors and walls. "Did you just move in?"

"I've lived here for three years."

Three years. Had he been living here when his wife died? No. The place showed no sign of a woman's hand, which meant he must have moved in immediately after his wife had died.

He'd been escaping. Running. And he was still running.

The place looked as if he'd jumped straight from that life into this one and brought nothing with him.

Her heart ached for him.

She tried telling herself his life was none of her business. She'd been employed to fix his apartment, not fix his life, and he'd made it clear how much he hated interference. The sensible thing was to leave right now, but if she left, he'd be alone and who knew what he might do? What if he picked up that knife? She was the only person who knew the truth. That Lucas Blade wasn't on a writing retreat in Vermont. He was holed up here in his apartment, alone.

If he did something, she'd feel responsible. She'd always wonder if she could have stopped it. Made a difference.

Her gaze met the fierce black of his and she knew she wasn't looking at a man who was dangerous. She was looking at a man who was desperate. Right on the edge. Holding it together by a thread.

Lucas Blade might write about horror, but she suspected that right now nothing matched the horror of his own life.

And there was no way she was leaving him alone.

CHAPTER THREE

Look before you leap. Or carry a first aid kit.
—Lucas

LUCAS HAD EXPECTED her to leave, but she was still standing there.

"I have work to do." And he was desperate to get started. The characters were coming alive in his head, becoming people with flaws and qualities. He could hear dialogue and picture scenes. For the first time in far too long he couldn't wait to sit down in front of his laptop. He wanted to escape into the fictional world that was waiting for him. It was like someone in chronic pain, contemplating a syringe full of morphine. He wanted to grab it and empty the barrel into his veins until the sweetness of oblivion numbed the agony that had been his constant companion for three years.

The only thing stopping him was the source of his inspiration who seemed stubbornly determined not to leave. He might have scared her, but apparently he hadn't scared her enough to send her running for the door.

"Your grandmother gave me this job, so either I

call her and explain, or I do the job she sent me here to do."

If she called his grandmother, any hope of being left alone over the Christmas period would vanish. He'd be required to explain why he was in New York rather than Vermont and, most awkwardly of all, why he'd lied about it.

"Look around you." He tried intimidation, his tone silky soft. "Do I look like a man who wants his apartment decorated for the holidays?"

"No, which is why your grandmother wanted me to do it. She doesn't think you should be living like this. She's worried about you. And frankly, having met you, so am I."

"Why would you care how I'm living my life?"

"Everyone deserves a Christmas tree in their lives."

"Only if you're trying to punish them."

"Punish? A Christmas tree is uplifting."

"What is uplifting about a fake Christmas tree, which is essentially a petroleum-based product probably manufactured in a Chinese factory?"

"Fake? Who said anything about fake? I don't do 'fake,' Mr. Blade. I don't do fake Christmas trees, fake handbags, or fake orgasms." Color streaked across her cheeks. "I didn't mean to say that last one. It slipped out. But my point is nothing in my life is fake." The words tumbled over each other and Lucas found himself struggling not to smile.

He didn't think he'd ever met anyone so deliciously indiscreet.

"You've never faked an orgasm?"

"Could you forget I said that?"

He imagined her in bed, naked and uninhibited. Heat raced over his skin and his thoughts were explicit enough to make him uncomfortable. Since his wife's death he'd had no shortage of offers, from sex to marriage, but had never once been tempted. It wasn't just that he'd left his bad boy days in his past. It was more that he no longer had the taste for it. Every time he looked at a woman he saw the expression on Sallyanne's face the last time he'd seen her alive.

But he was definitely attracted to Eva.

To take his mind off sex, he pondered on how someone of her build could murder a man twice her size.

"I'm a writer. Human behavior interests me."

She interested him.

He told himself that his interest was professional, but part of him recognized that as a lie.

She let her hands drop. "We were talking about Christmas trees. *Real* Christmas trees, which smell and look beautiful."

"And drop needles all over my floor." He remembered the way she'd felt underneath him.

"If needles drop you clean them up." She unbuttoned her coat. "It's not hard."

"I don't have time. I have a book to finish and I need to be left in peace to do that. If you decorate my apartment, you'll disturb me." It wasn't the noise that worried him, or the intrusion of having someone else in the apartment, it was *her.*

She made him feel something he didn't want to feel.

Maybe it was because she was nothing like his wife. Sallyanne had been tall and willowy. In heels, she'd matched his height. Physically, Eva was as different from Sallyanne as it was possible for a woman to be. He knew instinctively that losing himself in Eva's soft curves would be a whole new experience, with no flashbacks or reminders, but he knew that for a man like him to get involved with a woman like her would definitely be a crime, just not the sort he wrote about.

"You won't even know I'm here."

"You're not the type of woman who blends into the background."

"You don't need to worry about me disturbing you," she said quickly. "I understand that creative genius needs space to work. Also there's the fact that I don't find your company that thrilling, Mr. Blade."

The kitten had claws. "Tell my grandmother you changed your mind about the job."

"No. I'm being paid to decorate your apartment and stock your freezer in your absence. That's what I intend to do."

"I'm not absent."

"Which is inconvenient for both of us, particularly as you're not allowing me to disclose that fact to the person who gave me this job. I don't like lying."

He discovered that those soft blue eyes and mermaid-like hair concealed a woman with a stubborn streak a mile wide.

The thought that his grandmother might finally have met her match almost compensated for the irritation of failing to shift her from his apartment.

Almost, but not quite.

"Leave, and I'll match whatever she's paying you."

"It's not about the money, Mr. Blade. It's about my professional reputation. I take pride in my work."

"And what is your work, exactly? You're a Christmas elf? You decorate the apartments of unsuspecting Scrooge-like individuals, thus intensifying their loathing of this time of year?" His sarcasm seemed to slide right off her.

"I'm part of Urban Genie. We're an events and concierge company."

"Decorating my apartment is an event?"

"Your grandmother is one of our clients and this request came through her. We can do pretty much anything that's requested of us."

He bit back the obvious comment. He told himself that he didn't want to make cheap jokes at her expense, but the truth was he was trying hard not to think of her that way. "Anything, it seems, except leave when you're asked to."

"I'd leave if requested to do so by my client. You're not my client."

"Give me the name of your boss, and I'll call and explain that I no longer need your services."

"I am the boss. I run the business with two of my friends."

"How do you know my grandmother?"

"I met Mitzy earlier in the year when she requested a birthday cake. She was one of our first clients. We got talking, and since then she's used us a few times. When the weather is cold I walk her little dog, and sometimes we just talk."

No one but his grandfather had ever called his grandmother Mitzy. To everyone else she was Mary, or Gran. Clearly this girl was more to his grandmother than the face of an efficient concierge service. "What do you talk about?"

"Everything. She's an interesting woman."

"She pays you to chat? You charge an old lady for company?"

"No. I chat because I like her." She was patient. "She reminds me of my grandmother. She's a little lonely, I think."

Even though there was no accusation in her eyes or in her voice, he felt another stab of guilt.

"She calls you?"

"Occasionally. More often she uses our Urban Genie app."

"You're confusing her with someone else. My grandmother doesn't own a cell phone. She has always refused to have one." He thought of the number of arguments they'd had on that topic. He didn't understand how she was allowed to worry about him, but he wasn't allowed to worry about her.

"She didn't refuse me. And she regularly uses our app."

"She hates technology."

"She hates the idea of it, but she was fine once we'd given her basic training. She's very smart."

"You *trained* her?" How did he not know this? He thought back to the last time he'd seen his grandmother. The summer had been busy with an international book tour. He'd spent less than two days at home in July and August. Since then he'd been busy trying to find a way to start his book.

They were excuses and he knew it.

He could have found the time. He could have *made* the time.

The truth was he found it hard to be with his grandmother. Her intentions were good, but whenever she tried to soothe his pain she simply made it worse. No one could heal the wound that festered inside him, not his grandmother, and not this woman with eyes the color of a summer sky and hair the color of buttermilk.

He held out his hand. "Do you have the app on your phone? Show me." He took her phone from her and opened the app. *"Your wish is our command?"* He raised an eyebrow. "My wish is that you leave and tell no one you saw me. How do we make that happen?"

She snatched the phone from him. "We don't. Here's the deal, Mr. Blade. I don't know why you're not in Vermont, and I don't need to know. That's not my business. My business is doing the job your grandmother paid me to do. I will decorate your apartment, fill your freezer and then I will leave."

He would have been impressed if he hadn't been so exasperated.

Finally, after months of struggling, he was ready to write and he couldn't because this woman refused to leave him alone.

"I could have you removed."

"You could. But then I'd call your grandmother and tell her where you are. I'm sensing you don't want me to do that, so I'm sure we can reach a compromise we can both live with."

"You're *blackmailing* me?" After a decade spent exploring the darker side of human nature nothing ever surprised him, but this did.

Her eyes were kind, her mouth lush and perfectly curved. On the outside she was gentle and sweet. Inside she was solid steel. The contrast might have intrigued him, but right now all it did was aggravate.

He was about to find a way of forcibly ejecting her when he noticed the volume of snow falling past the windows of his apartment.

The sight chilled him.

He walked to the window in silence and stared at the world outside, transformed and remodeled by layer upon layer of snow. The thick curtain of flakes veiled his view of Central Park.

Memories rose in dark, menacing clouds, their presence blackening everything. He was yanked back in time to a night exactly like this one.

The same deceptively harmless swirl of snow had proved as deadly a killer as any he'd written into his stories. The unexpected twist had made it all the more brutal.

Time was supposed to heal, but he knew he hadn't

healed. He didn't know how to heal. His emotions were as raw and real as they'd been three years earlier. All he could do was cling on and survive. Get up, get dressed, get through another day. He wouldn't have thought there was anything that could make it harder, but one thing did and that was the pressure he felt from other people to "move on." The knowledge that he'd been unable to meet their expectations when it came to recovery added to his sense of failure.

He squeezed his eyes tightly shut, blocking out the images and the memory of the last time he'd seen Sallyanne alive. He wanted to be able to go back and think about the good times, but so far that hadn't happened. Like a misbehaving computer, his mind had crashed and frozen on that one single moment he would have chosen to forget.

"I love snow, don't you? It's like being wrapped in a great big hug." Her soft, dreamy voice cut through the nightmare playing out in his head and he opened his eyes, knowing that whatever his grandmother might have shared with this woman over cake and tea, she hadn't shared all the details of his wife's death.

Her innocent, optimistic comment grated on him, like sandpaper rubbed over raw skin.

"I hate snow."

She stood by his side, gazing out of the window, and he turned to look at her, aware of the false intimacy created by their circumstances.

He wasn't sure what he saw in her face. Wistfulness? Contentment? Either way it was obvious that she was as trusting of the weather as she was of people.

I'm a cup half-full sort of person.

Exasperation turned to resignation. He knew there was no decision to be made.

No matter how much he wanted to send her away, he couldn't do it. Not with the blizzard currently engulfing Manhattan. No one else was going to die because of him.

"Decorate the apartment if you must. Tie bows on the stairs, hang mistletoe from the light fixtures. I don't care." He knew he was being ungracious, but he couldn't help it. He felt trapped, cornered, even though she could hardly be held responsible for the weather. She probably thought he made Scrooge look like a man full of Christmas spirit. "I'm going to work. Do what the hell you like, but don't disturb me."

EVA FELT ABOUT as welcome as a rat in a restaurant.

She stripped off her coat and carried her bags through to the kitchen. Everything shone and she stood for a moment admiring the blend of gleaming metal and smooth polished countertops. She'd been in enough kitchens to know that this one was custom-built and expensive.

"I may feel like a rat in a restaurant," she muttered, "but at least it's a beautiful restaurant."

Keeping one eye on the door upstairs through which Lucas had vanished, she started to unload the food.

The refrigerator was huge. It was also mostly empty. He hadn't prepared for the blizzard?

She stared at the empty shelves, comparing it with the fridge in her own apartment. That one was half the size and twice as full, brimming with vegetables and the result of her creative experiments in the kitchen. This one looked as if the person who owned the apartment hadn't yet moved in.

Maybe he couldn't be bothered to buy furnishings, but what had he been eating?

She pulled open the cabinets and found a few jars, a few tins and some pasta. And six unopened bottles of whiskey.

On the far side of the kitchen one entire wall had been given over to wine storage, row upon row of bottles with only the tops visible. The only time she'd ever seen so many bottles of wine in one place had been in a restaurant. It was eye-catching and decorative, but she had a feeling its purpose wasn't to provide aesthetic appeal. Lucas Blade was either a collector or he was a big drinker.

No wonder his grandmother was concerned.

She was starting to have her own concerns, but mingled in with those concerns were other feelings. She paused and pressed her palm against her stomach, trying to subdue the butterflies. He was troubled and complicated. *Not* a man she should be looking twice at. Not that she was saving herself for Mr. Right, but at the very least she had to *like* someone and had to believe they liked her back.

She wasn't sure what she thought about Lucas

Blade. She felt sympathy for his situation, and she was certainly attracted to him, but as for whether she liked him—she needed more time before she could answer that. And he certainly didn't seem to like her.

Reaching for more bags, she carried on unloading the food.

Why didn't he just tell his family he was at home and didn't want to be disturbed? Why concoct an elaborate story that he was in Vermont?

She stowed a box of eggs and glanced up the stairs where Lucas had vanished. In the brief moment before he'd turned his back on her, his face had been like thunder. She'd been sure he was about to forcibly eject her from the building, or at least find some legitimate way to get rid of her and reclaim his territory but something, and she had no idea what, had caused him to reverse his decision.

She'd expected to be on her own here for a couple of nights. A few hours ago she would have rejoiced in the prospect of company, but now she wasn't so sure. There was something inexplicably lonely about being trapped in an apartment with someone who didn't want you there.

Maybe she should have done as he'd ordered and left, but how could she possibly leave a person who was suffering as he was? She couldn't, especially knowing that no one else was going to check on him. There was no way she could ever abandon another human being who was feeling that bad.

If something had happened to him she wouldn't have been able to live with herself.

And then there was the matter of the job itself.

Paige was the one who had so far won most of the new business for their fledgling company. She was a dynamo who had worked tirelessly to get Urban Genie off the ground.

This was the first significant piece of business Eva had brought in and she didn't want to lose it. Nor did she want to let her client down. And Mitzy had become more than a client. She was a friend.

Eva unpacked the rest of the bags, leaving only the ones that contained decorations for the tree.

Those could wait until the tree was delivered.

Trying to forget about Lucas, she pulled on her headphones and selected her favorite festive soundtrack from her playlist, reminding herself not to sing. She didn't want to disturb him while he was writing.

Two minutes into the song, Paige called.

"How are you doing? Is it weird being in an empty apartment?"

Eva glanced upward to the silent space above her. "It's not empty. He's here."

"Who is 'he'? And I'm putting you on speaker. Frankie is gesturing to me."

"Lucas Blade." She explained the situation, leaving out mention of the police.

There was no point in worrying her friends.

"Why would he pretend to be away?"

Eva remembered the look in his eyes. She glanced at the knife on the table. "I don't think he wants company." She suspected he didn't want his own company either, but that wasn't something he could easily escape.

"So you've seen him then? Hey, is he smoking hot or did they use a body double in that photo on the book jacket?" It was Frankie who spoke and Eva thought about those strikingly masculine features and those eyes. *Those eyes...*

"He's smoking hot."

"There you go." Frankie sounded triumphant. "You wanted to use up that condom before Christmas—this is your opportunity."

Eva thought about how his body had felt crushing hers and her stomach did a succession of flips. "He's not my type."

"Sexy as hell? He's every woman's type."

"I'm not denying he's sexy, but he's not friendly."

"So? You don't have to have a conversation. Just use him for great sex."

Her words must have set off alarm bells because Paige came back on the phone.

"What do you mean he's not friendly?"

"Nothing. Forget it. He doesn't want me here, that's all."

"But you're staying anyway? You are one of a kind." Frankie muttered something indistinct. "If a man didn't want me around, I'd be out of there so fast you wouldn't see me for dust."

"But you're an introvert. And you're weird around men."

"Do I need to remind you I'm in love and engaged?"

"You're weird around all men except Matt."

"In this case I agree with Frankie. If he makes you feel uncomfortable, you should leave." Paige was emphatic. "We have a rule, remember? If a situation feels wrong then we get the hell out, especially when we're working alone."

"I don't feel threatened. And I can't leave him." She lowered her voice. "There was almost no food in the place until I showed up. And it's not only food that's missing. There's hardly any furniture. No mess. It's as if he just moved in."

"Having you there will soon change that," Frankie said, but Paige didn't laugh.

"The more I hear, the less I like. How did he persuade you to stay?"

"He didn't. He wanted me to leave, until—" *Until he'd noticed the weather.* She turned and glanced toward the windows. That was it. He'd been pushing her to leave right up until the moment he'd looked out of the window and seen that New York was virtually shut down. "He didn't want me to travel in a blizzard. Don't worry, if he was planning to do away with me, he would have booted me out into the street and let the weather do the job for him." She strolled toward the windows and peered through the swirling wall of white. The streets and the park had vanished behind the ferocious fury of the storm. "I couldn't leave now even if I wanted to." The knowledge made her nerve endings tingle. It was just the two of them. Alone. Only this time the word *alone* conjured up different feelings. Her stomach felt jittery.

"Do you have everything you need?"

"Yes. I came equipped to turn his house into a winter wonderland with gourmet extras." But she hadn't expected the place to be quite so stark. She could decorate, but she wasn't a magician.

"Stay in touch," Paige said. "If we don't hear from you, we're coming down there, blizzard or no blizzard. Jake's here and he's staying over. And Matt's here with Frankie. We miss you!"

Eva felt a pang. Both her friends were in committed relationships. They'd found love and she was happy for them. But there was no denying it made her feel even more alone.

"Remember that self-defense move I taught you?" Frankie's voice came down the phone and Eva smiled.

"This guy is a black belt in you-name-it-I-do-it martial arts, so my single self-defense move isn't going to get me far." She remembered the skill with which he'd brought her to the floor. "I'm going to trust my natural instinct about people. I know he writes about bad guys, but he isn't a bad guy himself."

She tried to forget what he'd said about the man in the street hiding who he really was.

He was wrong about that. Perhaps some people hid who they were, but most people were kind. She'd seen it time and time again.

Damn the man for planting that nasty seed in her usually optimistic mind.

"So you're staying the night with a guy you never met before tonight?" Paige sounded worried. "I don't like the sound of it, Ev."

"I can assure you he has no interest in me." Eva glanced up the stairway again, but upstairs was still and silent. "What does it mean when a guy says you have good bones?"

"When a crime writer says it, it means you need to get out of there," Frankie muttered. "Lucas Blade writes scary stuff. The last guy he wrote about used to strip his victims."

"Of their clothes?"

"Of their skin."

"Ew." Eva wished she hadn't asked. "Why would you read that?"

"Because I can't *not* read it. Everything he writes is gripping. He gets into the minds of people. Exploits your fears. He is hugely successful and his books are getting better and better. Everyone is waiting for his next book, including me. Hey, if you get a glimpse, send me a couple of chapters. What's he like, anyway?"

Intimidating. "He wasn't expecting to see me here, so I don't think I've seen him at his best."

"If you can't find anything good to say about him then he must be truly bad," Paige said. "You always see the good in people."

"He isn't bad. He bought his grandmother a puppy."

"So? Psychopaths can be pet owners. Come home, Ev. He's not your responsibility."

"I'm the only one who knows he's here," Eva said simply. "And he's in trouble. Whether he wants me here or not, I'm not leaving."

LUCAS STARED AT the glow of the screen.

Do I look like a murderer to you?

Those words had triggered a flow of ideas in his head, but none of them had made it from his head to his fingers. There were still too many unanswered questions.

It was like looking at a tangled ball of wool. The threads were there, but so far he hadn't managed to untangle them and weave them into a pattern that would keep his readers turning the pages.

But he had something. He knew he had something.

He rose to his feet and paced to the window of his study.

It was his superpower, the ability to delve deep into the psyche of the average person and expose, and exploit, their deepest fears. If he hadn't been a writer, he would have been a profiler for the FBI. He had contacts, had developed a few close relationships over the years. If he'd thought about it for too long he might have been disturbed by the directions his mind took. Right now though it was going nowhere.

His agent would be calling again soon. And his editor.

Soon they wouldn't just want a few chapters, they'd want the whole damn book.

He was running out of time. The book was due on Christmas Eve. He had less than a month. He'd never written a book that fast. He was approaching the point that he was going to have to tell them the truth. He'd have to tell them that the book wasn't finished. It wasn't even started. He didn't have a single word on the page.

A scent rose up through the apartment and he turned his head to the door, trying to place it.

Cinnamon.

The moment he identified it coincided with a soft tap on the door.

He dragged it open and saw Eva standing there, holding a tray.

"I thought you might be hungry. I'll make supper later, but for now I made a batch of my special Christmas spice cookies. I was going to freeze them for you, but as you're here you might as well eat one now."

He stared down at the plate. The cookies were shaped like Christmas trees and specs of sugar dusted the golden brown surface.

"Aren't cookies usually round?"

"They can be any shape you choose."

"And you chose Christmas trees?"

"It's a cookie, Mr. Blade. Eat it or don't."

He eyed the tray in her hands. Next to the plate of cookies was a mug full of—

"What the hell is that?" A slice of lemon floated on the top of straw-colored liquid.

"It's herbal tea."

"Herbal—?" He shook his head. "I'm pretty sure you didn't find that in my cupboards."

"I didn't find anything much in your cupboards."

"I drink coffee. Strong. Black."

"You can't drink strong black coffee in the afternoon. It will stop you sleeping. Herbal tea is refreshing and calming."

He rarely slept, but he didn't tell her that. He'd seen enough of his life plastered across the press over the past decade to make him miserly with the personal details he shared.

Herbal tea. *As if that was going to solve his problems.*

"Take it away." If it had been neat whiskey he would have downed it in one, but he wasn't swallowing herbal tea for anyone. "Do I look like a guy who drinks herbal tea and eats cookies shaped like Christmas trees?" His tone was infused with a harshness a thousand times more unpalatable than the brew in the cup in front of him and she studied him for a long moment.

"No, but you can't tell much about a person by looking at them, can you? You were the one who taught me that. Has it occurred to you that maybe I'm not trying to sweeten you up, Mr. Blade. Maybe I'm trying to poison you." She pushed the tray into his hands and walked away, dismissing him with a swish of her golden hair.

He stared after her, reeling from the contrast between her sweet face and the sharp rebuke.

Poison him?

That was it.

Finally he was ready to type something, and he had his hands full.

He took the tray into his study and set it down on his desk.

It was already dark and the only light in the room came from the glow of his laptop and the strange, luminescent light reflecting off the snow beyond the windows.

He returned to the screen. So far there were only two words on the page.

Chapter One.

He sat down and started to write.

CHAPTER FOUR

You are what you eat, so keep it sweet.

—Eva

OF ALL THE RUDE, moody, irritable—|

Eva stomped around the kitchen, hurt and upset. She'd been raised to consider what might lie beneath the surface of a person's behavior. You didn't have to be a psychologist to understand what was going on with Lucas, but still his words had stung.

She told herself that he was grieving. He was in pain. He was—

Cold. Distant. Intimidating. Formidable.

And obviously not a lover of herbal tea.

Her brief glimpse inside his study had shown her that the room was nothing like the rest of the apartment. It smelled of wood smoke and leather, and had both personality and warmth. A warmth that came from more than the flickering fire. Unlike the rest of his apartment, his office space had been furnished with loving care and attention. Two worn, deep leather sofas faced each other across a low table piled high with books. Not coffee-table books chosen as a design accent, but real books, thumbed at the corners and stacked haphazardly as if they'd only recently been read.

There had been a desk, she remembered, dominated by what appeared to be a very expensive computer, and there was also a laptop. The room was graced with the same soaring glass windows that enveloped the rest of the apartment, but the image that remained with her was of the bookshelves. They'd stretched from floor to ceiling and were packed with more books than she'd ever seen in her life outside a library. The covers didn't match and leather-bound volumes were interspersed with the less durable paperbacks, the lines on their spines suggesting that they were well-read and well loved.

She was curious to know what Lucas Blade read when he wanted to escape from his own work and his own world. Did he read crime fiction or something different?

She'd had no opportunity to take a closer look. With a single glance and a few carefully chosen words, he'd made it clear that she was intruding on his space.

He didn't want her here. She wasn't welcome.

But before she'd turned away, she'd learned one other thing. Perhaps the most important thing of all. Whatever Lucas was doing in his office, it wasn't writing.

The computer screen had been blank. Had it been smaller, she might not have noticed but as it was she'd managed to read two words—*Chapter One*.

There had been nothing else.

What had he been doing up there in the weeks he'd supposedly been hiding away and writing? What had he been doing while she'd been familiarizing herself with his kitchen?

Not working, that she was sure about.

In the few awkward moments before she'd plucked up the courage to knock on his door, she'd heard silence. There had been no sound. Nothing. No rhythmic rattle of fingers on a keyboard. No tap of the space bar. No soft whirr of a printer.

If she hadn't seen him disappear inside, she would have assumed the room was empty.

She felt a pang of empathy.

After her grandmother had died she'd struggled to drag herself out of bed. If it hadn't been for her friends, she probably wouldn't have bothered.

Where were Lucas's friends?

Why weren't they banging on his door and bringing him hot meals? Why weren't they insisting he left the apartment?

Because they thought he was in Vermont. Everyone thought he was in Vermont.

Only she knew differently.

She glanced up the elegant curve of the stairs to the closed door, wondering how to handle the situation. She wasn't exactly in a position to criticize him for his lack of social life. She couldn't even get herself a date. She was hardly qualified to rekindle his flagging inspiration, or whatever it was that was preventing him from writing. All she could do was make sure he was well fed. That, at least, was within the scope of her experience.

What would tempt him? It had to smell good, be quick and easy to eat and not too heavy.

She opened the fridge, now fully stocked, and pulled out cheese, eggs and milk.

She'd whip up a soufflé, light and fluffy, serve it with some of the fresh salad leaves she'd purchased earlier. And she'd make bread.

Who could resist the smell of freshly baked bread?

For the next few hours she whisked, poured and kneaded. She rarely consulted a recipe and never weighed anything. Instead she relied on instinct and experience. Neither had failed her yet. She added rosemary and sea salt to the dough and made a few notes in the small book she always carried so she could add the recipe to her blog later.

She'd started her blog, *Eat with Eva*, as a way of recording and remembering all that her grandmother had taught her. To begin with she'd only had a few loyal followers, but they were growing rapidly and what had started out as an interest and a hobby had turned into a passion and a job. She'd been as surprised by the discovery that she could earn her living doing what she loved as she was by the surge in her own ambition.

She wanted this to be big. Not because she wanted fame and fortune, but because she wanted to spread the word about good, simple cooking to everyone. With that objective in mind, she tried only to use simple ingredients that could be easily sourced. She wanted people to use her recipes after a hard day at work, not just for the occasional dinner party.

She couldn't remember a time when she hadn't cooked. One of her earliest memories was of standing on a chair next to the stove, concentrating as her grandmother taught her how to make the perfect omelet.

At Urban Genie, she rarely did the cooking herself. Her job was to outsource catering, and she spent her days discussing menus, meeting with new suppliers, managing budgets.

It was a pleasure to be back in the kitchen, especially a kitchen as well equipped as this one. And part of that pleasure was the feeling of being close to her grandmother, as if this memory and the happy feelings were something that couldn't be erased by her absence. It was a way of keeping her alive, of remembering the touch, the smells, the smiles that had been exchanged during activities exactly like this one.

She'd discovered that a legacy wasn't money, it was memories. And inside her was a treasure trove of a thousand special moments.

She shaped the dough into rolls, scored the tops and placed them on a baking tray.

Out of the corner of her eye she spied the knife that Lucas had left on the table.

Having witnessed plenty of accidents in the kitchens where she'd worked, she was obsessively careful with knives.

After a moment, she picked it up and slid it into

the back of one of the drawers so that it was hidden from view.

It occurred to her that if he tried to harm himself with that knife it would now be covered in *her* fingerprints and she paused, horrified by her thought process.

She pushed the drawer closed, exasperated with herself and also with him because she knew exactly who had put that thought in her head. *He* had, with his comments about never really knowing a person. Even though she disagreed with him, his words had seeped into her mind and contaminated her usually sunny thoughts, like poison dropped into a clear mountain stream.

Unsettled, she slid the softly curved rolls into the oven. Hopefully Lucas would give them a more positive response than he had the herbal tea.

While she waited for them to cook, she tidied up. At home her untidy nature had been a source of argument between herself and Paige, who had shared an apartment with her for years. The only exception to her tendency to drop things where she stood was in the kitchen. Her kitchen was always spotless.

Timing it perfectly, she removed the rolls from the oven, leaned in to inhale the delicious fragrance and transferred them to a wire cooling rack. The magic of baking never failed to charm her.

While she waited for the soufflé to rise, she pulled out her phone and took a photo of the rolls, focusing in on the domed, crusty surfaces. She posted it to her Instagram account and noted that the number of her followers had rocketed since the day before. She'd been experimenting, working out what time of day attracted most traffic.

Frankie loathed social media. Paige, the business brain behind their company, understood the importance of building a connection with customers but had no time, so it had fallen to Eva to manage all Urban Genie's accounts as well as her own. The interaction suited her social personality, and she loved seeing increased interest in the company as a result of her endeavors. Encouraged by Paige, she'd started her own YouTube channel demonstrating recipes and it was gaining popularity.

Maybe she'd film herself making bread rolls while she was here. The kitchen would be a fabulous backdrop.

Finally the meal was ready, but there was still no sign of Lucas.

She was about to risk life and limb by taking up another tray when she heard the sound of the door opening and footsteps on the stairs.

Lucas had pushed the sleeves of his black sweater back to his elbows, revealing forearms that were strong, the muscles contoured. He didn't look like a guy who spent his day glued to a computer. He looked like a sexy construction worker. His hair was rumpled, his jaw dusky with shadow and he seemed distracted.

Was his mind on his book or his dead wife?

He glanced around the kitchen. "What are you doing?"

"Cooking. You need to eat."

"I'm not hungry. I came down for whiskey."

She told herself his drinking habits were none of her business. "You should eat something. Good nutrition is important, and you *are* hungry."

"And how would you know that?"

"Because you're moody and irritable. I'm the same when I'm hungry." She hoped she sounded kind rather than judgmental. "Of course it could be that you're moody because your work isn't going well, but you never know. Eat. If nothing else, it will make you nicer to be around."

"What makes you think my work isn't going well?"

"I saw the computer screen—there were no words on it."

"The process of writing isn't all about putting words on the page. Sometimes it's about thinking, and staring out of the window." But there was an edge to his tone that told her she'd touched a nerve.

"I have a friend who's a writer and she tells me that when the words are flowing it feels like magic."

"And when they're not, is that a curse?"

She served the meal. "I don't know. I'm not a writer, but I'm guessing it could feel that way. Is that how it feels?"

"Maybe I'm moody and irritable because I have an overnight guest I wasn't expecting and didn't want."

"Maybe, but why don't you eat something and we'll find out. Being hungry isn't going to help your mood or your brainpower." Eva pushed the plate in front of him and saw his expression change.

"What is that?"

"It's a perfect soufflé. Try a mouthful."

"I've told you, I'm not—"

"Here's a fork." She handed it to him and dressed the salad leaves with organic olive oil and balsamic vinegar she'd bought on her trip to Dean & DeLuca.

"Who goes to the trouble of making a complicated soufflé for supper at home?"

"Who goes to the trouble of buying an oven as beautiful as that one and not using it?" She pushed the salad toward him. "It's like buying a Ferrari and keeping it in the garage."

In some ways he reminded her of a Ferrari. Sleek. Beautiful. *Out of her league.*

"The oven came with the apartment. I don't cook."

And she had a feeling that everything in the apartment was the best. "If you don't cook, what do you eat?"

"When I'm working? Not much. Sometimes I order takeout."

"That's shockingly unhealthy."

"Most of the time I'm too busy to care what I'm eating."

She watched as he slid his fork through the light, airy soufflé. *Try it*, she thought, *and discover what it's like to care about what you're eating.*

He took a mouthful and nodded. "It's good." He took another mouthful and paused. "No, I'm wrong about that."

She was offended. "You don't think it's good?"

He took a third mouthful and a fourth and then

lowered his fork down slowly. "First she drugs her victims—"

"Excuse me?"

He stared down at his plate. He didn't seem to have heard her. "She invites them to dinner. A romantic evening. Soft music. Wine. It's all going well. He thinks he's going to get lucky—"

"And then she breaks the bottle over his head?"

He glanced up and blinked. "She would never do anything so unsubtle."

"But I would," Eva said sweetly, "if you insult my cooking."

"When did I insult your cooking?"

"You said it wasn't good."

"It's not good. It's better than good." He slid the fork into the fluffy soufflé, examining it closely. "It's perfect. Like eating a cloud."

His compliment thawed the frosty atmosphere and Eva watched as he cleared his plate. "In that case I forgive you." Although she wouldn't have admitted it, she was relieved to see him eating. The vast, empty fridge had worried her. Not eating was a bad sign. She knew. She'd lost fifteen pounds after her grandmother had died. Getting through each hour had been hard and every day had felt like a month. Sympathy swelled inside her.

He stared at his plate. "If you were going to poison someone, how would you do it?"

Sympathy evaporated. "Keep being obnoxious and you might find out."

He put his fork down slowly. "Was I being obnoxious?"

"You were questioning whether my food was poisonous."

"Are you always this sensitive?"

"Is it sensitive to be hurt when someone criticizes your professional abilities? If someone asked you how you choose to bore your readers, you'd be similarly offended."

"I never bore my readers."

"And I never poison the people I cook for."

"My question was abstract, not personal. I was speaking hypothetically."

"Then your timing was bad. Abstract is when you don't have a plate of freshly cooked food in front of you."

His gaze locked on hers and she noticed that his eyes weren't black, but a velvety dark brown. A slow dangerous heat spread through her body until her limbs had the liquid consistency of warm honey.

He was the first to lower his gaze. "You're right. I was hungry." He helped himself to another roll, his voice level. "And, for the record, I do own a Ferrari I keep in the garage."

Her heart was pounding. What just happened? *What was that look?* "You own a Ferrari in New York City?"

"Hence the reason it stays in the garage for most of the winter. Apparently it doesn't like idling in traffic or the bitter cold." He glanced across at her plate. "You're not eating?"

"I want to make sure you don't die before I take a mouthful."

He laughed, and in that instant she understood exactly why he had to fight off women. That smile held an indecent amount of seductive charm. She hastily started eating to take her mind off the direction her thoughts were taking.

"So tell me," he said, breaking off a piece of roll, "what hell do you intend to inflict on my apartment?"

"Excuse me?"

"At least spare me pine needles."

"I have a Nordmann fir arriving any minute."

"Cancel the order."

"You can't have Christmas without a tree."

"I've managed it for the past three years."

"All the more reason to have an extra big one this year."

"There is no logic behind that statement."

"I don't tell you how to write your book. Don't tell me how to decorate your apartment."

"The difference is that readers are waiting for my book. I'm not waiting for you to decorate my apartment." The smile was gone. "In fact, the last thing I want is for you to decorate my apartment, so why would I let you go ahead and do it?"

"Because it will please your grandmother."

"How," he asked, "does me treading on a carpet of pine needles while surrounded by pointless decorations please my grandmother?"

"You need to allow her to show you she cares. You are going to let me do what she's asked and then you are going to tell her it was a great idea that made you feel a thousand times better."

"She'll know I'm lying."

"Then you'll have to work harder to be convincing."

"Or I could be honest and tell her I don't want the apartment decorated."

"That would hurt her feelings and you wouldn't want to do that. You're a kind person." She said it firmly and saw his eyebrows lift.

"Since I almost knocked you unconscious you've accused me of being obnoxious, moody and irritable. And now you think I'm kind."

"I didn't say you were kind to *me*, but I know you're kind to your grandmother. And the reason I know that is because you bought her a puppy." Eva played her trump card. "She was lonely and spending far too much time in her apartment, so you bought her a dog. And she adores that dog and she gets out to walk it every day. Well, almost every day. Sometimes her arthritis is bad and she has to call for help."

"And then she calls you."

"Yes. Or she puts in a request through the app and we arrange dog-walking. We use a fantastic company on the Upper East Side. Not far from here in fact. They're called The Bark Rangers."

"You know I was the one who bought her the dog. What else has she told you about me?"

"Not much." Eva was intentionally vague. "She only mentioned you once or twice."

"Let me guess. While you were sitting there sip-ping tea and eating cake, she told you about her widowed grandson and how her greatest wish is to see him settled again." He leaned forward, his gaze penetrating and intense. "She sent you. And you expect me to believe that this is about my apartment?"

"It is." It was a good job she had nothing to hide because she would have confessed everything under the steady burn of his gaze. "Newsflash, Mr. Blade. I'm not a complicated person. Men think women are a mystery, but I'm straightforward. What you see is what you get. I've never been much good at hiding things. But that doesn't make me naive."

"If you believe my grandmother sent you here to cook and decorate my apartment, then you are naive." He returned his gaze to his plate and finished his food. "Is that why you're preparing delicious meals? Because you think the way to a man's heart is through his stomach?"

"I'm a cook, not a cardiologist. I can't think of a single reason why I'd be interested in your heart. And given that your grandmother doesn't even know you're here, I don't see how someone with your supposed powers of deduction can believe this is some sort of blind date." Flustered because she'd been having thoughts she knew she shouldn't be having, Eva stood up and cleared the plates, crashing the crockery as she loaded the dishwasher. "I can assure you I'm not part of your grandmother's plan."

Far from it. She and Mitzy had talked about it several times and Eva had always said the same thing. That she didn't think Mitzy should be pushing women toward him. If he was going to meet someone, then he had to do it in his own time at his own pace. "You can relax, Mr. Blade. You're not my type. You're a cynical crime writer who believes everyone is hiding a secret. Have you ever watched the movie *While You Were Sleeping*?"

"No."

"That's what I thought. It's my favorite movie so, as I said—" she waved her hand, finishing "—you're not my type."

"Now I'm intrigued." He leaned back in his chair, watching her. "What is your type?"

She thought of the few desperately unsatisfactory dates she'd had over the past year. "I don't date much and I don't have a type, although I do have a general wish list."

"Go on."

It was a standing joke between her and her friends. "Broad shoulders, abs, sense of humor, ability to tolerate my ancient soft toy and in possession of enough stamina to give my condom a decent workout before it expires like the last one I carried in my purse." She grinned and then saw the incredulous expression on his face. "It's a joke. Kind of. Never mind. Too much information. Let's move on."

"I'm starting to understand why you don't date much. You're a hopeless romantic and you're waiting for Prince Charming?" The faint hint of humor needled her, even though she was used to being teased for her rose-tinted view on life.

"No, but even you have to agree Prince Charming is a more appealing character than Jack the Ripper."

"But less interesting. And I'm sure even Prince Charming had a hidden side."

"I don't want to think about it." She finished clearing the kitchen. "It's late and if it's all right with you, I'd like to go to sleep. Which is your bedroom?"

"Why would you need to know that?"

She could almost feel the barriers coming up between them. "How else am I going to be able to come into your room and seduce you in the night, Mr. Blade?"

Something glimmered in his eyes. "Pick either of the rooms on the left at the top of the stairs. And if you're spending the night here, you can't keep calling me Mr. Blade. We should introduce ourselves properly. I'm Lucas, cynical crime writer."

"I'm Eva. Hopeless romantic. Pleased to meet you."

A smile tilted the corners of his mouth and the smile was so irresistible, she smiled back.

Oh holy crap, she was in trouble.

CHAPTER FIVE

One person's dream is another person's nightmare. It's all a matter of perspective.

—Lucas

HE FELT STRONGER than he had in days. Maybe weeks.
The dark images that had paralyzed him had faded,
like clouds receding after a storm. He'd been drawn
downstairs by the mouthwatering smells, but it wasn't
only the food that had replenished his energy, it was
the conversation. There was something about Eva that
fed his creativity. Every exchange, every conversation, unlocked another piece of the puzzle.

He had his murderer, and now he had her motivation.

She'd started her life full of hope, believing in true
love and happy-ever-afters.

All that had been crushed when she'd met—

Michael?

Richard?

He frowned, trying to decide on a name for his
murderer's first victim. It was a small role, but cru-
cial to the character motivation. Gradually life had

chipped away at her relentless optimism, tarnishing her shiny vision of reality.

Her victims were the people who had disappointed her.

His mind wandered to Eva.

Most people are simply what they seem.

Did she really believe that? In his experience people were rarely as they seemed.

Take her, for example. Was she an innocent, or an opportunist who had taken advantage of his grandmother? Had she used her relationship with a vulnerable woman to extract information about him?

And what about the rest of her life?

He wondered what secrets she was hiding because if he knew one thing it was that *everyone* had secrets.

He sat down in front of his computer screen and the words started to flow.

He rarely based his characters on real people. Instead he preferred to use them as inspiration, taking traits and crafting his own fully formed individuals. But in his head, his main character was taking shape, and that shape was uncannily like Eva. He imagined how Eva might change if she met the wrong people, if life dealt her a different set of cards. Imagined the damage that life could do to someone like her.

She'd been eight years old when she'd discovered that not all endings were happy. At the time, she'd been standing over the body of her stepfather. She hadn't known there could be so much blood in one person.

The words tumbled past the block that had stopped

him working. This was what he'd been waiting for. This feeling that the words were unstoppable, the story pouring onto the page.

The raw burning panic eased, but still he knew he faced a herculean task if he was to get the book written by Christmas.

THE TREE HAD arrived after dinner, considerably larger than expected, and she and Albert had set it up close to the window in the living room. Instantly the place looked lived-in and festive.

Eva hoped Lucas wasn't going to throw it down the elevator shaft.

Tiredness descended on her. It had been a long day. She'd get up early and decorate the tree, but right now she was going to take a shower, write her blog and update the Urban Genie social media accounts.

She chose the larger of the two spare rooms, and took a moment to admire the view. No matter where you were standing, this apartment was all about the view. It rendered paintings, or any other type of wall hanging, obsolete, because nothing could compete with the magical cityscape that lay beyond the expanse of glass.

She'd expected the bedrooms to have the same impersonal feel as the rest of his apartment, but that wasn't the case.

Two large lamps drenched the room in muted golden light and a soft, velvety throw flowed over the oversize bed and pooled on the hardwood floor. It invited the occupier to snuggle down and admire the winter white of New York City while cocooned in comfort.

Eva sank onto the edge of the bed.

She'd told herself that she was staying because it was her job and because she didn't want to leave Lucas alone, but she knew she wasn't being entirely honest. She was at least partly staying because *she* didn't want to be alone. What did it say about her that she'd rather spend the night in a stranger's apartment than back home in her own?

It said that she needed to do something about her life. She needed to make an effort to get out and meet people.

She sighed and sprawled on the bed, drawn to the comfort of the soft, velvety cover. It was a dark moss green, the same color as the forest floor.

When she and her grandmother had first moved to New York they'd lived in an apartment with no outdoor space and every weekend they'd worked side by side in the tiny kitchen and made a picnic. They'd packed it up and taken it to Central Park, always to the same spot. Not Sheep Meadow or the Great Lawn, but to the Great Hill in the northern part of the park where they'd eat at one of the picnic tables, surrounded by majestic elms. They'd watched people playing lawn games, dodged Frisbees and occasionally listened to jazz concerts while the sun faded.

Eva pulled the throw closer, snuggling deep into its comforting folds.

She felt as if she'd lost her anchor. Her security.

Even having wonderful friends didn't stop her feeling empty inside and horribly alone.

Sliding off the bed, she unpacked her clothes from her bag, took a shower in the luxurious en suite bathroom and changed into pajamas. They were a soft peach silk, an extravagant treat bought a few months before to celebrate the first six months of Urban Genie. She'd been with Paige, on one of their trips to Bloomingdale's. Paige had bought two dresses and a smart jacket, all suitable for business meetings. Eva had chosen pajamas.

It hadn't mattered that no one was going to see them except her; wearing them made her feel good.

She updated her blog, answered messages on Facebook and Twitter and then tried to sleep.

It was just over three weeks until Christmas, and this would be her second Christmas without her grandmother.

In the last few years of her life her grandmother had lived in an assisted living community in Brooklyn, not far from the brownstone Eva shared with her friends. Eva had visited regularly, sometimes cooking with her grandmother as they'd done when she was young.

If her grandmother had still been alive they would have been baking Christmas treats for the other residents and the staff about now, including her grandmother's favorite nurse Annie Cooper.

Every year Eva had helped decorate her grandmother's small apartment, and also the communal areas including the light-filled Garden Room that had views over the water. She'd gotten to know the staff well, and many of the other residents. There was Betty, whose only daughter lived in California. Betty had been a dancer, and she still liked to dance as long as her arthritis allowed. And then there was Tom who had grown up in Maine, not far from her grandmother, and spent his time painting watercolors, several of which had hung in her grandmother's living room.

Every Christmas, Eva had joined them for their Christmas party. It was something her grandmother used to talk about for months.

Restless, Eva glanced at her phone. It was three in the morning. The loneliest time. It was a time she'd seen almost every day since her grandmother had died. She hated the nights, when her mind raced wildly down paths that were banned during daylight hours.

Giving up on sleep, she wandered out of her bedroom, pausing as darkness engulfed her.

Retrieving her phone from the bedroom, she used the flashlight and made her way along the darkened corridor that led to the staircase.

Noticing that Lucas's office door was open a crack, she paused.

"You shouldn't creep around," a deep voice said, "or I might think you're a housebreaker and use you as an excuse to practice my jujitsu again."

Eva jumped. "Are you trying to give me a heart attack?"

"I was giving you a warning that I was here."

"Putting a light on might have been a better option. Why are you sitting in the dark?"

"Why aren't you asleep?" He flicked on a lamp and the room was illuminated by a soft light.

He was sprawled on the sofa. There was a bottle of whiskey next to him and his laptop was open on the table. His gaze moved over her slowly, and she wished she'd grabbed a robe. Knowing the way his mind worked, he'd probably think her silk pajamas were part of a master plan cooked up by her and his grandmother.

"You're not asleep, either." She pushed the door open. "How's your book going?"

"Better, thanks to you."

"I didn't do anything except feed you."

"Your words—helped. I made a start with the book."

She was ridiculously pleased. "Has this happened to you before?"

"If you're asking me if strange women often break into my apartment to cook and decorate, then the answer is no." He caught her eye and sighed. "You're talking about writer's block? Only at this time of year."

"But you wrote a book last year and the year before so you must have found a way to deal with it."

He leaned forward and sloshed more whiskey into the glass. "The way I deal with it is to make sure I've finished the book before now."

"But this year you didn't."

"I was touring. Six European countries and twelve US states." He set the bottle down. "I ran out of time."

"And now the book is due and you're feeling the pressure, which makes things worse. It's like trying to get to the top of Everest in a day when you're still at base camp."

"That's uncannily accurate." He downed the whiskey in one mouthful. "And now you can go and sell that story to the press. Call it a Christmas bonus."

"Oh *please*, do I look like someone who sells stories to the press?" She rolled her eyes. "Sorry— I keep forgetting you think everyone has a hidden side. Why do you write?"

"Excuse me?"

"Why do you write?"

"I have a contract, a deadline, readers—you need me to go on?"

"But before that—you didn't always have all that. What made you start writing in the first place?"

"I can't even remember back that far."

Without waiting for an invitation, Eva sat down on the sofa next to him and curled her legs under her. "My grandmother taught me to cook, and it was something we shared. Something we loved to do together. A hobby. I never for one moment thought that one day I'd earn a living cooking. It was pleasure, that was all."

He lowered the glass slowly. "What are you saying?"

"I know the world is waiting for your next book, but presumably it hasn't always been that way. There must have been a time before you were published

when you wrote for yourself, because it was something you loved to do."

"There was."

"How old were you?"

"When I wrote my first story? Eight. It all seemed
a hell of a lot easier then." He stared into his glass
and put it down on the table. "Ignore me. Go back
to bed, Eva."

"And leave you with your friend Mr. Whiskey Bottle? No. If you want company, you can talk to me."
Her gaze met his. His eyes were velvet dark and so
sinfully sexy they might as well have been designed
to tempt a woman to abandon self-control and live
in the moment. There was no way the human race
would ever die out while there were men like him
on the planet.

The flames flickered in the hearth, but she knew
the fire wasn't responsible for the sudden flash of
heat that washed over her skin. She saw the same
heat flare in his eyes and felt the sharp savage burn
of sexual tension.

His gaze slid to her mouth and for a wild, crazy
moment she thought he was going to kiss her.

She stopped breathing, paralyzed by the moment,
and then Lucas looked away, dragging his attention
back to the whiskey bottle.

"Hemingway said, 'A man does not exist until he
is drunk.'"

Released from that gaze, Eva let out her breath,
feeling as if she'd just come out of hypnosis. What
had just happened? Had she imagined it? Was she so

desperate she couldn't look at a man without think-ing about sex?

She reached for a spare glass and helped herself to a slosh of whiskey. It burned her throat and cleared her head.

"And F. Scott Fitzgerald said, 'First you take a drink, then the drink takes a drink, then the drink takes you.'" She put the glass down and intercepted his curious look. "My grandmother was an associ-ate professor of English before she took early retire-ment. Instead of drinking that whiskey, I could make you one of my famous hot chocolates. I guarantee you won't ever have tasted anything better. It might help you sleep."

"I don't have time to sleep. I need to write this damn book."

"I'm worried about you."

"Why? You don't know me." His tone held a warn-ing, but she ignored it.

"I know you're hiding out here. And I know I'm the only one who knows. That makes you my respon-sibility. I want to help."

"You're not responsible for my emotions or my work."

"If you don't finish your book, my friend Frankie will never stop complaining. I have a vested inter-ested in seeing you finish. So, you wrote your first story when you were eight, but when did you sell your book?"

"I was twenty-one. When I got the call from my

agent—well, let's just say I thought it was all plain sailing from there."

"But it wasn't." She chose her words carefully. "I think when we lose someone close to us, it can be very hard to find the concentration necessary to complete tasks that used to be simple. And when the holidays come around, everything feels more acute."

"Is this the part where you tell me you know how I feel, or that time heals all?"

"I wasn't going to say either of those things." She hesitated. "Maybe you're trying too hard. You've been injured, so you should take it carefully and slowly. Be kind to yourself. Writing is natural for you. Maybe you should just focus on writing a few words at a time rather than thinking of the whole book. Like making a grilled cheese sandwich rather than a gourmet meal." Seeing nothing in his expression that encouraged her to continue, her voice trailed off. "I'm shutting up now. Not another word on the subject from me. My mouth is zipped."

He gave a faint smile. "I haven't known you long, but I have a feeling that's hard for you."

"It is. I feel as if I might physically burst if I don't talk." She stared at his lips, wondering how they'd feel against hers. She knew instinctively that he'd be an expert kisser, and this time she was the one who swayed toward him.

The darkness created a false intimacy, cloaking common sense and facts that would be clear in the light of day.

"Go to bed, Eva. It's late." His voice was soft, but

it was enough to rouse her from her sensual trance and the fantasies she definitely shouldn't have been having.

"That's man-speak for 'I don't want to talk about it.'" She sat for a moment, feeling as if there was something else she should say. Something had almost happened here tonight. Were they going to talk about it or pretend it had never happened?

"Good night." There was a finality to his tone and she stood up.

It seemed they were going to pretend it had never happened. And that was probably best.

"Good night, Lucas. Get some sleep."

CHAPTER SIX

Be the sunshine, not the rain.

—Eva

THE FULL FORCE of the storm hit just after dawn. It swirled past the windows, dumping several more feet of snow on the New York streets.

Lucas didn't notice. He'd worked most of the night, snatching a couple of hours' sleep on the sofa when his brain was too tired to continue.

Despite the brevity of the nap, he'd woken refreshed and energized and ready to continue, and had carried on writing until he'd heard the sounds of Eva singing.

Not loudly, but enough to disturb his concentration.

He moved to the top of the stairs. From here he had a perfect view of the whole of the downstairs, including the kitchen.

When he'd moved, he'd brought nothing from his old life but his books. This place held no memories, nothing to remind him of the past. It was impersonal and it suited him that way.

Until now, when he barely recognized his own apartment.

A huge Christmas tree dominated the space by the window and several magazines lay open and abandoned on the sofa, alongside a sweater in a bright shade of green. A half-drunk mug of tea was growing cold on the low table and a pair of shoes lay strewed on the floor where they'd been kicked off.

The place looked...*lived-in.*

But the biggest change was Eva. She filled the place with her summery scent and with her voice. He could see the cascade of honey hair and the roll and bump of her hips as she danced to the music. There was no doubt that she knew how to move, and oh God how she did move. As if she was seducing the hell out of his kitchen as she confessed to Santa in a surprisingly tuneful voice that she'd been an awfully good girl.

She was chopping, dicing, crushing, all while putting on a one-woman show worthy of Broadway.

Turned out she could sing and dance as well as she could cook.

Lucas felt sweat prick the back of his neck.

If it was left up to him, she wouldn't be a good girl for long. He'd take her from good to bad faster than it took for Santa to drop a parcel down the chimney. Last night he'd come so close to kissing her, but fortunately for both of them something had stopped him.

He stared at those hips, feeling like a voyeur.

One word from him and she'd stop dancing. She'd stop swinging those hips like a pole dancer and singing in that throaty voice.

He opened his mouth but no sound emerged.

A man could be pretty much blinded by those hips, imagining what all that subtle movement could do. It was performing art. He remembered her in those peach silk pajamas, the peep of curves and the hint of cream. The pajamas had been replaced by the shortest skirt he'd ever seen, although to be fair she wore it with black tights that made it mouthwatering but perfectly decent. Her black sweater hugged her waist and hips, the color a dramatic contrast to the gold of her hair.

She turned to pick up a knife and saw him.

She froze, the knife in her hand, and for a moment he wondered if he'd picked the wrong murder weapon.

Maybe she didn't poison her victims. Maybe, as a skilled chef, she filleted them expertly.

Jill the Ripper.

He would have turned back to his study and carried on writing, but she was smiling at him and he decided that he could spare some time to talk to her, particularly as talking to her seemed to spark ideas in his head.

"Er—good morning." She put the knife down and tugged the headphones away from her ears. A smile dimpled at the corner of her mouth. "Did my singing disturb you?"

"No." *She* disturbed him. He almost wished she hadn't noticed him. Then she would have kept swinging those hips for a little longer and he could have stayed suspended in a world driven by nothing but elemental instincts. He gestured to the living area. "Were we burgled?"

"I made myself at home. I hope you don't mind. I'll clear it up later."

"I owe you an apology."

"What for?"

"Last night. I was rude."

"You have nothing to apologize for. This is your home and you weren't expecting visitors."

"Are you always this understanding?"

"Would you rather I was upset?"

It would have been the natural response. Years of experience and close study enabled him to predict with almost faultless accuracy how a person would react in any given situation. Eva seemed to defy all his expectations.

"Does anything upset you?"

"Plenty of things. Animal cruelty, cabdrivers who lean on their horns, men who talk to my chest and call me 'honey' when we've never been introduced, people who cough without covering their mouth—" She paused. "Do you want me to go on?"

"Good to know you're human. By the way, I owe you a thank-you. I took your advice and made a grilled cheese sandwich. Thanks to you, I've written twenty thousand words."

"In one night? That's not a grilled cheese sandwich, that's a nine-course tasting menu." She looked impressed. "How did you do it?"

"One grilled cheese sandwich led to another."

"As a lover of grilled cheese sandwiches, I can understand that. They've always been my downfall." She waved a hand toward the counter. "Sit down. In case it was my food that triggered your burst of creativity, I'll fix breakfast."

He knew the source of his motivation had nothing to do with food, and everything to do with her. The character she'd inspired was going to be one of the most complex and interesting that he'd ever written. "I don't eat breakfast."

"You don't seem to eat much at all. But I'm here to change all that." She started humming again and he decided it was a reflex.

"Do you know anything that isn't Santa-themed?"

"Excuse me?"

"I'm wondering if we could change the playlist. I'm not a lover of festive music."

She slid a tray of tomatoes into the oven. "Always happy to take requests from the audience. I know you love Mozart, so how about a little aria from *The Marriage of Figaro*?"

"What makes you think I love Mozart?"

"Aha!" She waggled the spoon in his direction, triumphant. "You're not the only one capable of spotting clues. You could put me in your next book. I'd make a cute FBI agent. Perhaps everyone underestimates me because of my blond hair and my impressive rack and then boom, I let them have it."

He decided this wasn't a good moment to tell her that aspects of her were certainly going to be in his next book, but she wasn't going to find herself on the right side of the law.

"Does that happen often?"

"People underestimating me? All the time."

"That must be frustrating."

"Mostly they're the ones who are frustrated." She flashed him a wicked smile. "Don't worry about me. I can handle myself."

"With that deadly move you keep warning me about?"

"That's the one. When you're least expecting it I'll take you by surprise and wham, you're history."

He'd come out of his study with the intention of asking her to keep her noise down. He'd had every intention of returning to work, but now he felt in no hurry to do so. Instead he joined her in the kitchen. Eva's energy and enthusiasm were infectious, filling every dark corner of his soulless apartment. And talking to her sparked ideas. His character was becoming clearer and clearer in his head, layer upon layer.

"So what powers of deduction did you use to discover my taste in music?"

"You have CDs next to your bookshelf. I saw a whole shelf of Mozart." She lowered the spoon. "You don't just stream the music like most people?"

"The CDs belonged to my father. He played principle cello for the Metropolitan Opera Orchestra."

"Lucky you. So I guess you didn't have to scramble for tickets like the rest of us mortals."

"You like opera?"

"Love it." She sang a few notes from *The Marriage of Figaro*, in Italian and pitch-perfect.

"Don't tell me—your grandfather was a music professor."

"In fact my grandfather was a lobster fisherman,

but he happened to love music. And he loved my grandmother. I grew up with singing and Shakespeare. If my singing is disturbing you, I'll try to remember not to do it, but you might have to keep reminding me."

"It's not disturbing me." The singing was nowhere near as disturbing as the bump and grind of her hips as she'd danced.

"Paige, who used to share the apartment with me, wore noise-reducing headphones most of the time. She needs silence to concentrate."

"Is that why she's now your ex-roommate?"

"No. She's my ex-roommate because she fell in love."

"Ah. True Love's Kiss?"

"I think it was closer to True Love's Steaming Hot Sex, but same principle."

"So now you live alone?"

"Yes." Her expression changed and then she tugged open the door of the refrigerator and looked inside, so he could no longer see her face. "Although not exactly alone, because my other friend lives upstairs with Paige's brother, Matt—he owns the whole brownstone—and downstairs is Roxy and her little girl, Mia, who is adorable. Roxy works for Matt and she found herself homeless back in the summer so he gave her a place to stay. Paige seems to spend almost as much time at our place as she does with Jake, so it's not exactly quiet. And then there's Claws." She talked without pausing for breath, painting a picture of her life. He'd expected a one-word answer, but by the time she stopped he knew more about her than he did about people he'd known for a decade. It took months of close questioning to get that quantity of information from most people.

"So Claws is your friend's psychotic cat?"

"Yes. You could put her in one of your books. She'd be a great murder weapon. She has a sweet face and a psychotic personality, but I don't blame her because she had a horrible life before Matt rescued her." She selected various items from the refrigerator and in the moment before she closed the door he caught a glimpse of color layered upon color.

"Are you planning on entertaining? Because if that's all intended for me I think you might have over-estimated my appetite."

"It's going in the freezer. The idea was that you could have access to the perfect meal whenever you need one. I discussed the menu with your grand-mother."

"You were discussing menus designed to help my libido?"

Her eyebrows lifted. "Food allergies," she said slowly. "Some people are allergic to peanuts, or wheat or shellfish. I needed to know if you were gluten-free or vegetarian. If you're likely to go into anaphylac-tic shock if I feed you nuts, that's something I need to know. Jabbing adrenaline into a half-dead client isn't generally one of the complimentary extras we like to offer at Urban Genie. Prevention is better than cure and all that. Dead people are bad for business."

She gave a half smile. "Except for in *your* business, of course. Your business is all about dead people."

"So you weren't discussing how to seduce me with my grandmother?"

"I love your grandmother, but if I want to seduce a guy I don't generally take advice from someone in their eighties." She studied him for a moment. "Does your libido need help?"

Not since he'd met her. "She would go to pretty much any lengths to see me married again," he said, skirting around the question.

"That may be, but as far as I'm concerned you're an adult, presumably capable of making your own choices. If you choose to stay in sexile, that's really none of my business."

"Sexile?"

"Sex exile. Sexile. I'm there through no obvious fault of my own, unless you count being picky as a fault." She frowned slightly. "But you're there on purpose. You've chosen to live in sexile."

He watched as she rinsed bell peppers. "What did my grandmother tell you about me?"

"I know you hate cucumber, love spicy food and prefer your steak rare. It's important that I know your preferences."

Right now his preference would be to have her naked and on top.

Her skin was smooth and creamy, like silk, he thought, and then dismissed the comparison as cli-chéd. He was a writer. He should be able to come up with something better than that. Her cheeks were flushed but he had a feeling that was the heat of the oven rather than makeup. He would have sworn she wasn't wearing makeup, but then recalled a conversation with Sallyanne where she'd mocked him for telling her how much he liked her without makeup. She'd told him in a tone loaded with amusement, that achieving the "no makeup" look had taken her forty-five minutes.

He wondered how long it had taken Eva to make herself look that wholesome and innocent.

"Show me the menus." He held out his hand and she handed over the pages she'd been working from. He scanned them quickly. "Chicken pot pie? I haven't eaten that since I was twelve."

"And when you taste mine, you'll be wondering why. It's the ultimate comfort food."

"It reminds me of school."

"Mine won't remind you of school. Mine will give your taste buds an orgasm."

"You seem fixated on orgasms."

"That's what happens when you don't get something." She took the menus from him. "It's the reasons diets don't work. The more you deny yourself, the more you crave the very thing you're cutting out. And before you say anything, of course I know I can give myself an orgasm, but there are some tasks I prefer to delegate."

"So you're on a sex diet?"

"It feels that way. Not self-imposed, I might add. I just haven't met any decent guys lately, but all that is going to change."

"It is?"

"Definitely." She diced the peppers. "It's Christmas. I'm going to get out and meet people. Party, party, party."

"Where are these parties?"

"My friends have invited me along to a few."

"You don't sound enthusiastic."

She put the knife down. "Honestly? It feels a little... awkward. Like online dating. I don't really want to be fixed up. It's like social media. You only get to see someone's best side."

"So you admit that people aren't always as they seem."

"You make it sound sinister, like a great big cover-up, but on social media it's just people trying to present the best of who they are."

"And you then ask yourself what the worst part is."

"Everyone has flaws," she said mildly. "It wouldn't be realistic to expect a person to be perfect, would it?"

"What are your flaws?" It would be like one of those interview questions, he thought, where the candidate was asked to name a weakness and they went with the classic "I work too hard" or "I care too much." No one voluntarily revealed their real flaws to strangers.

"I'm horribly untidy, apart from in the kitchen. I drop things where I stand and then I lose things and make an even bigger mess trying to find them. I'm truly terrible in the mornings and I'm generally a bit cowardly," she admitted. "I'm not good with scary stuff—blood, gore, menacing threats, things that go bump in the night."

He absorbed that, filing away the details. "I would have said your flaw was being too trusting."

"I don't see that as a flaw." She rinsed the knife. "It's hard to get close to people and have fulfilling friendships if you always suspect people are hiding things from you. That's probably your biggest flaw, isn't it? Not trusting enough."

"I would have said that's one of my good qualities. So when you tried online dating, what did you write on your dating profile?"

"I didn't write desperate, trusting blonde seeks wild sex, if that's what you're asking." She opened the oven and gave the tray of tomatoes a little shake. "In the end online dating didn't work for me. I need to be able to see someone in person to know if they're okay. I have good instincts. And although it's a perfectly valid way to meet people, especially in today's busy world, I would prefer to meet someone organically."

"You want an organic orgasm?"

She laughed. "That's the goal. And everyone needs a goal, don't you think? It's fine. I'm not going to meet anyone if I hide away inside my apartment, so I'm determined to get out. That's the first step. I want to go on a few dates."

"So you don't want to go straight for the orgasm and cut out the in-between stage?"

"No." She closed the oven. "I can't go to bed with someone I don't know. I've never had a one-night stand. For me, sex is tied up with caring about some-one."

"You don't hold much back, do you?"

"No. I'm not what you might call a mystery. I'm pretty much an open book—Jake says I'm an audio book, because everything I'm thinking comes out of my mouth."

The description made him smile. "Who is Jake?"

"Paige's fiancé. And now that's enough questions about me. What's your favorite food of all time?"

"I don't have one."

"Everyone has a favorite food. Either something that is delicious, or something that's associated with a wonderful happy memory. What were your favor-ites when you were a child? Something that takes you right back there and brings back all the warm feelings."

He thought back to family gatherings and his trav-els through Europe. "I enjoy good cheese. Particularly with the right wine. It was one of the benefits of my French book tour."

"Is that where you bought all that wine?"

"Some of it. Some of it I've been collecting for a while."

"Do you actually drink any it?"

"Of course, although some bottles are valuable. I'm saving them for a special occasion."

"If I had good wine, I'd drink it. But then I guess you'd say I'm more of a 'live for the moment' kind of girl." She pushed her hair out of her eyes and he tried not to think about which moment he'd like to live in with her right now.

"The soufflé you made last night was good."

"I'm glad you enjoyed it." She picked up her pen and scribbled on the pages in front of her. "I'm trying to decide what to make tonight. Any requests?"

"You choose. Which cookbooks do you use? Or do you rely on the internet?"

"Neither. I use my grandmother's recipes, or I make them up." She must have seen something in his face because she smiled. "Relax. I'm not making anything for you I haven't made a hundred times already. You're not a guinea pig and I'm not going to poison you. Have you ever written that in one of your books? A killer who poisoned his victims?"

He wondered why she thought the killer had to be a man.

"No, but it's something I'm considering."

"How do you decide on the crime?"

"It comes from the personality and motivation of the killer. Jack the Ripper was good with knives, which was what led people to speculate that he might have been a surgeon."

She returned to her cooking. "No wonder you have trouble sleeping at night. You spend your entire working day thinking about horrible things."

"I find them more interesting than horrible." He watched, transfixed, as she sliced some garlic, drizzled oil and added a pinch of salt. She was astonishingly skilled with a blade. "Who taught you to use a knife?"

"Not Jack the Ripper." She threw him an amused look. "My grandmother, and then I worked in a few kitchens straight out of college. It's a skill you develop pretty fast unless you want to lose a finger." She scattered the ingredients over a baking tray and slid it into the oven alongside the other tray. Strands of hair wafted down over her face and she pursed her lips into a round O and blew them away gently as if she was blowing out candles on a birthday cake.

"What are you making?"

"I'm roasting tomatoes and peppers, which I'll then turn into soup. When you're busy, you can take a portion out of the freezer, add a chunk of crusty bread and have something nutritious in less time than it takes you to open a whiskey bottle." She gave him a pointed look that he chose to ignore.

He decided that the creative process behind cooking was not so different from his writing. She started with an idea, added a bit of this and that, adjusted it according to instinct and then served up something intended ultimately to please.

"Now, for breakfast would you like my special eggs Benedict or buttermilk pancakes?"

He was about to tell her once again that he didn't eat breakfast but the sound of pancakes was too good to turn down. They took him right back to his childhood and family holidays spent in Vermont.

"Do the pancakes come with a side of bacon?"

"They could, if that's what you'd like."

"It is." It was the first time anyone had used the kitchen, and she'd used every available inch. The counters were piled high with glossy fruits and vegetables. It looked haphazard, but he had a feeling it wasn't. "Do you always sing when you cook?"

"Singing is good for the mood. So is walking, but it doesn't look as if the weather is going to let me do that anytime soon." She put bacon in the frying pan and made pancake batter without weighing anything or consulting a recipe. "I might go for a stroll later if it eases."

The relaxed atmosphere vanished. "You're not leaving the apartment in this storm. They've canceled bus services, announced a ban on driving and shut down the subways. The bridges and tunnels are shut and there are no flights leaving from any airport."

"I don't want to fly, drive or use the bus. Just walk."

"Have you even looked through the window today?" He stood up, found the remote control and flicked on the TV that was concealed in the living room.

The news channels were dominated by the blizzard as the news anchor warned everyone, in serious tones, to stay indoors. "The storm has flooded low-lying beaches, brought down trees and power lines leaving thousands without electricity…"

"Oh, those poor people." There was distress in her voice and Lucas flicked off the TV.

"Are you convinced?"

"Yes." She returned to her cooking. She whisked the batter and poured it into the hot pan, waiting while the surface bubbled.

After a few moments she flipped the pancake, timing it perfectly.

Finally she slid it onto a plate, added the bacon and handed it to him along with a bottle of maple syrup. The color reminded him of whiskey.

The pancakes were soft, golden and delicious, the sweet drizzle of warm maple syrup a contrast to the crispy perfection of the bacon.

He took a mouthful. "You asked me about my favorite food. This is my favorite food."

"You said you didn't have a favorite food."

"Now I do." He cleared his plate, wondering why he was suddenly so hungry when for so long he hadn't cared what he ate. "So you seem to spend plenty of time with my grandmother. Why not spend that time with your own?"

For the first time since he'd hauled her off the floor of his apartment, his words were met with silence.

"Eva? Why not just spend more time with your own grandmother?"

"Because she's dead." Her voice thickened and without warning tears welled up in her eyes and spilled down her cheeks.

CHAPTER SEVEN

In times of crisis, keep your lipstick red and
your mascara waterproof.

—Paige

"I'M SORRY. IGNORE me." Eva grabbed a napkin and
dabbed her eyes but it was as if she'd developed a
leak, as if her emotions had swollen and grown, pressing against the outer layer of her self-control until
gradually it had cracked, allowing her feelings to escape.

Through the scalding blur of tears she was vaguely
aware of Lucas watching her.

She expected him to make his excuses and escape
faster than a gazelle trying to outrun a lion, but he
didn't move.

"Eva—"

"It's perfectly fine." She blew her nose hard. "This
happens sometimes. I think I'm doing great and then
it hits me from nowhere like a horrible gust of wind,
and it blows me off my feet. I'll bounce back. Don't
look so alarmed. Ignore me."

"You want me to ignore the fact you're upset?
What sort of person do you think I am?"

"You're a horror writer. And a woman in tears is probably your own personal idea of horror." She took a ragged breath and got herself under control. "I'll be fine."

"But you're not 'fine,' are you? Talk to me."

"No."

"Because you don't know me? Sometimes it's easier to talk to a stranger."

"It isn't that. I don't want to be the dark cloud in anyone's day. It's better to be the sunshine than the rain."

"What?" Dark brows came together in a frown. "Who the hell told you that?"

"Grams." Tears spilled over again and he sighed and spread his hands in a gesture of apology.

"Sorry. I didn't mean to hurt you but, Eva, everyone gets upset sometimes. You shouldn't feel you have to hide it."

"You do. Isn't that why you haven't told anyone you're here?" She scrubbed her hand over her face and he gave a faint smile.

"Good point. Since you're now hiding here with me, why don't we agree that we don't have to hide how we feel, for the moment at least?"

"Sounds like a plan. Thank you. And now you should go and write. You have a deadline." His kindness cut the last threads of her control and she turned her back on him to hide the spill of tears. She expected to hear his footsteps on the stairs as he retreated to a place of safety, but instead she felt his hand close over her shoulder.

"When did she die?"

She was torn between desperately wishing he'd leave her alone and wanting to talk about how she felt. "Last year. In the fall, when the leaves were changing color. I kept wondering how everything around me could seem so vibrant when she was gone. And I feel guilty being sad because she was ninety-three. And she didn't linger or anything. That was great for her but hard for me because it was a shock." She still remembered the phone call. She'd dropped the mug she'd been holding, spilling scalding coffee all over the floor and her bare legs. "She'd be furious if she could see me now—" She blew her nose again. "She'd remind me that she'd had a great life, was very loved and had all her mental faculties right up until the end. She always focused on what was right in her life, not what was wrong, and she'd want me to do the same. But that doesn't stop me missing her. And now you're standing there thinking 'what am I supposed to do with this sobbing woman,' but honestly you don't have to do anything. Just go about your business. I'll be fine. I'll just be extra nice to myself for a little bit until I feel better."

But he didn't leave. What he did was turn her around and pull her into his arms.

It was so surprising that for a moment she didn't move. Then the unexpected sympathy tipped her over the edge and Eva dissolved into great choking sobs. She felt the strength of his hand on her head as he stroked her hair gently, while his free arm held her close.

He held her while she cried herself out, murmuring soft indistinct words of comfort. She breathed in male warmth and felt the reassuring weight of his arm supporting her and she closed her eyes, trying to remember the last time she'd been held like this. It shouldn't feel this good. He was a stranger, but there was something about the strong embrace that filled the emptiness inside her.

Finally, when she was drained of emotion, he eased her away from him so that he could see her face.

"What does 'being extra nice to yourself' involve?" The kindness in his voice connected straight to her insides.

"Oh, you know—" She sniffed. "Not telling myself I'm fat, or beating myself up for not exercising as much as I should, or for eating that extra square of chocolate."

"You do that?"

"Doesn't everyone?" She rubbed at the damp patch she'd made on his shirt, embarrassed but at the same time grateful. "I feel better. Thank you. I never would have thought you'd be such a brilliant hugger. You'd better let me go or I'll be crying all the time just to get you to hug me. Go and work."

"Tell me you don't seriously think you're fat."

"Only on a bad day, but that's because I love food and if I'm not careful I do become a little extra curvy."

"Extra curvy?" There was a seam of laughter in his voice. "Is that like extra strong coffee? In other words more of the part that's already good?"

"Now I know why you're a writer. You know exactly which words to use." She forced herself to step back. "Thanks for making me feel better."

"I know what it's like to lose someone you love." The laughter was gone from his voice. "You think you're doing fine, you think you have it all under control, and then suddenly it slams into you. It's like sailing on a smooth ocean and suddenly a giant wave hits from nowhere and almost swamps your boat."

No one had ever described the way she was feeling so perfectly.

"That's how you feel?"

"Yes." He lifted his hand and stroked her cheek gently. "It's supposed to get easier, so hang in there." His gaze held hers and there was a new intimacy, and a strange, unexpected heat that stole through her against her will.

Arousal.

He was comforting her, and she was aroused. She would have been embarrassed, except she saw her own feelings mirrored in the depths of his eyes.

"You should go and write."

"Yes." His voice was roughened at the edges and he let his hand drop and stepped back. "And you should cook."

They were both stiff and formal, both denying the moment.

Eva went back to the kitchen, trying to forget how it had felt to be held by him.

She cooked all day, stirred, whisked, simmered and tasted while on the other side of the huge glass windows the storm blew itself to a frenzy. New York was eclipsed by swirling white, the streets and the buildings blurred by snow. Restaurants, bars and even Broadway had closed.

Eva felt a pang of concern for the emergency services and people who still had to be out in that terrible storm. She hoped no one was injured.

Occasionally she glanced up the stairs, but the door to the office remained closed. Lucas, she knew, was dealing with his own injury.

At lunchtime she took up a tray, but heard the soft thud of computer keys through the door and decided writing was more important than food. She retreated downstairs with the tray and went back to her cooking.

Paige called twice, the first time to ask questions about the engagement party they were planning for a client based in Manhattan, and the second to check Eva's availability for New Year's Eve.

"I'm available." Eva turned the heat down under the pan she was using and reduced the sauce to a simmer. "I'm completely, totally available."

"Good, because I want you to meet someone."

"I want to meet someone, too." She tried not to think about how it had felt to be held by Lucas. He'd been comforting her, that was all.

"How are things going there? When will you be home?"

Eva glanced out of the window. "I'd planned on staying as short a time as possible, but the storm has changed that. Can I let you know? I've sent over some ideas for the proposal, and I'm working on the Addison-Pope engagement dinner."

She ended the call and with everything in the kitchen under control, she turned her attention to decorating the tree, trying not to think of the Christmas two years before when she had done the same thing with her grandmother.

It was early evening and Eva was on her way back to her room to shower and change when the door to Lucas's office opened.

He stared at her, unfocused, as if he was in another world.

Maybe she should have knocked on his door earlier. It wasn't healthy to work so long without a break, was it?

"How did it go? Did you make a grilled cheese sandwich?"

"I made another banquet." His voice was hoarse and then he smiled. "You're a genius."

"Me? I'm just a cook who talks too much." Her heart bumped against her chest. How could she ever have thought he wasn't her type? It had been easier to dismiss him when she'd thought he was just an insanely handsome face, but now she knew he was kind, too. And he wasn't one of those men who were uncomfortable with emotions.

"Your talking is the reason I'm writing."

Her tummy did a little flip. "That's good to know, and thank you for not yelling at me about the tree. It is a little bigger than I thought it would be. I've taken photos and sent them to your grandmother. I hope you don't mind. I didn't mention you, but I wanted her to know I'm doing my job."

"Right now you could give me a partridge in a pear tree and I wouldn't give a damn." He raked his fingers through his dark hair and Eva wondered how doing that made him even more handsome. If she ran her fingers through her hair she looked as if she'd made contact with an electric fence.

"Why is everyone so obsessed with poultry this week? I don't think they're the best indoor pets." Her nerves were strung taut and she knew it was because of that hug. She needed to pull herself together. "If you give me half an hour, I'll make us dinner. Unless you want to work more?"

"I need a break. I'll work later. I'm going to take a shower, too, and then I'll choose us a bottle of wine. We should celebrate."

Celebrate.

It sounded intimate. Personal.

She had to remind herself that this wasn't a date, it was her job.

Lucas stood under the scalding spray of the shower, feeling better than he had in months. He was still a million miles behind the place he should be this close to his deadline, but at least it was a start.

And Eva was the reason.

He pulled on dark jeans and a fresh shirt and paused as he moved to the stairs and heard singing from the kitchen. The singing stopped momentarily and he heard the whirr of a food processor. Then it started again.

Looking down, he saw she was wearing headphones again, but this time she wasn't dancing.

As soon as she saw him, she stopped. "Sorry. Was I too loud?"

Her comment made him think about sex, and he wondered what it was about her that triggered those thoughts in him. He wished he hadn't hugged her, because now he didn't just know how she looked, he knew how she felt.

"I have a love for Ella Fitzgerald. As long as you're not singing Christmas carols, I have no problem with your soundtrack." But he had problems with other things, like the way holding her had made him feel. As if he was missing something that up until this moment he hadn't even realized he wanted.

"What have you got against Christmas carols?"

"I think we already have enough festivity around here." He eyed the Christmas tree. Its lush branches were now trimmed with silver and interwoven with delicate lights. He wondered if its extravagant height was supposed to compensate for the lack of festive cheer in the rest of his apartment. "That is one hell of a tree. Clearly you're a woman who doesn't believe that less is more."

"Not when it comes to Christmas trees." She smiled, and he saw that her lipstick was candy-cane pink. It reminded him of the indulgent sweet treats he'd enjoyed as a child.

"Anything else?"

The irrepressible dimple appeared. "That's a personal question, Mr. Blade."

"You're living in my apartment and I've seen you in your pajamas. I think we've already ventured into personal." He didn't mention the fact that he'd held her. He didn't need to. He'd felt the shift in their relationship and he knew she had, too. A casual attraction had transformed into an intense awareness that electrified the air.

And it wasn't just physical. Each conversation with her revealed something new.

She was a treasure trove of inspiration.

He paused by the wall of wine. "What are we eating?"

"Roasted vegetable and goat cheese tartlet, followed by sage-and-pumpkin ravioli. I made something you could eat by your computer if you wanted to."

"I don't want to. I want to eat with you and a special meal calls for a special wine." He walked to the chiller and picked a white. "I first tasted this on a book tour in New Zealand and had a crate of it shipped over. It's spectacular."

"How the other half lives. Half a glass for me," she said. "I'm a cheap date. And if I drink before I've finished cooking, I can't vouch for the food. In fact, maybe I shouldn't drink at all. I don't want to lose my inhibitions."

"You have inhibitions?" He opened the wine. "Where are you hiding them?"

"Very funny. Some people like the fact that I'm

easy to read. But you, of course, are probably wondering about my evil side."

Maybe he wasn't with her, but he certainly was with the character he was developing. She was shaping up to be the most duplicitous character he'd ever written. And he'd rather think about her than the flesh-and-blood woman standing in front of him.

He poured, watching the wine swirl into the glass. "Try it. It's delicious."

"Are you going to dazzle me with a speech about tropical notes and an undercurrent of sunshine and all that jazz? Or do you save all your flowery words for your books?"

He thought of the gritty reality he'd been writing. "Something like that. Drink."

She sniffed and then sipped, slowly, cautiously, as if she wasn't sure he wasn't poisoning her. "Oh." She closed her eyes for a moment and then took another sip. "Why does the wine I drink at home never taste like this? Is it expensive?"

"It's worth the money."

"In other words, it *is* expensive. I guess you know a lot about wine."

"It's one of my hobbies."

She put her glass down and turned back to the food. "I'm guessing answering your mail isn't one of your hobbies." She put a plate in front of him. It was a work of art. The scalloped edges of the pastry were crisp and golden, the surface of the tartlet a swirl of color. "Are you planning on dealing with it?"

He picked up his fork. "I'm not here, remember? I can't open mail if I'm not here."

"But what if it's something important?"

"It won't be."

"But it could be." She was persistent. "Can I open it for you?"

"Do you really want to?"

"Yes. Someone might be waiting for an answer from you. Don't you have an assistant?"

"My publisher has a team who deals with all my professional communication."

She watched anxiously as he took a mouthful. "Well?"

"Spectacular." And it was. The pastry was buttery, crumbly perfection and the creamy goat cheese melded with the tang of peppers. "You've woken my taste buds from a coma."

She looked pleased. "Good. And I know you're great at what you do, too. Not that I've ever read any of your books, but my friend Frankie is addicted. She only reads vile stuff."

"Thank you."

"That didn't come out the way I meant it to." Her cheeks were pink. "I didn't mean that your books were 'vile,' more that the subject matter is vile. They are way too scary for me. I know I wouldn't like them."

"If you've never read one, how would you know?"

"The cover is a clue." She sliced into her tartlet. "The last one had blood dripping from the blade of a knife. Then there are the titles. *Death Returns* isn't exactly going to make me rush to pick it up off the shelf. I'd have to sleep with the lights on and I'd wake in the night screaming. Someone would dial 911."

"You might be gripped."

"I don't think the subject matter would thrill me. Tell me about the story you wrote when you were eight. Was that the same kind of thing?"

"The neighbors' cat was found dead on the side of the road. Everyone said it had been hit by a car, but I kept asking myself, *what if it wasn't?* What if something more sinister had happened to that cat? I drove my family crazy with all the alternative explanations I offered." He saw her expression change. "You would have rather gone with the car scenario?"

"I'd rather have the scenario where the cat lived, but I'm guessing if you're the one telling it, this story has no happy-ever-after."

"Afraid not." That statement was all he needed to remind him of the differences between them. "It was summer, and I shut myself in my room and didn't come out until I'd written the story. I figured there were at least nine different ways that cat could have died."

"Please don't list them."

Remembering the macabre ending he'd chosen, he gave a faint smile. "I gave the story to my English teacher and she said she'd never been so spooked by anything in her life. Said she had to check the doors and windows twice before going to bed and locked her cat in her bedroom. Then she suggested I consider a career as a crime writer. She was joking."

"But you took her seriously."

"She told me she'd had to read my story with the lights on. I don't think she meant it as a compliment, but to me it was the biggest compliment anyone had ever given me."

Eva looked unconvinced. "So you wrote your terrifying cat story, and then what?"

"I kept doing it. I gave stories to my classmates, chapter by chapter. I discovered that I liked keeping people in suspense. It carried on when I went to college, except that by then I knew I was serious about it."

"What did you do at college? Creative writing? English? History of the great American novel?"

"I studied law at Columbia, but I was more interested in why people committed crimes than I was in defending them. I finished my first novel, handed it to my roommate to read and he was up all night. I decided then that was what I wanted to do."

"Keep people awake all night?"

"Yes." He looked at the soft curve of her mouth and decided he would have no problem keeping her awake all night, and he wouldn't be relying on words to do it.

Maybe his grandmother was cleverer than he gave her credit for.

"Does anyone fall in love in your books?"

"Occasionally."

"Really?" She looked surprised. "But do they live to enjoy a happy-ever-after?"

"Never."

"That's why I don't pick your books from the shelf.

I'm a coward. Speaking of dialing 911—" She stuck her fork into her food. "Those officers that showed up here yesterday—they knew you and you knew them."

"That's right." He took another mouthful of food. It was delicious, the flavors fresh and intense.

"But you don't actually have a criminal background, you just write about it. So how do you know them?"

"They help me with research from time to time."

"So you plan a murder and then you call them up and say 'hey guys, what do you think of this?' And they tell you whether it would work or not."

"Close enough."

"Do you ever go out with them?"

"Ride along? In the past, yes. Now, not so much. When I'm not touring, I'm writing."

"Were the ride-alongs scary?"

"They were more interesting than scary. But most of what I write about is dealt with by the other departments. I write about—" he reached for the salt, buying time while he worked out how much to say "—complex cases."

"You mean you write about serial killers." She put her fork down, leaving half her food untouched. "Why would you want to write about terrible people doing terrible things?"

"The average serial killer wouldn't think he, or she, was a terrible person. And I write about it because it fascinates me. I've always been drawn to scary stuff. Doesn't make me scary, and doesn't mean I have small children locked in my closet, waiting for me to show up and torture them, as one interviewer seemed to think."

"That happened?"

"People assume because I write about crime, I must worship the devil. You should be scared to stay overnight here with me."

"I'm not scared." Her gaze held his for a moment and then she picked up her wine. "But I don't understand why people would want to be scared by choice."

The sexual awareness was building but she was ignoring it.

He followed her example.

"Books are safe. I think of what scares people and I use those fears. Some people like to be scared. They like to feel that emotion from the safety of their own lives."

"Don't you scare yourself when you write this stuff?"

"If the writing is going well, then yes." Mostly it was the research that spooked him, but he didn't tell her that.

"Is that why you do martial arts? So that you can protect yourself from the demons you've created?"

"I hate to shatter your illusions, but mostly it's an interesting form of exercise and mental discipline." He finished his food and sat back. "Enough about me. Now it's your turn. You don't read crime or horror, so what do you read? Classics?"

"Yes. And I read romance, women's fiction and cookbooks. I'm addicted to cookbooks."

"I thought you didn't use cookbooks?"

"I don't often cook from them, but I like to read them."

He reached for his wine and watched while she served the ravioli. "You ever consider writing one of your own?"

"I have my blog. And I have a YouTube channel. With the work I do for Urban Genie, that keeps me busy."

"You have a YouTube channel?"

"Cooking is visual. People like to see how things are made. And it turns out I'm pretty good at demonstrating. People like to watch me. That probably surprises you."

It didn't surprise him at all.

Who wouldn't want to watch her?

With those blue eyes and her sweet smile, he was willing to bet even without looking that she had a big following. He wondered how many of them were men and how many were genuinely interested in cooking.

Trying not to think about it too much, he took a mouthful of ravioli and momentarily stopped cursing his grandmother for her interfering tendencies.

"This is delicious."

"Good."

"Sage and pumpkin." He took another mouthful. "You don't cook meat?"

A hint of color appeared in her smooth cheeks. "I can cook meat for you if that's what you'd like."

"But you never eat it yourself?"

"Never. I'm a vegetarian. I don't like to harm animals."

His heart thudded. He put his fork down. His food lay forgotten in front of him. "How long have you been vegetarian?"

"Always. I was raised by my grandmother, and she had very firm views about respecting living things."

"So right from an early age you've been kind to all animals."

"I'm not a saint. I wouldn't cuddle a spider, but I don't tread on them if that's what you mean. If they're enormous I call for Matt and he does it."

"Matt is your friend's brother?"

"That's right. He lives in the apartment above mine. He's like family."

"Right."

"And speaking of family, are you going to tell your grandmother that you're back? At some point she's going to ask me about this job, and I don't want to lie."

He realized that he was putting her in a difficult position. "I'll tell her I'm back." His attention was caught by the smooth surface of the table in the living room. It took him a moment to realize what was missing. "What happened to the knife that was on the table?"

She didn't look at him. "What knife?"

"There was a knife on the table."

"Was there?" Her tone was innocent. "I probably moved it. It's dangerous leaving knives around. Everyone who has ever worked in a kitchen knows that."

He gave her a long look. "Why did you think the knife was there, Eva?"

She took a large gulp of wine. "I wasn't sure. But it seemed safer to move it."

"Did you think I might harm you with the knife?"

"What? No!" She looked horrified. "Not for a moment. Despite the blood dripping off the cover of your books, I can see you're a really good person."

Lucas felt tension prick the back of his neck. "So why did you move it?"

Her gaze returned to her plate. "Because I was afraid you might use it on yourself."

He stared at her in silence. "That's why you stayed? Because you were worried about me?"

"No. I stayed because I had a job to do and I made a promise to your grandmother. Even if she wasn't a client, I have great respect for grandmothers."

"Eva—"

"Okay, yes! Part of the reason I stayed was because I was worried about you."

"The knife was there to give me inspiration for the book. Nothing more."

"That's good, but when I saw it, I wasn't sure. You had these big shadows under your eyes and you looked so *alone*, and no one knew you were here and—" She took a large gulp of wine. "I had a bad feeling, that's all. You probably don't believe me. You thought I was staying because I had designs on your body, and why wouldn't you because you do have a *great* body. Crap, I told you not to pour me more than half a glass of wine."

The silence was heavy and loaded, cut through with rivulets of sexual tension.

Remembering the way she'd felt against him triggered another serious attack of lust.

He ran his hand through his hair, trying to control it. "I should probably get back to work."

"If you're panicking about my last comment, then don't. I already told you, you're not my type."

He was starting to think that she might just be *his* type, and the thought surprised him because since the death of his wife he hadn't met many women who had raised his interest levels.

"I thought you didn't have a type."

"I probably shouldn't. Given how long it is since I had sex, my type should just be anyone with a penis and a pulse, right?"

Lucas choked on his wine. "Did you seriously just say that?"

"In any case, haven't we established that prejudging people can be dangerous? Who knows what lies beneath the surface?"

He'd interviewed enough serial killers to know that most people were better off not knowing what lay beneath the surface.

"Do you ever edit your thoughts before they come out of your mouth?"

"It's your fault for pouring wine into me." She poked at her food. "But it's true that generally I'm a spontaneous type."

"How have you survived this long unscathed?"

"I'm not unscathed. I've dated some serious losers."

"But that hasn't damaged your faith in happy-ever-afters?"

"No. It means there are losers in the world, but I already knew that. There are also some great guys out there. I don't happen to have met too many of them lately, that's all. And I do know you're not going to meet the right person by hiding away in your apartment."

"Are we talking about me or you?"

"Both of us. I promised myself that this Christmas I wasn't going to spend my whole time alone in my apartment watching reruns of Hallmark movies and enjoying a threesome with Ben and Jerry." She eyed him. "The ice cream, in case you were wondering."

"I'm 'hiding' in my apartment, as you put it, because I'm working."

"We both know that isn't true, Lucas, but even it was you can't work all the time."

He thought about his deadline and how far behind he was. "I shouldn't even be sitting here talking to you." And yet he was. And he was in no hurry to change that.

"Go. The sooner you finish the book, the sooner you can get a life." She stood up, careful not to look at him. "I'll clear up. And I'll open your mail."

"Do what you want with it."

His mail was the least of his problems.

HAD SHE REALLY told him he had a great body?

She was going to have to tape her mouth. Or clamp

her jaw shut. Anything to stop herself babbling like an idiot when she was with him.

But it *was* partly his fault. Every time he looked at her she was scalded by the heat of sexual tension. Each smoldering glance fried her brain, burning away the last of her already inefficient filters.

It was no good telling herself he wasn't interested, or that he was unavailable. Her body wasn't paying attention.

Resolving to keep her lips sealed next time they were together, Eva cleared the kitchen, polished the stove until it shone, and then settled down at the island unit with the remains of her wine and a large stack of Lucas's mail.

She dealt with the junk first, carefully tearing through the address and disposing of it in the recycling. Then she turned to the rest.

Most were invitations. Four publisher parties, another author's book launch, nine charity balls, a night at the opera and two movie premieres. In addition there were twelve letters requesting charity donations.

She didn't even know people wrote letters anymore. And *nine* charity balls?

Eva surveyed the invitations spread in front of her with more than a twinge of envy.

Here, right in front of her, was evidence of an interesting life.

If her social life looked like his, her chances of meeting someone would have been significantly increased.

"Lucas Blade," she muttered, "for someone who

isn't a party animal, you're invited to a large number of parties." Parties he would, no doubt, refuse to attend.

And she knew now that the reason he wouldn't attend wasn't all to do with his deadline.

In his current mental state he found the company of strangers as unappealing as she did.

She grabbed her laptop and started with the letters.

Dear Caroline, she typed, thank you for your kind words about my books. I'm flattered to know that— She pulled a face, wincing slightly as she typed, wishing she could change the title—Death For Sure was your favorite read of the year.

She wrote at length and then signed off with Best wishes, Lucas Blade.

Too formal?

With a grin, she deleted *Blade* and added two kisses. She was willing to bet he'd never added kisses to any of his letters in his life.

Each letter was given the same treatment and then she turned to the invitations, politely declining each one until she reached the last one in the pile.

Darkness had fallen outside the windows and Central Park was bathed in the ethereal mix of moonlight and snow.

The final invitation was to the Snowflake Ball at the Plaza hotel.

The invitation was embossed in silver and shaped like a snowflake.

Eva stared at it. If she'd been sent an invitation as beautiful as this one she would have put it in a frame and hung it on the wall. He was lucky she'd sorted through his mail.

It was less than a week away. Was it too late to respond? No. Lucas was a VIP guest. They'd make room for him no matter how late his RSVP was.

She scanned the details. The proceeds were going to a charity that trained and provided therapy dogs for the elderly. Her heart melted. She knew how many elderly people were lonely.

On impulse, she picked up the phone.

"Hi, I'm calling for Lucas Blade… Yes, I work with him…" *That wasn't a lie, was it?* "Mr. Blade will be attending The Snowflake Ball. Yes, and a plus one. We'll let you know the name later. Thank you so much." She hung up, imagining what would have happened if she hadn't opened his mail.

He would have missed the ball, the social event of the New York calendar.

He would have been so mad at himself.

And he was going to be so grateful to her.

"YOU DID WHAT?"

"I called the Plaza and said you'd be attending the Snowflake Ball. Let that be a lesson to you to open your mail. You almost missed it."

"Eva—" Anger thickened Lucas's voice even though he knew it was wrong of him to take it out on her. "I don't want to go to the ball." The thought of it froze him to the bone. As always they saw things differently. She heard the word *ball* and thought of starlight and romance, whereas he knew it would be an evening filled with curious looks and sympathetic glances.

"I know you're busy, but it will be amazing and it's just one night. I turned down a ton of other invitations. This is the only one I accepted."

"You shouldn't have accepted that one."

She froze. "You told me to deal with your mail as I saw fit. I saw fit to accept one ball, the proceeds of which go to a very good cause."

"If I supported every cause I'm asked to give money to, I'd never get any work done and I'd be broke."

"But you're not broke, and we're not talking about *every* cause, just this one. It's an organization that provides therapy dogs, and—"

"But it isn't just this one, is it?" To take his mind off the damn ball, he scanned the letters she'd spread in front of him. "I'm sending signed books for auction? What makes you think I even have that number of signed books?"

"You wrote them. You must have copies. And maybe it seems generous, but it's less time-consuming than going to the auction yourself and you'll be raising money for lots of people less fortunate than yourself. I thought it was a perfect compromise. Why do these people write letters to your home address, anyway? Why don't they just email your publisher?"

"They do," he said wearily. "These should have been handled by my publisher, too, but they have a new assistant in the office and she sent them directly to me. Do you have any idea how many invitations we receive? We can't say yes to all of them, Eva."

"Not *all* of them, no," she said, "but you can manage these. I've checked them all out. They are really good causes."

"Is there anything you think isn't a good cause?"

"Of course. I'm more businesslike than you may think." She bristled. "I took a look at the financials and checked what percentage of their donations is spent directly on the cause, and what is spent on salaries, etc. These all came out well. All you have to do is sign the letters, sign the books and I'll do the rest."

Deciding that in this case surrender was quicker than a fight, he reached for a pen. "Have you ever worked in charity fund-raising?"

"I would be hopeless working for a charity. I'd be in tears the whole time. I don't have a very thick skin. Try not to scrawl," she added as she studied his signature. "They might not think it's you."

He signed with an exaggerated scrawl. "Normally my publisher just sends these with a compliments slip."

"I thought this was more personal. They'll treasure the letter."

He picked one of them up and read aloud. "*I enjoyed writing it and it is certainly among my favorites.* Anyone who knows me would know I didn't write that sentence. I never admit to having a favorite."

"Why not?"

"Because then it sounds as if you think the other books you wrote aren't as good."

"That's ridiculous. If I tell you I'm cooking you one of my favorite dishes, you don't automatically assume that anything else I cooked you would poison you, do you?"

He carried on reading. *"I agree it was a shame that such a warm, lovely character had to die in the second chapter."* He glanced up, exasperated. "You can't write that. I don't agree. That character had to die."

"Why? Couldn't they just have been injured or something and then made a full recovery after good medical care? Why do all your characters have to *die*? It's horribly depressing."

He lowered the letter. "Do I tell you how to cook? Do I suggest that the egg needs a little longer in the oven or that the cookie you baked would be improved with chocolate chips?"

"No."

"Then don't tell me how to write my books." He returned his gaze to the page. *"I agree that your charity is raising money for a most excellent cause.* I would never say that, either. I'm already inundated with sob stories about excellent causes."

"Which is why it's even more important to make your response sound personal. They'll appreciate it."

"And they will come back to me time and time again." He carried on reading, *"Although I am unable to attend your event on this occasion, it is my pleasure to enclose a signed book for you to include in your auction. I wish you every success with the evening and with your fund-raising.* You've signed my name with kisses. And asked them to stay in touch."

"The kisses were a joke. It was supposed to make you smile." She snatched the letter back from him and he felt a stab of guilt.

"If I sign my name with kisses my social media account will be jammed with readers wanting to marry me."

"Don't kid yourself. You're scary when you're moody."

"Because I don't want to go to a ball that makes me moody?"

"How was I to know you wouldn't want to go? This one is special. It's winter-themed, with snowflakes and Christmas trees. Silver." She stared down at the invitation and he had a feeling she'd forgotten he was in the room. "I would kill to go to this. There—that's a whole new motivation for murder you've never even thought of."

"But you're not the one going. I am. Thanks to you."

"You can't spend the whole of the festive season locked in this apartment."

"You're starting to sound like my grandmother."

"I happen to think she is right about certain things. Not trying to set you up with someone," she said quickly, "that never works. But the fact that you should start getting out again."

"Next you'll be telling me that it's been long enough." The words came out as a growl and she looked at him steadily.

"We both know I'm not going to say that. You're not the only one grieving, Lucas. You don't have the monopoly on that type of pain. Just because people want you to occasionally step outside and breathe in fresh air doesn't mean everyone thinks you should have 'recovered,' whatever that word means. Maybe you'd feel better if you went out."

"Or maybe I'd feel a thousand times worse. One thing I know for sure is that nothing I'm feeling is going to be 'fixed' by going to a ball. If you want to live in a fantasy world, go right ahead, but don't expect me to join you there."

"I wouldn't want you to join me. There's no room in my fantasy world for cynics." She picked up her bag and stuffed the last of her things into it. "You should go, Lucas."

"Why? Because there is a strong chance I'll meet someone, fall in love and live happily ever after? Is that what you were going to say?"

"Actually I was going to say that shit happens, and all we can do is carry on as best we can." She snapped her bag shut. "But locking yourself away isn't carrying on, Lucas. It's hiding. Your grandmother is right about that. You should go to the ball. It will be a wonderful evening."

"Call them back and tell them I'm not going."

"I will not."

"You are out of line." He heard the chill in his voice but was unable to stop it. "I don't tolerate interference from my family, so I'm certainly not going to tolerate it from strangers."

Hurt flashed in her eyes. "Maybe I am out of line, but I'm not calling them back." Her voice tight, she put the invitations carefully back on the table. "If you don't want to go, then you'll have to call them your-self." With that she walked away and up the stairs.

Lucas swore under his breath and dragged his hand over the back of his neck. He felt as if he'd kicked a puppy.

What was wrong with him?

He was deliberately goading her, seeing how far he could push her, and he didn't even know why. All he knew was that having her here unsettled him, and thinking about snowflake balls and happy-ever-afters unsettled him even more.

He heard the sound of her feet on the stairs and glanced up to see her standing in front of him with her backpack in her hands.

Shock rippled through him. "You're leaving?"

"I've left all the instructions for the food on the pad by the refrigerator." Her tone was formal and she didn't look him in the eye. "If you have any questions, you can call the Urban Genie offices. The number is on the pad, too."

He wondered how it was that someone so small and fragile could cause so much disruption to his life in such a short time.

"I'm not going to the ball, Eva, and you walking out isn't going to change that."

"You already made that clear. You also made it clear that you don't want my help so yes, I'm leav-ing. It's bad for my emotional well-being to be around people who are angry, especially when they're angry with *me*. I don't want to get stomach ulcers or hardened arteries, so I'm leaving while I'm still healthy."

Her words intensified the guilt and made him feel like an idiot. "Put your bag down. You can't leave. It's still snowing."

"I like snow a whole lot more than I like being yelled at. And if I don't have the right to be concerned about what happens to you, then you don't have the right to be concerned about what happens to me. They've lifted the travel ban and I've done everything I came here to do."

The truth was she'd done more. It was because of her that he was writing again. That he had a plot, a character and an idea strong enough to drive the story through to its conclusion.

The corkscrew of guilt gouged a little deeper.

He knew he should be thanking her, or at least apologizing, but the words jammed in his throat. This whole situation was like walking on emotional quicksand. It would be so easy for both of them to be sucked in deep.

"Eva—"

"Good luck with the book and try not to let all that dark stuff you write about color the way you look at the world. You seem to think that all interaction is manipulation or interference, but sometimes it's just because people care. Have a good Christmas, Lucas." She tugged her hat onto her head, hoisted her backpack onto her narrow shoulders and walked toward the door.

He reached out a hand to stop her and then pulled it back again. What was he going to say? *Don't leave.*

It would be better for both of them if she *did* leave.

He'd be able to get on with his book in peace and quiet. He'd be able to forget her soft curves and her sweet smile, her infuriating optimism and the way she sang while she cooked.

He'd be able to focus on his book, one hundred percent of the time.

Which was exactly what he wanted, wasn't it?

CHAPTER EIGHT

Everyone has baggage, but when traveling through life take hand luggage only.

—Frankie

MARY ELEANOR BLADE, known as Mitzy to her friends, of which she had many, sat in the winged Queen Anne chair that had been a gift from her son, and was now carefully positioned to make the most of the charming view from the window.

Right now, though, she wasn't looking at the view. She was looking at her grandson.

She might be ninety, but she could still recognize handsome when she saw it, and Lucas was most definitely handsome.

He'd inherited his mother's beauty and his father's strength. He topped six-four, and those wicked good looks, combined with an aura of strength and command ensured him a fan base of women who probably hadn't even opened one of his books.

Mitzy felt a twinge of envy as she admired his glossy dark hair. She'd long since made peace with her smooth bob of elegant gray, but she could clearly remember the time when her hair had been as black as his.

One less seriously minded magazine had described him as perfect, but Mitzy knew better. He was smart and had a sharp sense of humor, but he also had a fierce temper and a single-minded approach to life that some had described as ruthless.

Mitzy didn't see it that way. She knew he wasn't ruthless, so much as driven. And what was wrong with that? Who wanted perfect anyway? She'd always been suspicious of perfect. Never found it interesting. She and Robert had been married for sixty years, and she'd loved his flaws as much as his strengths. Lucas was the same. He was interesting. He was also troubled, and she desperately wanted to fix that. His mother, her daughter-in-law, would have told her to step back and let him find his own way, but Mitzy figured that if you couldn't try to fix things when you were ninety, there wasn't much point in being here. And the good thing about her age was that people were more indulgent of interfering behavior. They saw it as endearingly eccentric. Mitzy played along, even though her brain was as sharp as it had been when she was twenty. If it was interfering to try to help someone she loved, then yes she was interfering. It gave her purpose.

"How was Vermont?" She used her most casual tone but she knew from the incendiary glance he sent in her direction that she was going to have to work a little harder if she wanted to appear innocent.

"We both know I wasn't in Vermont."

"You weren't?"

"Gran—" his tone bordered on the impatient "—let's cut the crap."

She blinked. "You're a writer. I would have thought you could have found a more eloquent expression than that."

"I could, but not one that so perfectly describes what's going on here. Why did you do it?"

He towered over her, but she was too long in the tooth to be intimidated by anyone, least of all her own grandson. She'd driven ambulances during the war. It would take more than a black look from Lucas to make her lose her nerve.

"Do what? Would you like tea? I've discovered this new brand and it's delicious."

"I don't want tea. What I want," he said tightly, "is to understand why you would enlist someone like Eva in your plans. What were you thinking?"

"I was thinking that you needed to eat. And Eva is a most excellent cook, as I hope you've discovered." She kept her head down and poured the tea, resisting the urge to smile.

If she smiled now, all would be lost.

"Do you think I'm stupid, Gran?"

"No." She thought he was passionate, and she loved a man with passion. Her Robert had been the same. "Stubborn, and occasionally wrong, but never stupid."

"We both know you sending Eva my way had nothing to do with her cooking abilities. We know what you were hoping would happen and, by the way, it didn't. I didn't lay a finger on her."

Then you're a fool, Mitzy thought, but she kept the thought to herself.

"I'm glad to hear it. I didn't send that young girl over there for you to molest her. I would have felt dreadfully let down if you'd done that."

Lucas shook his head in exasperation. "We were snowed in together."

"No." Mitzy widened her eyes in horror, delighted that for once the weather forecast hadn't let her down. "How *dreadful* for her."

"For *her*?"

"Being closeted with you and your dark moods. We both know that when you can't write, you're like a bear with a sore head. Oh, dear—" She rubbed her chest dramatically. "I hope I didn't do the wrong thing. I thought she'd be fine. I didn't even think she'd see you."

"Why are you rubbing your chest, Gran? Are you in pain? Can I fetch you something? Call someone?" The concern in his voice warmed her.

Underneath that brooding exterior he was a dear boy. "I'm a little anxious, that's all. I hope you weren't unkind, Lucas." She saw something that looked like guilt flash across his face, and there was a brief pause before he answered.

"I wasn't unkind."

Mitzy stopped rubbing her chest. "You *were* unkind?"

"We didn't part on the best of terms." His voice

was tight and she wondered if her grandson's irascible nature might have proved too much even for her lovely Eva.

"If you hurt that girl in any way, Lucas, I swear you will discover that there is an end to my patience. Eva has become a good friend. I can't imagine not having her in my life." It was probably the most honest statement she'd uttered since he'd walked into her apartment.

"And what is she doing in your life? Have you asked yourself why a young woman of her age would—" He broke off and she raised an eyebrow.

"Would what? Want to spend her free time with someone old and boring like me? Was that what you wanted to say?"

Men could be so tactless, she thought. *It was a wonder the human race hadn't died out.*

"That wasn't what I was going to say. You're the most interesting person I know, but you have to admit that it's a strange way for a young, single, attractive woman to spend her time."

So he *had* found Eva attractive.

She hadn't got that part wrong.

"Only you would consider it strange that two people might find pleasure in each other's company, and that's because you insist on believing that all interaction is driven by some lower purpose. Your writer's imagination may have made you a fortune, Lucas, but in the real world it does you a disservice. When she's working, I insist on paying her for her time, but sometimes she visits after work, through her own choice. She bakes me cakes and walks Peanut if I've not managed to get out."

"And you don't wonder why she'd do those things?"

Because she's lonely.

Mitzy kept her tone level. "You find my company so boring you can't imagine why another might seek it? It's a good job my ego is as robust as yours."

Dark color spread across his cheekbones. "You're deliberately misunderstanding me."

"If you have to ask the question, then evidently you didn't spend much time talking to Eva."

"We talked."

"Then maybe your listening skills need work."

"My listening skills are—" He sighed. "What are you getting at? What did I miss?"

"You're the writer with deep insight into human nature. Far be it for me to tell you how to get to know someone. Is that why you didn't part on the best of terms? Were you only thinking about yourself? What did you do?"

"I didn't *do* anything," he said irritably. "And she's more robust than she looks, by the way. We argued, that's all."

Knowing how sensitive Eva was, Mitzy was sure a few sharp words from her grandson would have been all it took to hurt her.

"What terrible thing did she do?"

"She accepted an invitation to the Snowflake Ball at the Plaza on my behalf without asking me."

Mitzy gave him a long look. "A heinous crime indeed."

"I don't need sarcasm, Gran."

"She probably didn't need your anger, either." It annoyed her, thinking of it.

"Are you trying to make me feel guilty?"

"No. If you're the man I know you to be, you're already feeling guilty." Watching him jam his fingers into his hair, she almost felt sorry for him. He looked so much like the little boy who had once stolen the last slice of chocolate cake from her kitchen.

He had a good heart, she knew, but that heart had been so badly bruised, so damaged, he didn't dare let anyone near it.

He thought she didn't know how he felt, but she knew.

She knew everything and she ached for him. She'd waited for him to talk to her about it, but he never had. She wondered if he'd ever told anyone how he'd felt after Sallyanne's shocking death. Probably not.

"So now she's gone. And presumably that's what you wanted, so what's the problem?"

He raked his hand over the back of his neck. "I need her back."

Mitzy's heart flew, but she kept her expression neutral. "If you sent her away, why would you need her back?"

"I just need her. And I need you to give me her home address."

Mitzy couldn't remember a time when he'd sounded so desperate. She almost took pity on him. Then she thought of sweet, dear Eva. "I'm not sure I have it. Or maybe I do, and I've forgotten. You know what my memory is like."

"Your memory is perfect, Gran."

She made vague sounds. "Could you pass me my reading glasses and my smartphone?"

Lucas found both on top of the piano and handed them to her. "You always keep your addresses in a book."

"Eva taught me to use the contacts in this wonderful phone." Should she help? If she was wrong and this didn't go the way she'd planned, two people she loved dearly could be hurt.

He held out his hand. "Could I look?"

"No. You'll press something, or do something clever, and I'll never be able to find any of my numbers again."

"Gran—"

"Why do you need her home address?"

"Because this is—" He broke off, breathing heavily. "Personal. It's better discussed face-to-face."

"Personal?" Oh, this was perfect. And people said that interfering was a bad thing. "I never had a granddaughter as you know and I would have loved to have one. I'm surrounded by men." *Men who invariably said the wrong thing.* "Eva fills that space in my heart. Why is it personal? Are you taking her to that ball?"

His expression was shuttered. "No. I'm going to call the Plaza and cancel."

Mitzy stared down at the phone, thinking hard. "No. I don't have her address."

He looked at her in exasperation. "There was never

any expectation that I would take her to the ball. Even she wasn't expecting that."

"Maybe not, but it's always nice when a man exceeds our expectations. If you want me to find out her address, you'll have to promise you'll take her to the ball."

"I will not be blackmailed."

Mitzy put the phone down. "Then you'll have to call her office."

"I've told you, this isn't something I wish to discuss on the phone."

"Then you'll have to *go* to her office." Better and better, she thought. The office was open plan and there was a strong chance he'd be making his speech in front of Eva's two friends and business partners, who were two of the strongest women Mitzy had ever met. "Good luck, Lucas."

"I'm not going to the ball, Gran."

Oh, the boy was handsome. Handsome, strong and decent. So a part of him was damaged, but that could be healed, she was sure of it.

Yes, Eva was a lucky girl, no doubt about it.

Eva sat in a meeting with Paige and Frankie, trying to concentrate as they ran through their new business plan for the next quarter. Her mind refused to cooperate, unengaged by talk of growth and client gains. Instead her thoughts were stubbornly preoccupied by Lucas.

Part of her was still upset and offended. She'd been *caring*, for goodness' sake. She'd actually thought they'd achieved a level of closeness, but he'd pushed her away and made it clear that any closeness was in her head only.

But even so she couldn't stop worrying. She hadn't been able to resist looking him up on the internet, and what she'd read had swiftly diffused her own anger. It turned out that the day she'd shown up at his apartment had been the anniversary of his wife's death.

He'd been hiding away like an injured beast, and she'd disturbed him.

Right at the point where he'd wanted to be alone with his pain, she'd shown up.

What was he doing now? Had he even left his study? What if he wasn't bothering to eat the food she'd prepared? It made her heart ache to think of him all alone there.

"Ev, are you listening?"

Eva jumped guiltily. "Of course."

"You don't look as if you're listening." Frankie was squeezing a stress ball shaped like a can of soda.

Eva forced herself to focus. "I'll make a list of the top wedding planners and make contact with them."

"That's new business finished." Paige closed the file. "Any current business anyone needs to discuss?"

Who would persuade him to leave the apartment? As far as she knew, even his grandmother still didn't know he was there.

Something thudded gently into her forehead and she looked up and saw Frankie with her hand raised, grinning.

"Did you just throw your stress ball at my head?"

"I did. The great thing about running your own company is that we can be as immature as we like and no one can fire us. What's going on in that head of yours?"

"Nothing. Even less since you smacked me in the forehead." Eva forced herself to concentrate. "Everything is set for Laura's proposal. I emailed you the plan."

"I saw it. It's excellent. One perfect Christmas proposal. I envy Laura. It's a day she's going to remember forever." Paige gave her a grateful look. "I can't believe you've put this together at such short notice. You're so good at fixing things for people."

Other people, Eva thought. *Never myself.*

And she hadn't fixed Lucas. She'd filled his refrigerator and decorated his apartment, but he was still hiding away from the world.

"We should probably add 'dating agency' to our list of capabilities." Frankie retrieved her stress ball. "Remember when we used to work for Cynthia?"

Paige frowned. "It's something I try to forget."

"She seemed to think that if you were having fun in your working day, it meant you weren't working hard enough." Frankie sat back, put her feet on the table and grinned. "And here we are, working hard *and* having fun. So come on, Ev, the hard work is done and now I want the truth about why you're so distracted. Debrief on your time with Lucas Blade. Did you steal any signed books? Was he working crazily hard? I can't wait for his next one."

She'd given her friends an edited version of her

time with Lucas, leaving out the fact that he had writer's block. That was his secret. Not hers to share.

"I spent my time in the kitchen," she said truthfully. "And he was in his office."

"So you ate separately?"

"We ate dinner together."

"So you must have talked about something."

"Not really." Eva was deliberately vague and Frankie exchanged glances with Paige.

"Ev." Frankie's tone was patient. "This is you we're talking about. You can't go five seconds without saying something. Remember that sponsored silence at school? You raised no money at all. None. Not a single cent."

Eva flushed. "We made small talk. I don't remember what about."

Paige put her pen down, her gaze warm. "You like him, don't you?"

Frankie frowned. "Of course she doesn't like him. He yelled at her!"

"That was my fault," Eva said. "I shouldn't have accepted that invitation without asking him first."

"How were you born so forgiving?" Frankie swung her legs off the desk. "The guy was rude. You should have punched him and walked out."

"She did walk out," Paige said and Eva felt a stab of regret.

"I'd finished the job." But she could have found an excuse to stay on, and part of her wished she had. How could you miss someone you'd known for only a couple of days? "He's hurting. He lost the love of his life. They met when they were just kids."

"How do you know that?"

Eva felt her cheeks burn. "I just do." She didn't tell her friends that she'd read the media reports. His wife had slipped on the ice while climbing into a cab. Her head injury had been massive. She'd never woken up from the coma. It had happened just a few weeks before Christmas.

Now she understood why he hadn't wanted her to leave that night. Why he'd stared out at the weather as if it was repugnant. And she'd made all those guile-less comments about the magic of snow.

"He made it clear he didn't want to go to anything. I made the decision for him and it was wrong of me. I hate when people do that to me."

Frankie gave her a speculative look. "Is there more than your marshmallow heart going on here?"

"What? No. Of course not." Eva felt the flush start at her neck and travel slowly up her face. "He's had a horrid time, that's all."

"So this is pity we're seeing?" Frankie gave her a long look. "Come on, Ev. Tell us the truth. Paige is right. You liked him, didn't you?"

She gave up pretending. "Yes, I liked him. He was smart and good company. And interesting."

"I thought you didn't say anything to each other?"

Paige smothered a smile and returned to her desk. "Leave the girl to her secrets, Frankie."

"I will not. Eva wants love, which makes her vulnerable. It's my job to vet any man she falls in love with."

"I'm not in love!" Eva's protests went ignored.

"I'm vetting raw lust, too, because there's a high likelihood that you'll fall in love with whoever you sleep with."

"Not true!"

Frankie waggled her eyebrows. "So there *was* raw lust? Because if he looks anything like the picture on his book jacket, I'd have struggled not to rip his clothes off."

Eva remembered that breath-stealing moment in the dark when she'd thought he was going to kiss her.

It had probably been her overactive imagination. The chemistry had almost fried her alive. She'd never wanted a man so much in her life. She'd backed away before she could be tempted to do something stupid. She could just imagine what he would have said if she'd grabbed him and kissed him.

"He wasn't *that* hot in real life. You know how it is," she lied. "Photoshop can make anyone hot. A man looks different when he hasn't shaved."

"Sexy stubble makes some men hotter."

"Not him." She broke off as Lara, their receptionist, walked into the room.

"We've had a ton of requests through the app," she addressed the three of them. "I dealt with the easy ones, the others I sent through to you, Paige. There's a full report in your inbox. We're getting more dog-walking requests. Some elderly clients who don't want to risk going out in the snow."

Paige was all business, Lucas forgotten. "More than The Bark Rangers can handle? Do I need to think about researching additional suppliers?"

"Not yet. The Rangers are thinking of taking on another person. I spoke to Fliss yesterday." Lara put a can of diet soda on Frankie's desk, and a mug of coffee in front of Paige. "I didn't make you anything, Eva, because you already made yourself green tea and you said you were— Oh, crap." She broke off, staring through the glass wall of the office.

"I'm certainly not crap," Eva said stoutly, and then realized Lara wasn't paying her any attention. "What? What are you staring at?"

"Him," Lara said faintly. "I'm married with two children. I'm not supposed to look at men and want to strip them naked."

"Nothing wrong with wanting," Paige said. "It's the doing that causes a problem." She glanced up. "Is that—?"

"Lucas Blade." Eva knocked over her mug of tea. Liquid spread across her desk, soaking everything in sight.

"I guess that answers our question about whether he looks as good as he does in his author photo. I was going to say play it cool," Paige said, "but I guess I'm too late." She stood up, rescued Eva's laptop, grabbed a bunch of napkins left over from an event and tried to stem the flow.

"Not at all hot in real life." Frankie gazed through the glass to the man standing at the reception desk.

"Not even warm. And you're right—that dark stubble is just, well, there are no words for it."

"Shut up." Eva bent down, her face scarlet as she tried to undo the destruction she'd wrought on her desk. "What is he doing here?"

"I don't know, but I think we're about to find out because they directed him this way." Paige disposed of the napkins.

Frankie, who was never flustered, looked flustered. "I'm going to fangirl all over him."

"You? You are Miss Cool. And I've got a massive damp patch on my skirt. I look as if I wet myself." Eva dabbed ineffectually at the fabric and made it worse. "I could hide under the table and you could say I wasn't here."

"Stay seated," Frankie advised. "I'm not usually starstruck, but would it be horribly crass of me to ask if I can take a selfie with him? Seriously, I can't believe I'm meeting the mind behind the books I love."

"His mind is a weird thing," Eva muttered. "What's he doing here anyway?" Her heart was racing. Her hands shook a little. "Does he look angry? Is this about the ball at the Plaza? Maybe he tried to cancel and they're going to bill him anyway. I'm glad he finally left his apartment, but part of me wishes I wasn't the reason."

"Who says you were the reason? There could be a million reasons why he's out and about in Manhattan. Calm down." Paige rose to her feet, her smile warm and professional. "Mr. Blade. I didn't realize you had an appointment."

"I love your books!" Frankie stumbled over the words and Lucas flashed her a smile.

"That's good to know."

Frankie dug her hand into her bag and pulled out one of his books. "I don't suppose you'd—"

"You carry that around with you?" Paige gaped at her. "Don't you get a backache?"

"I couldn't put it down. I've been reading it under my desk when you weren't looking."

"Seriously?" Paige rolled her eyes. "Take a reading day or something, and then come back and concentrate."

"You want me to sign it?" Lucas held out his hand for the book and Frankie handed it over like a person in a dream. "To Frankie, yes?"

"Yes. Anything is f-fine."

Eva and Paige exchanged glances.

Frankie was stammering?

Lucas signed with a flourish and handed it back. "My price is five minutes alone with Eva."

Eva felt her insides turn to the same consistency as melted snow, but then she remembered the way they'd parted.

"If this is about The Snowflake Ball at the Plaza—"

"It isn't. I'm going to call them and explain that it was a mistake." He breathed deeply. "Is there somewhere we can talk?"

She felt a flash of disappointment. She'd hoped that he would find it easier to turn up at the ball than cancel.

"Whatever you need to say, you can say it here." Paige's tone was pleasant but firm. "Don't mind us."

He held Paige's gaze for a moment and then turned back to Eva. "I need you to come back."

"Excuse me?"

"I need you to come back to my apartment."

"Why? Has the Christmas tree dropped its needles?" Eva dug her nails into her palms. "Is there some problem with the food I prepared?"

"The food is delicious and the tree was intact last time I looked. It's a great tree. If you like trees."

"Which you don't."

A ghost of a smile flickered at the corner of his mouth. "I'm growing accustomed to it."

"So if it's not the tree and it's not the food, then what do you need?"

"I need you." His voice was soft. "I need you to come back."

Confusion rushed through her. "In what capacity?"

There was a taut silence. A muscle flickered in his lean cheek. "Inspiration."

"Excuse me?"

He drew in a deep breath. "As you know, I was having some issues writing—"

"I thought you'd fixed that."

"I thought so, too, but it turned out that the moment you left, I could no longer write."

"I don't understand."

"I don't understand either." There was a gleam of frustration in his eyes. "Something about having you there, our conversations, triggered ideas. This time of year is tough for me, and you were a distraction."

"You're asking me to come back and distract you? I don't know anything about writing or the writing process," she said. "I don't really see how I could help. Shouldn't you be talking to your editor? Or your agent? Or if you need another writer, then my friend Matilda is more likely to empathize and understand what you're going through."

"Forget it." Frankie waved a hand. "She and Chase are in the Caribbean making babies."

Lucas shook his head. "I don't need empathy, I need creative inspiration. You gave me ideas for a certain character in my book. While you were there, I can clearly see her, imagine her, see her actions. When you left, she disappeared for me."

"I'm a character in your book?" Warmth spread through her. She couldn't breathe. "You've put me in your book?"

"Not you, specifically, but certain aspects of a character are inspired by you. I thought I had enough to write to the end of the book, but it turned out that wasn't true. The moment you left, I found the writing hard."

Her heart was pounding. He'd thought about her. *He'd put her in his book.* She wasn't going to read anything into that. No. She definitely wasn't. "So I'm the inspiration for one of your characters."

He hesitated. "In a manner of speaking. Loosely."

"I've never been in a book before, loose or otherwise." She was immensely flattered. She told herself it was that and nothing else that was making her heart sing. "I'm honored, but I can't come back. I have to work. I'm the creative side of this company and we're horribly busy."

"I'll pay you." He named a figure that made Frankie choke on her drink.

"It isn't just the money." Paige was calm. "Eva is right. She plays a key role in Urban Genie. She's the creative brain and clients adore her. They always ask for her personally. Even if we could reassign some of her face-to-face meetings, we'd still need her to be available for phone consultations. Would you be happy for her to do that from your apartment?"

"The third bedroom can be easily converted to an office. She can work there."

"In that case I'll give you a rate." Paige tapped on the keyboard. "You want her until Christmas? That's three weeks, not just days but nights, too—"

"Hey, this isn't *Pretty Woman*," Eva protested but Paige ignored her and named a figure that made Eva's jaw drop.

"Done." Lucas didn't hesitate. "You drive a hard bargain. I can see why your business is thriving."

Paige gave him a cool smile. "We charge a fair rate for our excellent service and our business is thriving because we're the best at what we do. You want Eva full-time, in person, and she isn't cheap."

Eva blinked. "I—"

"You have yourself a deal." Lucas stood legs spread, arms folded across his chest, a study in male magnetism and arrogant assurance.

"Wait a minute." Eva stood up, her legs shaking. Saying yes would mean it had all happened on Lucas's terms. He was a man who was used to getting his own way, but she needed to see him flex a little. On principle. "If I'm doing this for you, then I want you to do something for me."

One dark eyebrow lifted. "The amount I'm paying could buy you a small Italian sports car."

"I don't want a sports car."

His gaze locked on hers and tension shimmered between them. "Then what," he asked softly, "do you want me to do for you?" There was an intimacy in that gaze that made her heart kick hard against her ribs.

"I want you to go to the Snowflake Ball."

There was a long, loaded silence.

His expression was unreadable. "Why does it matter to you if I go to the damn ball?"

"Because *I* want to go, and I'm not walking in there on my own. You're going to take me."

At least then she'd be one step closer to achieving her goal of getting out of the apartment.

"And if I say no?"

"Then I won't come and work for you."

His eyes narrowed. "I hardly think your partners would allow you to turn down a piece of business that significant."

"I'm an equal partner. It's my decision," Eva said quietly. "So what's it to be?"

"You're serious?"

"If I'm stuck indoors in your apartment for the next

three weeks, at least I'll have this one opportunity to get out and meet people."

"So you don't plan on being my date. Your plan is to use me shamelessly to gain entry into the ball and then abandon me?"

"Yes. And that shouldn't bother you because I'm sure you'll be mobbed by gorgeous women the moment you set your foot inside the place. With luck, you'll meet someone, too."

"Too?"

"Yes. I'm going to get lucky. I feel it." What she really wanted, of course, was to get lucky with him, but she knew that wasn't going to happen. He wasn't ready for a relationship, and she wasn't prepared to get involved with someone who wasn't ready. She needed a straightforward relationship that made her happy. She didn't have the emotional resilience to cope with more trauma, no matter how scorching the chemistry.

"Have you been talking with my grandmother?"

"No. I planned to stop by to see her tomorrow on my way home. So what's your answer, Mr. Blade? Will you take me to the Snowflake Ball?"

"If that's your price, then yes." A sardonic smile touched his mouth. "You were the one who got me into it. Seems only fair that you have to endure the evening with me."

"Endure?"

"Oh, yeah, the Snowflake Ball at the Plaza will be a real hardship for her," Frankie muttered. "Torture in a tux."

Eva shot her friend a quick glare before turning back to Lucas. "We have a deal?"

"We do. But what happens when this ball doesn't live up to your expectations? I know that top of your Christmas list is meeting someone, but your list of requirements was pretty specific."

Paige frowned. "You know about her list?"

"I do. What were your criteria again?" He ticked them off on his fingers. "Broad shoulders, abs, sense of humor—ability to tolerate your ancient teddy bear and enough stamina to give your condom a decent workout before it expires like the last one you carried in your purse."

Paige glanced at Eva in disbelief. "Ev—?"

Eva felt her face burn. Why did she have such a big mouth? "I don't see anything wrong in being honest, although I admit I didn't mean to tell him all that. It sort of slipped out. And it isn't a teddy bear, it's a kangaroo."

Frankie dropped her head onto her desk. "You're not safe to be let out. If you go to that ball, what's to stop you going home with some sleaze?"

"I am a very good judge of human nature."

Frankie lifted her head and gave Lucas a long, hard look and he gave an almost imperceptible nod, as if they were in perfect agreement on something.

"She'll be safe with me. I promise not to let her go off with anyone unsavory."

"You think you can tell what someone is like by just looking?"

"No." His response was immediate. "That's why

you should know she'll be safe with me. I have no illusions about human nature."

"He doesn't." Eva confirmed it. "It's very disturbing. And I wish you'd all stop talking about me as if I'm some abandoned puppy that needs a home. I can bite when I need to, thank you."

He turned back to her. "So now I've agreed to this, you'll come back and work for me?"

"Yes. I need to pack a few things, though. I'll come over tomorrow."

"Tonight. Time is tight." He checked his watch. "Give me your home address and I'll send a car for you. I don't want you traveling on the subway."

"We'll email the contract over to you right away." Paige was brisk and businesslike and Lucas gave a brief nod and left the room.

Eva stared at her friends. "You just sold me. To the highest bidder."

"He was the only bidder," Frankie said cheerfully and Paige grinned as she opened up their standard contract on her computer.

"I didn't 'sell' you. I cut a very good deal for Urban Genie."

"You sold me for the same price as that small Caribbean island Matilda and Chase are currently staying on."

"And you still get to work while you're there. This is the deal of the century. I love my job. And you, Miss Jordan, are very good at yours. I've pulled up your schedule. We'll reassign your external commit-

ments and the rest you can do from Lucas's apartment. Just check in here with us from time to time."

"I've never been a character in a book before," Eva
said with a hint of trepidation in her voice.

"It's exciting!" Frankie dismissed it with a wave
of her hand. "I want that book! He's the only author
that makes me prioritize reading over sleep. You're
his inspiration. His muse. Whatever. He's obviously
made you his sweet, vulnerable victim. It's cute. I
can't wait to read how he plans to murder you."

"Victim?" The thought made her uncomfortable.
"I was hoping to be the smart, sassy FBI agent or
something. If I'm the victim I'm definitely going to
fight back. I'd use that deadly move you taught me."

Frankie sat back in her chair. "I only taught you
one? A couple more might be useful."

Eva had a vision of Lucas, his body hard on hers
as he pressed her into the floor.

"You think he is going to have me murdered?"

"In his story, Eva. This is fiction. I don't know
anything about how a writer's mind works, I just read
the stuff. And whatever it takes, right? If he needs
you as his muse, then go."

"I don't want to die horribly. Maybe this is a mistake."

"It isn't a mistake. Apart from the fact he's paying
you enough money to ensure that none of us has to
work for the first six months of next year unless we
want to, he's taking you to the ball, Ev. You're going
to love that. Think of all the Prince Charmings you
could meet."

CHAPTER NINE

On the road trip of life, be the driver, not the
passenger.

—Frankie

HE'D BEEN WELL and truly manipulated. He didn't
know whether to punch something, laugh or admire
her.

She was so much tougher than she looked.

And now he was going to the ball, which was the
last thing he wanted to do with his time. He'd been
desperate enough to agree to anything.

His writing, which had flowed smoothly while Eva
had been staying in his apartment, had stopped the
moment she'd left. It was like slamming the brakes
on a car.

As someone who had never required anything
other than a pen and a blank sheet of paper in order
to write, it exasperated him, but after struggling and
wasting an entire day that he could ill afford to waste,
he'd bowed to necessity.

He paced the length of his apartment, keeping his
eyes averted from the snowy expanse of Central Park.

They'd agreed that he would take her to the ball,

but hadn't agreed how long he had to stay. He'd stay ten minutes and leave. And he'd send a car to bring her home when she was done.

Having found a satisfactory solution, he returned to his work.

It was hours later when he heard the tentative knock on the door.

"Lucas?" Her voice came from outside the door and he stood up suddenly, guilty that he hadn't at least been there to welcome her when she arrived.

He opened the door to his study, his mind still in the fictional world he'd created.

She was standing there smiling at him, holding a tray.

He looked at the sweet curve of her mouth.

He was sorely tempted to haul her inside and do what he'd wanted to do that night she'd shown up wearing the peach silk pajamas, but that would lead to more complications than he was ready to handle. He knew enough about her to know they didn't occupy the same fairy-tale land.

"Please tell me that isn't herbal tea."

"You said that my presence inspired your writing, and since we don't know exactly which part of what I did cured your writer's block, I thought we'd better keep doing the same thing. Last time you drank my herbal tea."

"Last time I tipped your herbal tea down the toilet."

"Oh." There was the faintest hint of reproach in her voice. "You're not that careful with people's feelings, are you?"

"You didn't know I tipped it down the toilet."

"Until now."

He gave a half smile. "Honesty seemed the only way to break the flow of herbal tea that's likely to come in my direction otherwise."

"Another way would be to drink it."

He leaned against the door. "So is this how it's going to be? If you're staying here you're going to make my life hell?"

"Not hell—heal*thy*. The word you're looking for is *healthy*." She pushed the tray into his hands. "You drink too much caffeine and alcohol."

"Do I have any other sins you plan to reform while you're here? What about my work ethic?"

"There's nothing wrong with hard work. I admire your dedication."

Her answer surprised him. He was used to being lectured on working too hard. "How about meat? Aren't you going to lecture me on my red meat intake?"

"I'm not feeding you red meat. Dinner tonight is my special vegetarian risotto."

"I'm starting to regret the impulse that drove me to invite you here."

"You're going to love it. And you didn't invite, you demanded. And you already paid up front so you can't back out now."

"You're telling me I've lost all leverage."

"That's right. I'm in charge." She smiled. "Enjoy your herbal tea."

TRYING TO BLOCK out the image of smoldering eyes and that sexy-as-hell body, Eva set to work the next day in the place that was most natural for her. The kitchen.

She'd already planned to add two new festive recipes to her blog, and Lucas would be the beneficiary because he'd get to eat the spoils.

She cooked all afternoon, recorded a new YouTube video, skillfully edited the result and posted it online. Not once in all that time did Lucas emerge.

Occasionally she glanced up the sweep of stairs, but his office door remained firmly closed, which confused her a little. It seemed that needing her for inspiration didn't require him to lay eyes on her.

Darkness fell, cloaking the silvery-white of the park in moonlit shadows. Still there was no sign of him and the silence stretched her nerves to the breaking point.

Eventually she took the stairs that led to the upper floor, knocked on his office door and paused, listening.

There was no sound.

She was about to walk away, when the door opened.

Lucas stood there. "Yes?"

He was the type of guy who could carry off a tux or jeans with equal confidence. Today it was jeans and he filled them well, the denim skimming the powerful muscles of his thighs. His shirt was open at the neck revealing a hint of dark chest chair.

A ripple of sensation skittered over her skin. "Hi."

He looked preoccupied. "Did you need something?"

Her mind blanked.

Confronted by sexy male, she couldn't remember why she'd knocked on his door.

She stared into his eyes and felt her knees go weak and her tummy flip.

"I wondered if you were hungry." She glanced over his shoulder and was ridiculously pleased to see a screen covered in type. "You're writing again? It's working, having me here?"

He blinked and finally focused on her. "Yes," he said. "It is."

"So having me clattering downstairs is inspiration enough. I mean, you're not like an artist who needs his subject sitting in the chair to be able to create? I'm your muse, but you don't need me in the room doing anything muse-like." She thought she saw amusement light his eyes.

"The conversation we had when you brought my tea was enough."

"You refused to drink it, I threatened you. How was that inspirational?"

"I decided that my character would drink herbal tea, and be vegetarian."

"She's vegetarian like me?" Eva was delighted. "And kind to animals?"

He gave her a long speculative look. "She's kind to animals."

"Good. Frankie said you didn't write books with likeable characters, but this book is obviously different. Maybe I should read one of yours after all. Is there one you'd recommend?" She strolled past him into his study, scanning the rows and rows of books and thinking how Frankie would drool if she could see this room. There was never any hardship in choosing a gift for Frankie. All she ever wanted was books and it seemed Lucas was the same.

Close up, she could see that one wall was dedicated to his own work, both English language and foreign editions.

"If you're looking for a happy-ever-after, you won't find it on those shelves."

She paused and admired a photograph on the wall. A log cabin framed by snowy pine trees, nestling in a forest by a lake. "That's idyllic. Where is it?"

"Snow Crystal, Vermont."

"That's where you told people you were on your writing retreat? It looks blissful." She took a closer look, studying the snowy peaks behind the forest. She could imagine it would be the perfect place for someone who wanted to get away from it all. "Romantic. I might have to put it on my bucket list." She turned and saw something flicker in his eyes. Something that made her heart rate surge into overdrive. Sexual awareness uncurled inside her, sliding through her limbs and turning her bones to liquid.

Could he see the effect he had on her? She hoped not, but she knew she wasn't good at hiding either her thoughts or her feelings.

She was here to offer inspiration, and to cook. She was supposed to salivate over the food, not the client.

"I've been going there for decades. It's a family-owned resort. Do you ski?"

"I've never tried it, but I love snow—" She broke off, aware that she'd been tactless. "Sorry."

"Why are you sorry?"

"Because—" She licked her lips. "I know you don't like snow."

His face was expressionless. "You've been reading about how my wife died."

Oh, crap.

"Yes. Not because I'm nosy, but because I was afraid of saying something that might make you feel bad. I didn't want to do that. I know how much you loved her."

There had been surprisingly few photos of them together online, but the ones she'd found had shown them almost glued together, bodies touching as if they couldn't bear to be separated, so close and wrapped up in each other that it had almost hurt to look at them.

Looking at the photos, she'd understood why he hated this time of year. It had robbed him of the love of his life and there was no doubt in her mind that Lucas Blade had loved his wife. Truly loved her. Loved her so much that carrying on without her was almost unbearably hard.

Despite the obvious pain he was feeling now, Eva dearly wanted to love, and be loved, that deeply.

"We haven't discussed the terms of our contract." His voice was cool and formal. "I'll be working most of the time, but I hope you'll treat the apartment as your own."

"If I did that, you'd throw me out within a day. I'm

horribly untidy, remember?" She smiled, desperately hoping to see at least a glimmer of a smile in return, but the mention of his wife had sent him back behind the wall of protection he'd erected between himself and the world. "I'll try to remember I'm a guest, and not drop things where I stand."

"I've watched you in the kitchen. You're meticulous and organized."

"I'm at my best in the kitchen. The rest of my life runs away from me sometimes. It's one of my major flaws, along with talking too much and being terrible in the mornings."

"You're not a morning person?"

Eva shook her head. "I've tried. I've tried cold showers, leaving my alarm clock on the other side of the room—pretty much everything. Nothing works. I don't wake properly until around ten. I try never to use knives before then." She pulled a face. "This is terrible. I'm telling you all the worst things about myself. It's Flaw Friday." Finally she saw a glimmer of a smile.

"Those are the worst things about you? That you drop your clothes where you stand and hate mornings?"

"Thank you for making it sound like nothing, but believe me it drives my friends insane. We all used to work for the same company before we lost our jobs, and I would have been late every day if they hadn't dragged me onto the subway in the mornings. There were days when I didn't even remember the journey."

"I didn't know you'd lost your job."

"We all worked for a company called Star Events. They lost a big piece of business and we were the casualties." Eva remembered the horrible, churning panic of that day. "As it turned out, it was the best thing that could have happened. We decided that we could do what we did for Star for ourselves. That happens in life sometimes, doesn't it? Something terrible happens and you think it's the worst thing ever and then it turns out to be the best." Realizing how her words could be interpreted she closed her eyes. "I didn't mean—"

"I know you didn't. And you don't have to tiptoe around me, Eva."

"It's another of my flaws," she muttered, "my lack of filter between my brain and my mouth. I do have some good qualities, but you must know that or you wouldn't have put me in your book. What are your worst flaws? Apart from the fact that you drink too much and like to lock yourself away on your own."

"I consider both those elements to be lifestyle choices rather than flaws." He seemed to relax again. "I'd say my flaws were that I'm single-minded. When I want something, I go after it and not much gets in my way."

"I don't see that as a flaw." She flopped onto his sofa without waiting for an invitation. "I wish I was more focused. I'm very good when it comes to work and cooking, but the rest of my life is a haphazard mess. I have very good intentions, but most of them don't happen."

"Like what?"

"Exercise. Paige and Frankie both run, but they run in the mornings when I'm still in a coma. Besides, I can barely walk, let alone run. I always promise myself I'll go later when I'm properly awake, but then of course I'm busy and the day happens and I come home exhausted and I'm in a coma again. So mostly I just collapse on the bed with Netflix."

"The upstairs room has been converted into a gym. You're welcome to use it while you're here. I'm usually in there at five thirty, but there's plenty of room for both of us and I have several cardio machines and plenty of free weights."

"Five thirty? That remark tells me you have a lot to learn about me. The heaviest thing I can lift in the morning is my eyelashes so we won't be competing for the weights." But now she knew what was at the top of the curl of stairs. The one part of his apartment that she hadn't seen. A gym. Not for Lucas Blade the sweaty cram of a public gym, or the bitter cold of a run on the New York streets. "No need to ask if you're a morning person."

"I don't sleep much. I've always had a haphazard work pattern. Routine office hours don't work for me. Writing that way doesn't work for me. I'm better writing fast."

"That's good, given the time you have left to write this particular book. Can it be done?" It sounded like an impossible goal to her.

His mouth slanted into a smile of self-mockery. "I guess we're going to find out."

"How can I help? I don't want to knock on your

door and disturb you in the middle of a sentence, but neither do I want you to discover that your muscles have atrophied because you haven't moved from the chair for days."

"You can help," he said, "by not insisting I go to this ball."

"I'll agree to anything except that." She walked to the door. "Get back to work. I'm going to use your gym."

The gym turned out to be a prime room in the apartment, with glass on three sides opening onto a roof terrace.

She could imagine sitting there in the summer months, staring out across the expanse of Central Park with the buildings of midtown framing the park.

Maybe if she had access to somewhere like this, she'd even feel like working out regularly, although she was unlikely to be tempted at five thirty in the morning.

Shuddering at the thought, she pulled her hair into a ponytail and stepped onto the elliptical.

Switching on her favorite playlist, she worked up a sweat, took a shower and then went downstairs to prepare dinner.

They were having risotto, and perfect risotto required one hundred percent attention.

While she gradually added stock and stirred, she thought about his book.

She was desperate to read a snippet, to see what he'd done to the character that was based on her.

He joined her halfway through her preparations

and sat at the counter, watching. "That looks labor-intensive."

"I find it calming. Other people might choose to use a relaxation app, but I make risotto." She adjusted the heat and went back to stirring. "What do you do to relax?"

"I used to write to relax, but that was before I was published."

"I guess it must be different when it becomes your job."

"Risotto is your job."

"True." She added a little more liquid. "But I chose to make this. So how do you choose to relax now?"

"I work out. I find that relaxing. And martial arts. There's a place I go close to here."

"Fighting is relaxing?"

"It's not really fighting." He selected a bottle of wine and opened it. "It's discipline, both mental and physical."

"I've never been big on violence. That's probably why I hate horror movies." She tested the rice to see if it was cooked while he poured wine into two glasses.

He handed her one. "When did you last go to a horror movie?"

"It was a long time ago. My date thought it would be a great way to get me to snuggle close to him. He hadn't reckoned on the fact I might scream." She turned off the heat and took a sip of wine. "Mmm, delicious. So you work out, you do martial arts—what else do you do to relax?"

"I walk the streets of New York, people-watching. You really screamed?"

"I made more noise than the heroine who was getting her throat cut. The woman in the row behind me started screaming too because I scared her so much."

He laughed. "I wish I'd been there."

"Trust me, you don't. If I ever find myself unemployed again, I might try to get a job as a scream artist, if such a thing exists. I have a scream that could make Hitchcock shudder."

"I want to hear your scream."

"I save my best screams for genuine moments of terror. If you don't use screams judiciously, people pay less attention. They'll be thinking, 'oh, Eva is screaming again,' rather than 'quick, something's wrong with Eva.'"

"When did you last scream?"

"Last week when I discovered a very big spider in the bathtub. This is ready." She spooned creamy risotto into two bowls, added a few shaves of fresh parmesan and placed a bowl in front of him. "Enjoy. If you're going back to work after this, I might go for a walk. Given that you didn't poke your head around the door once all afternoon, I presume my absence won't impact on your creative flow."

He paused, fork in hand. "You can't walk alone this late."

"This is New York City. It's almost impossible to find yourself alone, and it isn't *that* late. I don't plan to go into the depths of Central Park. Just wander along Fifth Avenue."

"The stores will be closed."

"That's the safest time." She forked up some rice. "When they're open, I'm dangerous."

"Shopaholic?"

"Not really. More that my taste exceeds my bank account."

"Speaking of taste, this is delicious." He ate and then accepted an offer of second helpings. "Do you have a favorite store?"

"Tiffany's." She didn't even need to think about it. "I like looking at the people who are looking in their window. And sometimes you see a man proposing and the woman's face lights up and it's pretty perfect. Real-life romance."

They'd finished eating and he stood up.

"Let's go."

"Together? Now?" She stared at him. "I have to clear up."

"Leave it."

"You don't strike me as someone who is addicted to retail therapy, and you have a book to write."

"I need a break. And I like hearing you talk."

"Most people want me to talk less."

"You have some interesting observations on the world."

She tried not to be flattered. It was probably more of his research. "So your character is going to take a trip to Tiffany's? Does she fall in love and get married?"

He opened his mouth and then gave a smile. "I

haven't worked out the precise details of her journey yet."

"Well, I can tell you that a trip to Tiffany's would be the perfect ending to any woman's journey."

THEY WRAPPED UP warmly and strolled along Fifth Avenue, their breath clouding the freezing air. The snow had stopped and the snowplows were finally winning the battle. Snow and ice glazed the sidewalks and lay piled in mounds and New York was enveloped in an almost ethereal calm.

The windows of Tiffany & Co. were decorated for the holidays. A cobweb of glowing lights framed the windows and the sparkle of decorations blended with the dazzle of diamonds.

Lucas watched as Eva huddled deeper into her coat and gazed at the tray of jewelry closest to the window.

Then she glanced at a woman who was doing the same thing at a different window.

After a moment the woman walked away and Eva gazed after her.

"That's sad."

"She was doing the same thing you're doing. What's sad about it?"

"She was upset. You couldn't see that? My guess is that the love of her life broke up with her."

"Maybe she broke up with him."

She shook her head. "Then she wouldn't have been staring wistfully in the window of the most romantic jewelry store in the world. She'd imagined herself coming here with him and choosing a ring."

Dragging his gaze from Eva's mouth, Lucas turned his head and watched the woman disappear into the darkness. "And yet you still believe in true love."

"Why not? I can believe in true love without thinking that all relationships are perfect."

He leaned against the wall, sheltering her from the vicious bite of the wind. "Where did you grow up?"

"Puffin Island, Maine. It's a small island the size of a postage stamp—"

"—off the coast of Penobscot Bay. I know it. So you're a small-town girl in a big city."

"I suppose, although I left the small town behind a long time ago."

He didn't agree. She had that trusting view of humanity that came from living in a small-town community where people relied on each other.

His heroine would have the same quality, he decided. She'd arrived in the big city full of hope and then all her illusions had been shattered.

"Do you still have family on Puffin Island?" It was only because he was watching her reactions closely that he saw her breathing change.

"I don't have family at all. Since Grams died, it's just me." She turned and gave him a bright smile. "Shall we walk?"

"You miss her a lot."

"She raised me. She was a mother and a grandmother rolled into one. Let's talk about something else or I'll start sobbing again and it was embarrassing enough the first time."

A few moments before he'd been desperate to

get back to the apartment and write, but now all he wanted was to find out more about her. It was something he'd been born with, this desire to always know more, to look deeper, but he knew that in her case there was something more personal driving him.

"What happened to your parents?"

"I never knew my dad. My mom was eighteen and about to start college when she got pregnant. I guess he thought I'd ruined his life. He wanted her to have an abortion and when she wouldn't he went off to college, and Mom stayed at home with Grams and Gramps. She died when I was born, from some rare complication during delivery. Grams took early retirement so she could stay home with me."

Lucas rarely thought about his own childhood. He'd been raised in the supportive cobweb of close family that included parents, grandparents, aunts, uncles and cousins. His memories were of large gatherings, always noisy because his family was nothing if not opinionated, and of time spent with his brother, of scraped knees, secret hideouts and arguments. There had been nothing there to inspire the darker fiction he wrote. Nothing as lean and spare as the family life she was describing.

"I'm sorry."

"Don't be." Her voice was level. "I never knew my mom and I couldn't have had a happier childhood. My grandmother always said I was the one who saved them. She and Gramps had lost their only child, but they didn't have time to fall apart because I was in neonatal intensive care with issues of my own. They virtually lived at the hospital with me and after about six weeks they brought me home. Grams said I was their most precious gift." She stopped and gazed into a store window, as if she hadn't just revealed something deeply personal.

It was a huge revelation, and it left him stunned. Because she was so refreshingly open, he'd assumed he knew everything there was to know about her. She was someone who shared everything, and yet she hadn't shared this. "I had no idea you lost your mom so young."

"It was hard on Grams."

"And on you."

This new information changed his view of her. It was as if he'd been standing in a shadowy room and someone had suddenly thrown open the shutters and let in the light. He understood now why her grandmother had been everything to her and why she was struggling so deeply with the loss. It explained the seam of vulnerability that he'd sensed within her, and why this time of year, with its emphasis on family and togetherness hurt so much.

"It didn't feel hard to me. In my fairy-tale world, Planet Eva as my friends call it—" she flashed him a brief smile "—family isn't so much about the individual people as what they represent. Family is about love, isn't it? And security. And that doesn't have to come from a mother. It can be a father, or an aunt, or in my case, a grandmother. What a child needs is to grow up with the knowledge that they're loved and accepted for who they are. They need someone who will be there for them no matter what, who they can depend on absolutely so that they know that no matter how many times they screw up, or how many other people have walked away, their family is always there. My grandmother was that person for me. In every way that mattered she was my mother. She loved me unconditionally."

And she'd lost that.

He remembered his grandmother's words.

Maybe your listening skills need work.

He felt a tug of guilt. His grandmother had been right—he hadn't listened properly to Eva. He'd seen the happy smile and he, who prided himself on always looking deeper, hadn't looked deeper. He hadn't seen how lonely she was.

He found himself wanting to say something reassuring, but what could he say? That the love she was searching for came with a price?

"Look at that. It's like a mermaid dress." There was a note of wonder in her voice and he followed her gaze and saw a long evening dress in graduating shades of blue and turquoise, shot with tiny strands of silver.

"You believe in mermaids?"

She lifted her hand like a stop sign. "This is *not* your cue to say something sarcastic or cynical. And I think the person who gets to wear that dress would definitely believe in mermaids." She pulled out her phone, took a picture and then sent a quick email.

"You're sending it to your fairy godmother?"

"I'm going to pretend I didn't hear that. I'm sharing it with Paige because I know she'd appreciate it."

"If you love it, you could come back when they're open and buy it."

"Are you kidding? I couldn't afford a dress like that in a million years. And even if I could, where would I wear it? I think I'd be a bit overdressed wearing it to watch Netflix while eating grilled cheese sandwiches. But that doesn't mean I can't dream."

He looked at the dress again. It was a deceptively simple sheath of fabric, but the strands of silver shimmered under the lights. "You could wear it to the ball you're making me attend."

"I already have a dress." She said it without enthusiasm and he searched her face for clues.

"But?"

"But nothing. It's a great dress. I got it on sale in Bloomingdale's a couple of years ago when I had a black-tie event to attend." She looked away from the window. "I've had enough dress envy for one night. And you should go back. You have a book to finish."

"I'll go back when you go back."

"I'm happy to be left. I walk around New York on my own all the time."

"Maybe, but right now you're with me and I don't want you to walk on your own."

"So underneath that cynical exterior, you're a gentleman."

"It's because of my cynical exterior that I don't want you to walk on your own. And now you'll probably accuse me of being sexist."

"I don't think it's sexist. I think it's good manners. My grandmother would have liked you." Her hair flowed from under the wool hat she wore, honey and buttermilk, with strands of gold catching the light. He wanted to catch it in his hands and feel the texture slip through his fingers.

"So will you come back with me?"

"If that's what it will take to get you writing." She turned and immediately slipped on a patch of ice.

He caught her easily, steadying her before she could hit the ground.

"Careful."

Her hand was locked in the front of his coat and he could smell the scent of her hair. It had been a long time since he'd wanted to kiss a woman, but he wanted to kiss Eva. He wanted to kiss her until neither of them could breathe properly, until he didn't know what day it was and could no longer remember why he'd stayed away from women for so long.

She was the one who pulled away first. "Are you really not looking forward to the ball?"

"About as much as I look forward to completing my tax return."

"That's sad. It's going to be full of wonderful, interesting people."

"What's sad is you believing you can find love in a place like that."

"We're not all lucky enough to meet the love of our life in kindergarten."

He knew she was talking about Sallyanne.

He thought about that first day of school, when

Sallyanne had stolen his apple. She'd charged him a ransom to get it back.

He'd been six years old.

"You really want to go that badly?"

"Yes." She was emphatic. "I promised myself that this Christmas I'd get out. I want to dance until my feet hurt. And meet people. Cinderella wouldn't have met the prince if she'd stayed in the kitchen."

He sidestepped a patch of ice, tightening his grip on her. "He tracked her down across the land. That makes him a seriously disturbed stalker. With a foot fetish."

She laughed. "Only you could put that interpretation on it. Go ahead and laugh, but I really want to meet someone and I'm not going to come across anyone trapped indoors. That ball will be full of people like me, having fun, hoping they might get lucky."

"It will be full of strangers. You won't know anyone."

"I'll know you." Her gaze grazed his and then she looked away quickly, as if she'd put her hand in a flame that was going to burn her. "Everyone is a stranger the first time you meet them."

"Take some advice from someone who knows more about human nature than you do—be careful how much you reveal."

"You don't have to worry about me. I'm not stupid and I've lived in New York City for a decade."

"Your honesty scares me. It's going to get you into trouble."

She gave him an impish grin. "I'm planning on

it. I've written my letter to Santa, confessing that I intend to be a really, *really* bad girl this Christmas."

"You're not safe to be let out. Let's cancel." They were talking, teasing, both of them ignoring the undercurrent of tension.

"No. And when it comes to flirting and relationships, you're as out of practice as I am, so I'd be pretty stupid to take advice from you." She patted his arm. "Relax."

He couldn't relax when she was standing this close to him. "You're not serious about being a bad girl?"

"Oh, I'm serious about that part. But I promise I'll be careful."

"Because you'll filter what you say?"

"No, because I'll use my condom."

CHAPTER TEN

The best accessory is confidence.

—Paige

"HEAD STRAIGHT FOR the best-looking guy in the room." Paige's voice echoed through the speaker on Eva's phone. "Text me his name and Jake will do a background check and see if he has any hidden habits you need to know about."

"How can he do that? Actually, forget it, I don't want to know." Wrapped in a towel, Eva leaned closer to the bathroom mirror as she stroked mascara onto her lashes. "Why are you all so suspicious? You and Frankie are worse than Lucas, and that isn't a compliment." She slipped the mascara back into her bag and checked her reflection.

She already knew who the best-looking man in the room would be, but he was off-limits. There was chemistry, but he seemed to have no problem resisting it.

He didn't want what she wanted. And that was why she was resisting it, too.

"You can't be too careful, Ev."

"Being too careful is probably the reason I haven't

had sex in so long. I'm happy to make a mistake once in a while." But there was one mistake she wasn't going to make, and his name was Lucas. Her hand hovered over her choice of lipsticks. "I will not be texting you and you will not be conducting illicit background checks or whatever else you have in mind. Tonight I am using that old-fashioned method of doing a check on someone. It's called using my instincts."

"Not sure that's foolproof in a place like New York City."

"Relax." She went with a shimmery pink. "And now I have to go. I still have to get dressed."

"What are you wearing?"

"I don't know why you're asking me that when we both know I only have one dress suitable for a black-tie event."

"The black one? You look great in that."

"We both know it's boring, but I couldn't afford to splurge for just a few hours. I'll talk to you tomorrow." She turned and gave a gasp of fright.

Lucas was standing in the doorway watching her, the expression in his dark brown eyes stealing the breath from her lungs.

"Holy crap, you scared me." She pressed her palm to her chest. "Is this another of your horror-writer party tricks? Lurking in the doorway and giving your victims a heart attack?"

He was already dressed, the fabric of his dinner jacket hugging the dense muscle of his shoulders.

"I knocked. You didn't hear me."

The fact that he was dressed made her all the more aware of her own seminakedness.

She clutched the towel self-consciously. "So you thought you'd come right on in anyway and make me jump out of my skin. An innovative way of skinning your victims."

His smile connected straight to her insides.

She tried to hitch the towel higher but realized that just revealed more of her thighs. The bathroom felt too small and there was a tension in the air that hadn't been there earlier. A slow, lethargic heat spread through her. Her nerve endings tingled and her stomach contracted into a tight knot. It was the same feeling she always had around him, but she knew she had to ignore it. "What do you want, Lucas?" Frustration made her unusually irritable.

"I bought something for you. It's on the bed."

She walked past him into the bedroom and stopped.

There, carefully spread out on the bed, was the blue dress she'd admired in the window.

"It's the mermaid dress." Her heart in her throat, she turned to look at him. "I told you I couldn't afford it."

"But I can, and it's a gift. Not that I'm an expert in the whole fairy-tale approach to relationships, but when a girl meets Prince Charming," he drawled, "I'm guessing it's probably best not to do it while wearing a wet towel."

He'd bought her a dress? "I already have a dress."

"A dress that didn't make you excited. If we're

going to this damn ball, then at least you're going to feel excited. I'll leave you to change." There was a raw, sexy quality to his voice that suggested that if he didn't he'd be helping her undress.

She stared after him for a moment and then shook her head to dispel the dizzy clouds of longing.

He'd bought her a dress. Not just a dress but *the* dress.

She should probably refuse, but it was *gorgeous*. Easily the most gorgeous thing she'd ever owned. Refusing would be rude, wouldn't it? And the fact that he'd seen how much she wanted it, and bought it for her—

Her imagination raced, taking her pulse with it.

Why? Why had he bought it? *What did it mean?*

She hadn't even realized she had tears in her eyes until she had to blink to clear her vision.

Crap.

It didn't mean anything except that he was generous. She absolutely couldn't get soppy about Lucas. The point of going to the ball was to meet someone, not fall for a man who didn't want a relationship.

LUCAS POURED HIMSELF a drink. He knew it was going to be the first of several if he had any hope of getting through the evening ahead.

His tux felt uncomfortable, as if it belonged to someone else, but he knew the problem didn't lie with the clothes. It lay in the woman in the next room.

"How do I look?" Eva's voice came from behind

him and he downed the whiskey in the glass and turned.

He was grateful that he'd swallowed before looking.

"You look—" His mouth dried and he licked his lips. What the hell had he done? He was finding it hard enough to keep his hands off her, and he'd just made it even harder.

"What? You were going to say something?" She stroked her palms over the curve of her hips and gave him a shy smile. "It fits perfectly."

"Yes." His voice cracked and he cleared his throat. "Good."

"How?"

He tried to absorb the question but his brain had ceased to function normally. "How what?"

"How does it fit so perfectly? Did you drug me and measure me in your sleep? Did you steal one of my dresses and send it to the store?" She lifted her hand to her mouth, her eyes wide. "Listen to me! I'm starting to sound like you. You've turned me into a suspicious cynic in less time than it takes to bake a cake. Are you proud?"

He wasn't sure what he was, but it was very uncomfortable.

"Say something." Her hand dropped. "It isn't easy finding clothes to fit me. I'm a weird shape. How did you do it?"

Her shape looked perfect to him.

"I called your friend Paige. As I'm officially now a client of Urban Genie, it entitles me to full concierge services. I can ask you to send flowers to my grand-mother, bake me a cake or walk my dog."

"You don't have a dog and I just spoke to Paige a few minutes ago. She asked me what I was wearing."

"I guess she was trying to work out if I'd given you the dress."

She twirled, throwing him a cheeky look over her shoulder. "So what do you think? Am I going to get lucky tonight?"

He looked past the dazzle of blue to the irrepress-ible smile. It was a sure thing. What man in his right mind wouldn't want to go home with her?

"I think it could happen." And he felt a flicker of unease, because she was so willing and ready and open to love. She had no barriers, no fears, no filter.

Had he ever been that way? Maybe, before life had ripped at his hopes and sprinkled the remains around him like confetti.

"I expect you to introduce me to everyone you know. And if you're going to score tonight yourself, you need to look extra handsome." She stood on tip-toe and adjusted his bow tie, the soft scent of her perfume enveloping him. She smelled like summer, like a bunch of freshly picked flowers, like sunshine and long lazy days. He wanted to bury his hands in her hair and taste her mouth. And he didn't want to stop there.

He could do it right now. He could take this thing to its natural conclusion and he was confident she'd be right there with him.

And then what? What happened afterward?

Heat rose inside him and he tried holding his breath, hoping that whatever she was doing to his bow tie, she'd get it done fast.

"I gave up 'scoring' in my teens."

The backs of her fingers brushed against his throat. "I'm sure. But maybe that's the first step forward for you."

"Maybe I don't want to take that step." He couldn't stop looking at her mouth. The lipstick she'd chosen was barely more than a shimmer, but it was enough to hold his attention. "Maybe I'm happy staying where I am."

"Not an option, Blade. Now smile."

"I'm going to a ball. Why would I smile?"

"Because your smile is sexier than your scowl, and for you, tonight is all about pulling women."

"I can't believe you're saying that."

"I'm your wingman. My job is to help you get the girl." Her husky voice curled around his senses like wood smoke.

"I don't want the girl, so I don't need a wingman."

"I know you're scared, but I'm right here for you cheering you on."

"I'm not scared. I'm uncomfortable, and that's because I don't like dressing up to make conversation with people who have no more interest in me than I do in them." And because she was standing so close he couldn't concentrate.

"You're going to be fine, Lucas." The kindness in her eyes took his breath away. His heart, frozen for what felt like a lifetime, started to beat.

"I'm the writer, not you. What does 'fine' even mean?"

"Before you continue with your insults, I should remind you that you had writer's block until I came along." She nudged him. "I'm going to find you a gorgeous blonde with a pretty smile who will make you forget your fears."

"I've told you, I don't have fears." Hell, he didn't want this. He didn't want the emotions stirred up.

"Everyone has fears and some people are afraid of showing them, which in fact makes you doubly scared. You're scared, and you're scared of being scared. That's a whole lot of scared."

"Are you done psychoanalyzing me?"

"I'm just getting started. Why *are* men so afraid of admitting fear?"

"I don't know. Maybe because I'm not afraid. And blondes aren't my type." He kept his gaze away from her blond hair. "I prefer brunettes."

"Then I'll find you the perfect brunette."

"Don't waste your time. I won't talk to her."

"Because you're scared."

"Fine, I'm scared. Is that what you want to hear? I'm so scared I'm thinking of staying here."

"You said 'fine.' And you can't stay here. We had a deal, Blade."

"You're a sadist."

She covered his lips with the tips of her fingers. "Quiet."

All it would take was the slightest movement of his lips and her fingers would be in his mouth.

He lifted his hand and closed his fingers around hers. "Why are we talking about me when tonight is all about you?"

She seemed to be barely breathing. Her fingers shook slightly in his.

He'd had no idea there could be so much tension between two people who weren't even looking at each other.

Gently she eased her hand away. "You're right. Tonight is all about me, and we should go." Her voice was bright and she kept her eyes away from his. "This is a once-in-a-lifetime evening. I don't want to miss a single moment. It's going to be amazing."

A once-in-a-lifetime evening where he got to watch her flirt with other men.

Lucas reached for his jacket, wondering how in hell that was going to be amazing.

THE PLAZA HOTEL was decorated like a snow palace, complete with towering ice sculptures lit by a dazzle of fairy lights.

It was like entering a grotto. Sensing that Lucas was about to turn around and walk out, Eva quickly handed her coat to a waiting attendant.

"It's like something from Narnia, although it's funny to think they're using fake snow when there is so much of the real stuff right outside the door."

"I guess they didn't want the gray slush or the inconvenience of ice and cold."

To anyone listening, their conversation would have sounded comfortable, as if they'd had a thousand similar exchanges over the course of their relationship. What wouldn't be so easy to detect would be the undercurrent of tension that had simmered between them since that shared moment in the apartment. They were dancing around each other and it wasn't the sort of dancing she'd had in mind.

In the end Eva had chosen to pretend it hadn't happened. That nothing had changed.

Nothing *had* changed, had it? They'd had a moment, that was all. And it wasn't the first time.

She walked through the doors into the ballroom, noticing the way heads turned toward Lucas. Despite his reluctance to attend, he looked more the part than anyone else in the room.

She felt a deep ache in her chest. She couldn't afford to want what she couldn't have.

"All right." She injected enthusiasm into her voice. "We should separate."

Lucas turned, his gaze intense and unsmiling. "Separate?"

"If people think I'm with you, no one is going to ask me to dance, let alone anything else." She saw his mouth tighten.

"I'm not leaving you alone."

"Lucas, you have to leave me alone. That's the idea."

"This place is a meat market."

"I hope not, because I'm vegetarian." She glanced at him, wondering if any man had ever looked this good in a dinner jacket. *He was temptation in a tux.*

"Would you smile? You look as if I've dragged you to the dentist."

"I promised to accompany you. I didn't promise to enjoy myself."

"Let yourself go a little. It's so long since you've been out, you might be surprised how much fun it is to talk to real humans. You spend too long in the world of serial killers." She gestured with her head. "Do you know that guy over there? The one smiling at me?"

"That's a fake smile. You can tell by the way his lips pull over his teeth. He's hunting."

"Hunting?"

"For his next victim. Look at the focus in his eyes."

Eva was finding it hard to focus on anyone but Lucas. "You think he's a serial killer?"

"More like a serial adulterer. He's been married four times. His last wife was eight months pregnant when he left her."

"You can tell all that by looking at the way he smiles? That's impressive."

"I can tell all that because I know who he is. His name is Doug Peterson and he's a partner at Crouch, Fox and Peterson. They're a law firm. Do *not* under any circumstances be tempted to smile back."

"The purpose of tonight is for me to get out and meet people."

"Not people like him. He's coming over. I'll deal with him."

She was about to protest that she was perfectly

able to deal with him herself, but Doug Peterson was already standing in front of them.

"Lucas. Good to see you back in the saddle." He grasped Lucas by the hand, kept eye contact for a fraction of a second and then turned to Eva. "And who is your charming date?"

If only. "I'm not—"

"This is Eva." Lucas clamped his hand around her wrist in a possessive gesture. "We won't keep you, Doug. I'm sure you have a busy night ahead."

Doug's gaze lingered on the dip in Eva's neckline and then he smiled, flashing perfect white teeth.

Like a shark before a meal, Eva thought, resisting the temptation to tug at her dress.

"Got to hand it to you, Lucas, when you come back, you do it in style." He walked away and Eva stared after him in disbelief.

"You let him think that we—"

"Yes."

She could feel the firm grip of his fingers around her wrist. "You didn't need to do that. I could have handled him."

"I handled him for you."

"Don't do it again. If you keep 'handling' people, I'm not going to meet anyone. Everyone is going to think I'm with you." And being with Lucas was something she was trying not to think about. Each time he touched her, each time he looked at her, it was getting harder.

"If that's what it takes to keep you safe."

"I don't want to be safe! I want to *live*."

"When we find someone I think can be trusted, I'll make it clear we're not together."

"If we're waiting to find someone *you* think can be trusted, we're going to be here all night. You don't trust anyone." She glanced down at her wrist, still encircled by his strong fingers. "Are you going to let me go?"

He didn't loosen his grip. "I'm keeping you out of trouble."

"That's why I'd like you to let me go. I'm trying to get into trouble, and you're preventing it." She scanned the room and saw a pretty brunette on the far side of the dance floor. "She has a nice smile. How about her?"

"You're bisexual?"

"I was thinking of you. She's your type."

"How do you know?" There was an edge to his voice. "You saw the pictures of Sallyanne, and you thought you'd find someone just like her, is that it? The perfect replacement?"

"No. You told me you didn't like blondes, and that you prefer brunettes." She saw a muscle flicker in his jaw.

"I apologize."

"Don't apologize for feeling sad and for finding this whole thing difficult." There were people milling around, but neither of them paid any attention.

"I shouldn't have come. It was a mistake."

"I think the fact that you find it hard is a good reason to have come. It will be easier next time." She slid her hand into his. "I'll stop matchmaking. Don't be mad. My intentions were good, just as yours presumably were when you sent that guy packing just now."

"That's not the same thing."

"It is. We're both interfering in each other's lives, so here's the deal. I'll butt out of yours, if you butt out of mine."

His gaze was fixed on the dance floor. "What if you decide to leave with a sleaze?"

"I have a PhD in dealing with sleazy men. Ask that woman to dance. She has a lovely smile."

"You said you weren't going to interfere."

"I lied." She poked him in the arm. "She looks nice."

"Nice? What sort of word is *nice*?"

"Don't mock me. If you made me a scrambled egg and it wasn't perfect, I would simply say thank you. I wouldn't point out all the ways you could have made it better."

"You're right. I apologize."

"It's okay. I know that it's being here that's making you moody and it's my fault because I forced you to come. But we're here now, and I'm going to enjoy it so stop scowling."

He turned to look at her, his eyes glittering dark under the lights. "Maybe I'm not afraid. Maybe I just don't want what you want. Has that occurred to you?"

"You don't want friendship and love? Well, of course you don't, because those two things are pretty horrible. Having someone who cares about you and brings out the best in you? Yuck. Much better to be lonely and unloved, that way you know for sure you're never going to get hurt."

"Sarcasm doesn't suit you."

"No? I thought it was the perfect accessory for your scowly face."

"*Scowly* isn't a word."

"Well, it should be. And don't be superior." But her mind wasn't really on the argument because she was thinking about what he'd said. "Are you serious?"

"That *scowly* isn't a word? Yes."

"I meant, were you serious about not wanting love?"

He paused just long enough for her to know that she had her answer.

Her heart ached for him. "It hurts that much?"

He stared across the room, his gaze fixed on the dance floor. "Yes."

She wished they weren't having this conversation here, surrounded by people.

"When something is hard, the best thing is to just get out there and do it."

He turned to look at her. "Have you ever been in love?"

"No, but it's on my bucket list."

"If you haven't been in love then you're not in a position to judge whether it's something a person would want more than once in a lifetime."

"I wasn't suggesting you go out there and fall in love. I was thinking smaller. Start with a dance. Even if you're not going to, then I am. I'd like to spread my feathers."

"You mean your wings. Feathers are ruffled." But the light banter held new layers of intimacy. It was superficial because they chose to keep it superficial, not because they didn't each have a deeper understanding of the other.

"I'm starting to understand why you're still single. If you keep correcting people it makes them want to slap you, not seduce you. At least talk to a few people. There isn't a woman in this room who isn't secretly hoping you'll dance with them."

"That's because they know I have money."

"It's more likely to be because you're pretty hot when you don't scowl. Being your wingman is hard work. I might have to charge you overtime." She nudged him. "Smile. Try it and let's see if you're mobbed. I'll stand on the other side of the room and watch."

He frowned. "No. Eva, you can't—"

She forced herself to walk away, even though all she wanted to do was stay by his side. He needed to meet someone who interested him and that was never going to happen while she was standing there. And she wouldn't meet anyone either, if only because while Lucas was close by he was the only man she noticed.

She was going to forget the fact that he was better-looking and more interesting than anyone else there. She was going to forget the way he listened so attentively and the way he made her feel.

She was going to meet someone who actually wanted a relationship.

WHY HAD HE agreed to come?

On the far side of the room he could see Eva, laughing up at a man who had his back to him. Was it someone he knew? The raw, gut-wrenching jealousy was something he'd never felt before and he certainly hadn't expected to feel it tonight.

"Lucas! It really is you." A female voice interrupted his thoughts and he turned to see a beautiful redhead smiling at him.

"Caroline." He leaned forward and dutifully kissed her on both cheeks. He could smell the alcohol and see the extra bright glitter of her eyes.

She'd been an acquaintance of Sallyanne's, although not one of the inner circle.

"I didn't expect to see you here. Are you alone?" She slipped her arm through his. "We should dance. Celebrate being young and alive." Her expression froze as she realized what she'd said.

The look in her eyes took him back to the time of his wife's death, when everyone had walked on eggshells and he'd found himself comforting those who had no idea what to say to him. His role had been to convince them that he was all right, and then to make them feel all right.

Social situations were almost invariably fake, but since Sallyanne's death they'd become even more so. Fake smiles, fake jollity.

And Caroline, having put her foot in it, now seemed determined to make up for it by being extra concerned and caring. "How have you been, Lucas?"

Her hand stroked over his sleeve, lingering just a little too long for friendship.

Across the room he saw Eva laugh again and watched as the man turned slightly and moved closer to her.

Now he had a better view, and—

Shit. It was Michael Gough. Single man of the town. Eva wouldn't stand a chance against him. However good her radar was, she was unlikely to detect the flaws in Michael. On the surface he was a charmer, but Lucas knew with one hundred percent certainty that he'd use that condom of hers and then break her heart.

"Lucas?" Caroline was still next to him, standing a little too close.

"Have a great evening, Caroline."

"Oh, but—"

He didn't hear the rest of her sentence because he was striding across the ballroom, half-blinded by the sparkle and dazzle of the dance floor and the light, avoiding spinning couples. The music was nothing more than a faint background noise, barely audible through the pounding of blood in his head.

He reached Eva just as Michael leaned closer.

"You," he purred, "are the most interesting woman I've met in a long time. You have the most incredible breasts. And beautiful hair. I want to see how it looks on my pillow."

Anger misting his vision, Lucas opened his mouth, but before he could speak Eva reached up and tugged out a strand of blond hair.

"Here." She handed it over and her voice was kind. "You can take this one and find out. Unfortunately my breasts are attached to me, so I can't give you one of those to take home."

Lucas stilled. He knew Michael was considered a catch and he'd expected Eva to fall hook, line and sinker for his smooth patter.

Instead she'd done what few women did. She'd rejected him.

Michael recognized the snub and his mouth tightened, but he wasn't about to give up, particularly when he realized Lucas had overheard. "Let's dance."

Eva shook her head. "No, but thank you."

"You're a very beautiful woman. I'm interested in getting to know you better."

"Are you?" Eva studied him thoughtfully. "How about my brain? Are you interested in that part of me? Or my feelings? What makes me laugh and cry?"

Michael looked mildly alarmed. "I—"

"I didn't think so. When you say you're interested in me, what you *really* mean is that you're interested in taking me somewhere dark and having sex with me. There's nothing wrong with that, except that I'm not interested." She smiled up at him. "Thank you for the compliment. Enjoy your evening."

With that she turned and walked slap into Lucas.

"My turn for a dance, I think." He took Eva's hand in his and hauled her against him, ignoring her startled look.

Michael's brows rose. "Lucas? Didn't realize you two knew each other."

"We're living together." Lucas saw Eva's eyes narrow in a warning and Michael smiled, the anger gone from his face.

"That explains everything. You always were a man of excellent taste. Enjoy the ball." He walked away and Eva turned back to Lucas.

"Why did you do that? Why did you *say* that?"

"He was making a move on you."

"And I handled it! But now he assumes that the reason I refused him is because I'm with you, not because he was behaving like a douche bag."

"It's better that way. He's a man whose ego means a lot to him. I know him, Eva."

"You know everyone! Unfortunately I don't, and I never will unless you stay on the other side of the room."

"I'm watching out for you. I'm here to save you from yourself." He ignored the little voice inside him that told him his intervention had little to do with her and everything to do with him.

"Did I look as if I needed saving?"

"Eva, he's a serial heartbreaker. And he has a wife."

"I know."

"You do? How?"

"He has a pale ring of skin on the finger where his wedding ring should be. Proof that he only takes it off when it is no longer convenient to be married." She sighed and slid her arm into his. "I'm touched that you cared enough to come shooting over here to save me. It's a lovely trait, but I've been dealing with guys like him since I was a teenager. Guys who stare at my chest and my hair and assume I can't string a sentence together."

"A first meeting in a place like this is almost always predicated on sexual attraction."

"True, but I can tell when a guy just wants to get inside my pants and when someone actually likes me enough to want to know me better." Her smile dimmed. "It's probably the reason I've been celibate for so long. The sad truth is, most men don't want to know me better, so that probably makes me an idealist."

He thought it made them idiots, but didn't say so.

He didn't want to think about them at all.

He let go of her hand, and slid his hand around her waist. "Let's dance."

"You hate dancing. You only suggested that to get me away from Marauding Michael."

"But you love dancing."

"I do. That's the main reason I wanted to come tonight. I want to dance until my feet hurt and my head is spinning."

He could think of a hundred ways to make her head spin that had nothing to do with dancing, but he pushed the thought down quickly. "So let's dance."

Several men were looking at her and Lucas swept her onto the dance floor before one of them had a chance to claim her.

He wasn't sure he wouldn't have punched them and laid them out cold.

Eva put her hand on his shoulder, keeping a respectable distance between them. "I love dancing. I took ballet classes until I was fourteen."

"I bet you danced the part of the Sugar Plum Fairy?"

"Yes, but how did you—?"

"Never mind."

"Grams used to take me to watch the New York City Ballet every Christmas. It was our routine, and I loved it. Snowflakes, glitter and beautiful music. It always put me in a Christmassy mood. I used to come home and twirl and wish I was a proper ballerina."

He looked down at her, imagining her in pink tights and shiny ballet shoes, dancing in a dream. And he wondered how she'd made it to adulthood without losing those shiny illusions about life and people.

She danced as she had in the kitchen, her movements smooth and fluid, her hair spinning around her bare shoulders, her megawatt smile lighting her face.

"This is so much fun."

He didn't disagree. "It's certainly a lot better than making small talk with boring people."

"You're very rude."

"I am. You'd probably be well-advised to avoid me."

"I tried that. But apparently you can't resist interfering with my love life. And I have to watch you closely so that you don't end up being tomorrow's headline."

Their efforts to talk above the music brought them closer.

"Do you blame me? You're reckless, and I made a promise to your friend Frankie."

"I'm an excellent judge of character."

"If you research homicides, you'll discover that most people are killed by someone they know."

She pulled away slightly, her eyes bright with exasperation. "We're at a ball, Lucas. A dreamy, romantic ball. And you're telling me I'm going to be murdered by one of my friends?"

"I'm telling you that if you *were* murdered, it would, in all likelihood, be by someone you knew. I'm trying to educate you. Encourage a little caution."

"You have a twisted view of life. And we're having one dance, that's all. First because if I talk to you for too long I'll have to sleep with the lights on, and second because if I'm dancing with you I'm never going to meet anyone. And neither are you."

The music slowed and Lucas expected her to pull away but instead she leaned her head on his chest and slid her arms around him. Awareness flowed over his skin and seeped into his bones. His mind emptied. His brain felt slow and heavy and he couldn't find any words that seemed to fit the occasion, but fortunately Eva had plenty to say.

"Have you made a New Year's resolution yet? Because if not, I have the perfect one for you." She was soft and pliant, her body melting into his.

"I can guess what it is," he managed to respond, which he saw as an achievement given that he could hardly breathe.

"I'm sure you can't." She rested her palm on his chest, over his heart, and looked up at him.

"You want me to promise to get out there and start dating."

"Wrong. I want you to stop always looking for a person's hidden bad side."

"It's the way I'm made. It's not something I can turn off."

"Of course it is. Your work has made you that way. You need to make a distinction between work and real life."

They swayed together, eyes locked, insulated from the people around them.

"If I told you to start being more suspicious of people, could you?"

"Maybe, but I don't think it would be a very nice way to live." She snuggled closer and he tensed and then let his hand slide to her back.

He felt the warmth of her skin through the thin fabric of her dress.

The dress he'd bought her. *Silk and sin.*

Giving up on restraint, he drew her closer still, molding the soft curves of her body against the hard planes of his. She slid her arms around his neck and rested her head on his shoulder. Easy. Natural.

Desire rushed through him, brutal and sharp. He reflected on how a person could want something so badly even knowing it was a mistake.

He should let her go. He should make some flippant comment about needing to talk to people and mingle, but he didn't. He held her closer, blanketing

himself in her warmth, taking what he could, while
he could. He didn't hear the music and he didn't see
the people dancing close to him. He didn't care what
other people thought or what they said. He didn't want
to think about them, or about Sallyanne.

All he cared about was dancing with Eva and making this moment last as long as possible.

It was like lighting a candle in the dark. He didn't
know how long it would take for the flame to burn
out, but until it did he was going to savor every moment of the light.

Beams of light played over the ceiling of the room,
turning Eva's hair to shiny gold.

Her head was bowed and all he could see of her
face was the sweep of her upturned nose and the soft
curve of her mouth.

The music changed again but she showed no sign
of wanting to move away and he had no intention of
letting her go, so they danced on, locked together,
the rhythm of their bodies following the rhythm of
the music. He wondered why he'd never before realized that dancing could be almost as intimate and
personal as sex.

He felt the light touch of her fingers on the back
of his neck and the warmth of her body against his
palm, and he knew in that moment that he didn't want
her to go home with anyone else.

He wanted her to go home with him. And it had
nothing to do with protecting her. Those reasons
would have been selfless and his were all selfish.

Because they were wrapped together so intimately,

he was aware of the change in her, too. He could feel it in the way she held herself, in the almost unbearable tension of her slender frame.

"Let's get out of here." He murmured the words into her hair, half hoping she'd resist. "Unless you want to stay? This ball was your dream." He asked the question and felt her still in his arms.

She lifted her head and he felt the warmth of her breath on his cheek.

"You want to leave?" Her words were a whisper in his ear. "I wanted you to meet someone interesting."

There was a long silence while they both wordlessly admitted what they already knew.

Finally, when the tension had almost suffocated them, he eased away from her and looked deep into her eyes. "I'm with the only person who interests me."

She swallowed. "Me, too."

Pretense, humor, reticence all fell away and were replaced by naked honesty.

They were no longer moving, no longer pretending to dance or be part of the party that swirled around them. They were in their own secluded, private world. Separate. Apart.

Rose pink spread across Eva's cheeks and her eyes sparkled sapphire blue under the lights. "Let's go." She took his hand but still Lucas paused, held back by the knowledge they were about to do something that couldn't be undone.

"Are you sure?"

"Sure? Oh, Lucas—" She touched his face with her palm. "I've never been more sure of anything."

CHAPTER ELEVEN

Always be good, unless being bad looks like more fun.

—Eva

THEY KEPT A distance from each other in the car, neither of them trusting their ability to control what they were feeling.

Visibly tense, Lucas loosened his bow tie and flicked open the top button of his shirt.

Eva's gaze slid to his throat. She wasn't able to look at him without wanting him. "Are you hot?"

The look he gave her was so intimate her insides melted. "Something like that."

She wondered if they could ask the driver to go a little faster. It was hardly any distance to Lucas's apartment. They probably could have run there faster than he was driving.

Her hand wandered across to Lucas and he took it in a firm clasp, pressing her palm against the hard muscle of his thigh.

Every touch increased the anticipation. Longing made her shaky and weak.

By the time they eventually arrived at his building she was so desperate to kiss him that she was almost ready to drag him into the park and risk frostbite rather than wait the extra few frustrating minutes while they took the elevator to his apartment.

The moment the elevator doors closed they came together like magnets.

His hand cupped her head and his mouth crushed down on hers, and all she could think was finally, *finally*. After that, everything blurred. She felt the erotic stroke of his tongue and the urgency of his hands as he shoved her back against the wall of the elevator, trapping her body against his. It was intense, impelling, and so exciting that all she could do was snatch in a breath and hold on.

His kiss bordered on the rough but she didn't care. She speared the silky strands of his hair with her fingers and drew him closer, desperately trying to drink in more of him. Somewhere in the distance she heard a muted ping and Lucas nudged her out of the elevator without releasing his hold on her.

They fumbled their way into his apartment and as the door swung closed, all restraint left them.

Breathing heavily, he dragged his mouth from hers and trailed his lips over her jaw and down her throat, his fingers peeling down the tiny straps that held her dress in place. The dress slithered to the floor and she felt the rush of cool air against her heated skin.

With a groan of appreciation, he cupped one of her breasts in his palm, dragging his thumb over the straining peak. She arched into him, feeling the thickened hardness of him pressing against her. Sensation showered on sensation. It was like being caught under a waterfall with no opportunity to catch her breath.

His lips followed his hands and he drew her into the heat of his mouth, the skilled flick of his tongue driving her wild.

"Wait—my purse—" She tried to focus, tried to find the place she'd dropped her clutch, but her head was spinning.

"You don't need your purse."

"My condom—"

Swearing under his breath, he drew away from her just long enough to locate and rescue her purse. He pushed it into her hands and then swung her and the purse into his arms.

"Where are we going?"

"Bed."

"The wall works just fine for me." Her need for him eclipsed everything.

She couldn't have said how they made it from the door to his bedroom, as she was too busy kissing her way down the roughness of his jaw, exploring hard lines and male textures.

He lowered her to the floor, the power of his body steadying hers as she stood on shaky legs. She felt him, hard and ready, through the thin fabric of her underwear and closed her fingers in the front of his shirt.

"Now. Now. Now—" She repeated the word over and over again like a mantra and he crushed his mouth to hers to silence her, his rough "no" muted by the pressure of his lips on hers.

She ran her hands down his back. "Don't make me wait. It's been a while."

"All the more reason why it's worth doing this properly." His hands were in her hair, his mouth on hers and they kissed, both of them insatiable, as if the erotic dance of tongues and the heated exchange of breath were necessary for life.

It was the first time she'd been inside Lucas's bedroom, but she didn't even look at it. She could have been anywhere, for all the attention she paid to her surroundings. Her whole world was him, and she couldn't look away from the molten burn of desire in his eyes.

She slid her hand down his body and covered the thickness of him with the flat of her hand. The intimacy of that touch seemed to shock him from the frenzy that consumed them both.

"This is crazy." He groaned the words against her mouth. "You want true love, and I'm not Prince Charming."

"Prince Charming was a weird stalker guy with a foot fetish." Breathless, she locked both hands behind his neck to stop him pulling away. "You taught me that."

"But he married the girl."

"I don't want to marry you. I just want you to give me an orgasm."

"Just the one? You have low expectations." His mouth was back on hers, his kiss skilled and deliciously explicit.

Had a kiss ever felt like this before? No. Never.

She tugged his shirt from the waistband of his trousers and he caught her hand, his breathing ragged.

"Eva—"

"I want this." And then it occurred to her through the mists of desire that perhaps he was looking for a reason to stop. "How about you?"

"Yes." He didn't hesitate. "Yes, I want this."

"In that case—" She hooked her leg behind his and a second later he was on his back on the bed staring up at her.

"What the hell was that?"

"That," she said proudly as she straddled him, "was my deadly move." She reached down and fumbled with the buttons of his shirt. "I need you naked." Her fingers slid on the fabric and she gave a growl of frustration and lowered her hands to his zipper instead. "Forget it. Naked is overrated."

She heard him swear under his breath and then he covered her hands with his and helped her finish the job. His clothes hit the floor and she felt another stab of desire as she ran her hands over powerful male muscle.

It had been so long since she'd had a relationship that had gone beyond a conversation and a kiss. So long since she'd been naked with a man. *Since she'd touched and been touched.*

Maybe she should have been nervous, but she wasn't. She'd never wanted anything more in her life.

He flipped her onto her back and shifted himself over her, pinning her there with his weight.

Breathless, she slid her hand over his shoulder. "What's wrong? Can't stand a woman on top?"

"It's the only way I can slow this down. You wanted an orgasm. I'm here to make sure it's the best orgasm you've ever had."

"Honestly, any orgasm would be good." She was squirming under him but he pinned her flat, holding her still.

"You need to lift your ambitions, sweetheart. Never settle for good when you can have great."

"Okay, but could you just—"

"No." He silenced her with his mouth. "How we do this is my decision. You're delegating."

Just to be sure she got the message, he held both of her hands trapped in one of his as he worked his way down her body, intent on exploring every inch of her.

She decided he obviously knew a lot about torture.

"Lucas—please—"

His response was to peel away her underwear and spread her legs.

He ignored her muted protest just as he'd ignored her plea for haste.

He explored her, the intimate stroke of his tongue arousing her to a peak she'd never known before. It was almost impossible not to move, not to squirm, but he held her trapped, totally at his mercy.

She felt the gentle slide of his fingers inside her and held her breath as he drove her higher and higher with a relentless patience and skill that left her writhing and desperate.

She came in a shower of blinding pleasure, her cries filling the room.

Afterward she felt weak and limp. Emotion overwhelmed her. Tears filled her eyes and she kept them tightly shut, not daring to look at him in case the swell of feeling spilled over.

She felt him shift up her body, felt the rough hair on his chest graze the sensitive tips of her breasts.

"Look at me." His soft command made her open her eyes.

She hoped he couldn't see the shine in them. "Thank you—"

"Don't thank me yet. I'm just getting started." He brushed his lips over hers one more time and then leaned across to grab something from the nightstand.

She tugged at his shoulder. "Is that my condom?"

"No, but don't worry, we'll get to that one later. We have all night." His voice was husky and raw with desire and her stomach flipped.

All night.

"Lucas." She breathed his name, her heart racing as she felt the thickened length of him brush against her intimately. "I know you like keeping people in suspense, but—"

"Suspense can be overrated." He slid his hand under her bottom and entered her slowly, taking his time, his gaze holding hers as he filled her, coaxing her body to take all of him.

He paused, giving her time to adjust, murmuring soft words into her hair, and she stroked her hand down his back, feeling the ripple of muscle under her seeking fingers. She hadn't thought anything could feel this good, but she'd been wrong about that, just as she'd been wrong about so many other things.

She arched under him, wrapping her legs around him and he thrust deeper, his slow rhythm creating an avalanche of sensation. She felt the brush of his leg against the sensitive skin of her inner thigh, the warmth of his mouth, the strength of his hand and she felt *him*. Felt the pulsing thickness of him filling her. And with each delicious, perfectly timed stroke, he drove her toward pleasure until finally she felt herself shatter again, and this time the ripples of her body coaxed his to the same conclusion.

EVA WOKE IN the dark to find herself alone in the bed.

Her body ached in ways she hadn't felt in a long time. Maybe never.

She turned her head to see if Lucas was in the bathroom, but there was no sliver of light under the door.

Dragging herself from the delicious clouds of sleep, she sat up and focused on the room.

Part of her wanted to snuggle back down in the nest of bedding and sink back into the deep delicious sleep, but another part of her needed to find him.

She thought about the intimacy and the discoveries they'd made about one another, not just the first or second time, but afterward. There had been a tectonic shift in their relationship. Neither of them had held anything back.

Was she the first woman he'd slept with since his wife?

Was he regretting just how much they'd shared?

The thought of it marred what, for her, had been a perfect night.

Eva slid her legs out of bed and reached for Lucas's shirt, pulling it on to keep the worst of the night chill away.

The arms fell past her fingers and the hem to midthigh. Rolling the sleeves back, she walked barefoot out of the bedroom in search of him.

The door to his office was open, but at first glance the room appeared to be empty. The light was out and the laptop lay closed on his desk. She was about to turn away and search for him downstairs when she saw his figure sprawled on the sofa. He had a glass of whiskey in his hand.

Something about the way he sat, the utter stillness, tugged at her heart.

She'd never seen anyone who looked more alone.

Everything about his body language told her that he didn't want to be disturbed, but how could she leave him? Particularly as she was the likely cause of his current agony. Because he was in agony, she was sure of that.

"Lucas?"

He didn't lift his head. Didn't look at her. "Go back to bed, Eva."

"Are you joining me?"

"No." He shut her out as effectively as if he'd closed the door.

All that intimacy, the closeness they'd shared, evaporated like morning mist. If she wasn't still experiencing the delicious and unfamiliar aches and tingles, she might have thought she'd imagined the whole thing.

She wished she could turn the clock back to those incredible hours where neither of them had been aware of anything but each other. But that time had passed.

Making a decision, she walked into the room. "Talk to me."

"You don't want that."

How could he possibly think that? "If you're regretting what we did, then this involves me, too."

"Why would I regret it?"

She swallowed, aware that she was on very, very delicate ground. "You loved her. It probably feels like a betrayal, but—"

"Eva, you don't want to have this conversation."

Her heart was thudding. "You mean, you don't want to have it."

He swung his legs to the floor. His eyes glittered in the darkness. "No. I meant what I said. *You* don't want to have it."

Why would he think she wouldn't want to talk?

Was he assuming that she'd been hoping for more from him than just a night of great sex? Was he afraid she'd read more into the night before than she should have?

"Do you think it will hurt me if you talk about your wife? I'm not naive, Lucas. I don't think last night was about love or anything like that." She ignored the tiny voice in her head that told her how much she really did want it to be about love. She wasn't going there. She didn't *dare* go there. "But I'd like to think we're friends. I want you to talk to me. I want you to tell the truth."

"You're not ready to hear the truth." He stared at the whiskey in his hand and then at her. "You want love so badly, but what if it doesn't turn out the way you hope it will? Have you ever wondered whether you might be better off without it?"

Her heart felt swollen and heavy. "You're saying that because you lost the love of your life, but I still believe it's better to love that way than never to love at all. You'll love again, Lucas. I know you will. It may not feel that way now, and I know you'll never forget her, but one day you'll find someone who makes you happy."

She clamped her mouth shut. She probably shouldn't have said any of that. It was too soon. He wasn't ready to hear it. He didn't believe it.

There was a long silence and when he finally spoke his voice was harsh. "You're such an idealist. Such a dreamer. You have no idea what you're talking about. Love is nothing like the vision you have in your head. It isn't some glowing, perfect thing where everyone dances under sunshine and rainbows. It's messy and untidy and it hurts like hell."

"You feel that way because you lost her, but—"

"I feel that way because it's true. You think I'm grieving because we shared the perfect love? Then let me shatter your illusions once and for all. There was nothing perfect about our love. But I *did* love her, and that made everything so much harder."

"I know, but—"

"You don't know. You have no fucking idea." The raw anger in his voice shocked her.

"Lucas—"

"The night she died, the night she left all dressed up and stepped into that cab, she wasn't going out for the evening." His fingers were white on the glass, his grasp so tight it was a wonder it didn't shatter. "She was going to join her lover. She was leaving me. So how's your image of our perfect love looking now, Eva?"

CHAPTER TWELVE

It's better to lead than follow, but if you must
follow, follow your instincts.

—Paige

HE'D EXPECTED HER to walk out, and he wouldn't have
blamed her. Maybe it was even what he wanted.

Why else would he have told her the truth?

For a long moment she said nothing and he watched
a range of emotions cross her pretty features. Only
a few hours before he'd seen ecstasy and passion in
those eyes. Now he saw shock and confusion, followed by compassion. Of course, compassion, because this was Eva and it wasn't possible for her not
to feel compassion.

It was the last thing he wanted.

He stared down at his hands, disgusted with himself for spoiling her perfect night but instead of walking out, she sat down next to him.

"But she—" She stumbled over the words. "She
was the love of your life. You knew her from childhood—"

"That's right." He watched her process all this
new information. Watched as her glowing picture of

the perfect love affair, the perfect marriage, changed shape into something distorted and ugly.

"I saw pictures of you together—at premieres, walking through Central Park. I saw the way you looked at each other."

"And that simply proves that you can tell very little about a person by looking at them. A point I've been making since you first broke into my apartment."

She didn't appear to hear him. "You say you loved her and I saw her in the photos. She loved you, too."

"She loved me. As well as she could. But love is complicated, Eva. That's what I've been telling you. It isn't all hearts and smiles. It can be pain. Sallyanne couldn't handle being in a long-term committed relationship. She kept waiting for it to self-destruct, and when it didn't she destroyed it herself."

"I don't understand."

"Neither did I." And he blamed himself for that. For not looking closer. He, who prided himself on always digging deep, had failed to even scratch the surface of what was going on with his wife.

"Does anyone else know the truth?"

"That she was leaving me? No. If she hadn't slipped on the ice getting into the cab, the world would have found out that night, and it would have been as much of a shock to them as it was to me."

Look, Lucas, look what I did to us. I took what we had and I broke it. I always told you I'd break it.

He reached for the bottle of whiskey but his hand was shaking so much he missed the glass.

Eva quietly mopped up the amber pools with

a napkin left over from one of the lunches she'd brought him.

Then she took the whiskey bottle from him and poured two fingers into the glass.

"Aren't you going to lecture me on drinking? Tell me it isn't going to help?"

"No." There was no judgment there, only kindness and friendship. "What happened that night, Lucas?"

He'd never talked about it. He'd never wanted to. Until now.

Why? Why now?

Was it because she made it easy to talk? Or was it because there was a new intimacy between them? Evidence of that intimacy was visible in the faint reddening of the skin on her neck and the tumbled strands of her hair. And then there was the invisible. The connection, the closeness that hadn't been there before. It had cracked open something that had been sealed inside him for three years.

"She told me she was leaving. We had an argument. I told her I loved her, and her response was to tell me she was having an affair. At first I didn't believe it—" He broke off, unsure how to describe the magnitude of his confusion. "I thought I knew her so well. I'd known her since she was five years old. We lost touch for a while when we went to college. I stayed on the East Coast, she went West. I wanted the adventure of the big city. I suppose you would have called it my bad boy phase. We met up again by chance at a reunion and this time she was interested. Turned out she liked my bad boy side. We were together when I sold my first book. We celebrated by getting blind drunk and having sex on—" He glanced at her. "Never mind."

She took his hand. "You don't have to edit what you say, Lucas."

"We renewed our friendship and it was as if we'd never been apart. Marriage seemed like a logical step to me. She was reluctant. She didn't see why we should change what worked, but I persuaded her. I never even questioned whether it was the right thing for her."

"But you knew her really well."

"I thought I did. Her parents separated when she was young, and it was a bitter, acrimonious divorce. It left her with a deep-seated belief that marriage couldn't last. I didn't know it at the time, but the moment I put that ring on her finger, I signed the death warrant to our marriage. It was over before it had begun."

"But you never suspected she was having an affair?"

"No. She didn't love him, she told me that." He lifted the glass and drank, trying to block out the memory of that last conversation. "She did it because she thought it would drive me away. She wanted to 'set me free.' She told me she'd done me a favor. She thought by making me hate her, I'd find it easier to move on. It was her 'gift' to me."

"Oh, Lucas—"

"I'm not sure what would have happened if she hadn't slipped on the ice that night. Maybe she was hoping I'd make a grand gesture and win her back to prove my love. Or maybe she really did mean to leave. What happened would have been tough to fix. She said a lot of things she shouldn't have said, and so did I. I was angry. So damned angry—" And the guilt gnawed at his insides like acid.

"Of course you were."

"She tried to make it as bad as possible, to stop me loving her, but it didn't work that way. After she died, the feelings were almost intolerable because I had no way of talking to her and getting to the truth. I truly believe she did love me, but she was too scared to trust it. It was as if she was so afraid of how she'd handle the ending, she wanted to just get it done and control it herself. But I still loved her. I'm not sure if that makes me crazy, delusional—" He put the glass down, saying, "possibly both."

"Loyal." Eva's voice was quiet. "I think it probably makes you loyal. Love isn't something that you can switch on and off. At least, it shouldn't be."

"I wanted to." It was something he'd never admitted to anyone before. "When you're wrong about someone, you go over it in your head. You think back to everything you ever did together, you examine everything that person ever said and you try to work out if anything at all was real. You unpick it, like a sweater, stitch by stitch, until it all falls apart and all you have in your hands is a pile of wool. Loose ends. And you have no idea how to put it together in a way that makes sense. Do you have any idea how it feels to think you know someone, really know someone, and then realize you don't know them at all? All those facts, those moments that you thought of as intimacy, suddenly blur and you don't know if you were ever really close or if you imagined it all. If you can't trust the person in life who is supposed to be closest to you, who can you trust?"

"You should be able to trust the person closest to you. That isn't asking too much." She moved closer to him, instinctively offering comfort.

Her thigh brushed against his and then she took his hand and cupped it in between hers.

"I thought," she said slowly, "that it was your work that made you so suspicious of people. I thought it was because you spend your days delving into the darker side of human nature. I never thought the reason stemmed from your own experience. I never suspected it was personal. I hate the thought that you've been carrying that all by yourself."

"I didn't want her memory to be all about gossip. I had her family to think about. Her parents and her sister were devastated. There was nothing to be gained by telling them the truth."

"But how did you keep it a secret? What about the guy she—"

"He was married. He never would have left his wife for her. That's probably why she chose him. She didn't want the commitment, just the adventure. Or maybe she really did just use him as a tool to destroy what we had. I'll never know. He was only too happy to keep it quiet because the truth would have put his marriage at risk." He heard her soft sound of sympathy and felt a flash of guilt. "I've destroyed your shiny view of love."

"No. I know love can be flawed, and messy. I know all those things."

"And you still want it?"

"Of course. Because in the end, love is the only thing that matters." She made it sound simple, and he'd only ever found it to be complicated and painful.

"I disagree. There have been so many days since she died when I wished I'd never met her." He lifted his head and looked at her. "I couldn't handle that she'd hid so much from me. I was as deluded as you were when you looked at those photos. A picture can be faked, but I was living with her and I thought what we had was real. If you can't trust a person you've known for more than twenty-five years, who can you trust?"

"It's no wonder you've steered clear of relationships ever since."

"Fortunately people make allowances for grief. I focused on my work. My output tripled and the stories I was writing were darker and deeper. My sales numbers rocketed. Critics said my writing had reached a whole new level. Sallyanne would have said it was her last gift to me. Ironic, don't you think? I'm a global bestseller because my wife screwed me up so badly." He picked up the glass and drained it, the whiskey scalding his throat. "So that's love, Eva. That's how it looks. You should go back to bed and I should write."

"Write? It's four in the morning."

"I won't sleep. But you should. You're bad enough

in the mornings without having hardly any sleep." He reached out and tucked a strand of hair behind her ear, wondering what would have happened if he'd met her at a different time of his life. He dismissed the question because the answer was that there hadn't been a single time in his life when he would have been the right man for a woman like her.

"Will you come with me?"

Part of him wanted to, but he reminded himself that at the moment all they'd shared was one night. That was all. People walked away after one night all the time. He didn't intend to let one night become two nights and two nights become three.

"No." He curled his fingers into his fist so that he couldn't be tempted to touch her again.

Her gaze searched his and then she straightened her shoulders and stood up. "Don't."

"Don't what?"

"Don't regret what we did. Don't start examining it and unpicking it. And don't start worrying about where I might think this is going. I know what last night was. So don't feel you have to give me explanations, or excuses or, worse, apologies. I'm going back to bed now. With no regrets. And I'd rather you didn't have any, either."

She walked away, leaving him to his self-imposed solitude, and he stared after her, seeing her slim curves silhouetted through his shirt and wondering how it could feel so bad when someone had just done exactly what you'd asked them to do.

He'd sent her away, but now he wanted to follow her. He wanted to thaw his frozen heart on her warmth, but he fought the impulse because he knew it was wrong of him to use her as a sanctuary when there was no way in a million years he could live up to her dreams.

If he didn't care about her, it would have been easier. But he cared. He cared too damn much for his own piece of mind. So he forced himself to stay where he was, his only companions regret, guilt and a whole lot of other emotions he couldn't begin to unravel.

EVA LAY CURLED in a ball in the cold bed, staring into the darkness.

She'd contemplated going back to sleep in Lucas's room, but decided that would be intrusive, because where would *he* sleep if she was in his bed?

Someone is sleeping in my bed and she's still there.

She didn't want to be like Goldilocks, so she'd returned to the room she'd been using as her own.

The bed felt huge, cold and empty, filled with just her and her thoughts.

It had been an incredible night right up until the point she'd found Lucas in his study and he'd shared his secret. And now that secret lay inside her, heavy as stone. It had never once occurred to her that his relationship, his "perfect" marriage, might not have been so perfect.

She rolled onto her back and stared up at the ceiling.

He was right when he'd said he'd tarnished her dreams. In a way, he had. She'd looked at those photographs, at the depth of his grief, and envied what he'd shared with Sallyanne.

She hadn't thought to look deeper. She'd thought that once you found the right person, love was simple.

He probably thought she was a dreamy fool.

She thought she was a dreamy fool.

No wonder he shut himself away. No wonder he rejected people's calls for him to move on. He wasn't just dealing with the loss of someone he loved, he was dealing with the discovery that something he'd believed in had never existed. She was beginning to understand why he never judged by appearances.

He'd lived it, discovering that what he'd seen on the surface didn't reflect what lay underneath. It wasn't just fiction, it was his reality.

And it was no good wishing things were different, or pretending that *she* was going to be the one to drag him from the past into the present. Maybe she was a dreamy optimist, but she wasn't stupid. He had a lot to process, and until he did that he wasn't going to be able to have a relationship with anyone. And the last thing she wanted was to lose her heart to an unavailable man.

She felt a tearing, aching pain in her chest and knew it was already too late for that. She was falling for him, and it was hopeless.

She could cook him delicious food, and make his apartment festive, but she couldn't do anything about the way he was feeling. Only he could fix that.

But that didn't stop her wishing she could fix it for him.

CHAPTER THIRTEEN

You can't step into the future if you keep one
foot in the past.

—Paige

LUCAS WOKE WITH an aching neck from having slept
awkwardly on the sofa.

Through the floor-to-ceiling window he could
see the golden fingers of dawn spreading across the
sky. The snow had stopped falling, but the past few
days had turned Central Park into a glossy winter
wonderland. Snow lay thick on the paths and trees
were draped with a sparkly coating of magical winter white.

The bottle of whiskey was still open in front of
him, and next to it the empty glass, a reminder of
the night before.

He remembered the dancing, the champagne, that
tense ride home in the car and the incredible sex that
had followed. Eva had been so open and willing, so
generous and honest in her affections, giving without
hesitation or qualification. And afterward, during the
conversation in his study, she'd been equally generous. Instead of being annoyed or insecure that he was

talking about his relationship with another woman when only an hour earlier they'd been wrapped together in the most intimate way possible, she'd listened carefully, paying attention.

Swearing softly, he swung his legs off the sofa and dug his fingers into his hair.

She'd gone to bed with him as a woman who believed in happy-ever-afters and emerged the next morning with her illusions shattered. That's what a relationship with him did to a person.

What the hell happened next?

He couldn't walk away because he was in his own apartment. And he couldn't send her away because he needed her here so that he could work.

Trapped by a dilemma of his own making, he walked into his bedroom, braced for conversation, and saw that the bed was empty. The shoes she'd worn the night before were half-hidden under the bed, a reminder of those few heightened hours of excitement at the ball.

He should have stopped it then.

Instead of dancing with her, he should have let her go home with one of the other men there. He should have stood back and let it happen.

It would have been better for both of them. Instead, he'd destroyed her fairy-tale moment.

He eyed the tangle of sheets and wondered if she'd slept in her own room. Either that or she'd packed and left. And he couldn't blame her for that, could he?

The thought disturbed him more than it should

have, as did the relief that followed when the delicious smells of sizzling bacon wafted up from the kitchen.

She hadn't gone home.

Trying to work out what that meant, he walked into the shower, hit the jets and closed his eyes as the hot water pummeled out the last of the sleep from his body.

Lifting his hand he stroked the water away from his face, trying to clear his head.

He'd known her for less than a week, and yet he'd told her things he'd never told anyone before. Deeply personal information he'd long ago promised himself would never see the light of day. But there had been something about the way Eva had looked at him, something about the kindness in her eyes and the lightness of her touch that had unlocked secrets he'd kept firmly to himself.

He wouldn't blame her for misreading the signs and thinking that this was more than it was.

He cursed softly and reached for a towel, knotting it around his waist.

There was no sense in delaying what was inevitably going to be an awkward conversation.

Better to get it over with so both of them knew exactly where this was going.

He dressed quickly and then walked downstairs to the kitchen.

She was wearing his shirt again, and her hair was piled haphazardly on top of her head. He heard the sound of sizzling and a delicious smell enveloped him, waking his taste buds. He noticed that today she wasn't singing and he felt another stab of regret and guilt.

No doubt he was responsible.

"Do I smell bacon?" He decided it was up to him to breach the awkward morning-after moment, although he wasn't exactly sure which part of the night before would make her feel most awkward. The sex or the confession. "I thought you were vegetarian?"

Without looking at him, she reached for a plate. "The bacon is for you. I've heard it's the perfect cure for a hangover."

"I don't have a hangover." It was a lie and they both knew it, but instead of arguing she turned back to the pan and left him to contemplate why she'd be going to so much trouble.

"Eva—"

"Don't talk."

"Because you're upset?"

"No, because I'm not awake yet. It's early, Lucas. I've already told you I don't function well at this hour, especially after the limited sleep I had last night." Yawning, she plated the bacon, added a toasted English muffin and a poached egg and placed it in front of him. "Don't talk to me. I'll be fine." She'd basically excused him from having a conversation he'd been dreading. He should have been relieved.

"I don't need breakfast."

"I got up early to make this for you, so if you don't eat it I *will* be upset. And you need to replenish the calories you used up last night."

"About that—"

"Eat." She handed him a knife and fork and turned back to pull a tray of something that smelled delicious from the oven.

He scanned her long, bare legs and forgot what he'd intended to talk about. "You stole my shirt."

"I wanted to make breakfast before taking a shower. Do you mind?"

What was one more intimacy stacked on top of the others they'd shared?

He took a mouthful of food. Then another, and instantly felt better. The bacon was crisp, the muffin lightly toasted and the egg perfectly cooked. She always seemed to know exactly what to serve him. Mood food.

"When you weren't in the bedroom, I thought you'd left."

"I slept in my own room." She poured herself a coffee and leaned against the counter. "You should have slept in yours. You must have a terrible neck ache after a night on the sofa."

"Eva, what happened between us last night—"

"We're not going to talk about this now."

"Yes, we are."

She sighed. "Well, if we are, I need more coffee and I won't be held responsible for anything I say while in a sleep coma." She topped off her mug and handed him one, too. "Last night was perfect, Lucas. The dress, the ball, the dancing, the sex. All of it was perfect."

He'd been trying hard not to think about the sex, but now she'd mentioned it he couldn't think of anything else. Eva, naked, those incredible breasts pushing into his chest. Eva, eyes closed and lips parted as he'd kissed her.

Eva, listening without passing judgment—

Shit.

"You're ignoring the part where I destroyed your dreams."

"You mean the part where you told me the truth about your marriage? No." She sipped her coffee and then put her mug down slowly. "I'm glad you were finally able to tell someone, because carrying that around on your own must have been a heavy burden. I'm sorry you've been living with that and I can understand now why you're so reluctant to believe that anyone is the way they seem."

"Eva—"

"You always look for deeper meanings, so I'm going to save you the trouble and tell you what's in my head. Was last night incredible? Yes, it was. Do I wish it could be more than one night? Yes, part of me does."

So did he. He wished she'd dressed in something other than his damn shirt. It would have made it easier to concentrate. "Part of you?"

"The part of me that wants to ignore the truth, which is that you have a lot of baggage to deal with before you're ready for a relationship with someone else. Getting involved with you would be like driving a car over nails or broken glass. It could only end badly and I prefer not to start something when I can already see trouble in the distance. So you don't need to worry about me. We'll call it a one-night stand."

He should have been relieved she was being so sensible. He *was* relieved, so the kick of disappointment made no sense.

"You don't like one-night stands."

"They're not my preference, but that doesn't mean I can't enjoy one if that's how it turns out." Her voice was light, but he knew it barely revealed the surface of her feelings.

"I'd understand if you decide to leave."

She lifted her coffee and took another sip, studying him across the rim of her mug. "Do you want me to leave? You asked me here so that you could finish writing your book. Unless you've finished, or my presence is no longer helpful, then I'll stay until the job's finished. Do you need me or not?"

His mouth was dry. He had to remind himself she was talking about work. "I need you."

"Then I'll stay." Her mouth curved into a smile. "And I promise not to pounce on you in the night, so you don't need to take refuge on the sofa. And now we've got that out of the way, we can carry on as if nothing has changed."

He wished it was that simple.

He wished he could pretend nothing had changed, but it had. It was like trying to close the door on an overfull closet. Everything stored there was pushing back, trying to escape after years of being locked inside out of sight.

Maybe she thought this was one-sided. Maybe she

didn't understand how hard he was struggling not to push aside everything decent inside himself and take sanctuary in her warmth and her generosity.

He said nothing as she served him another helping and made him a coffee that was exactly the way he liked it.

Everything she did was exactly the way he liked it.

The only way to deal with it was to go back to work.

After finishing his second helping, he stood up and loaded his plate into the dishwasher with a clatter. "Thank you for breakfast." His tone was rougher than he'd intended but she didn't seem offended. He was coming to the conclusion that she was one of those rare people who had an intuitive grasp of another's emotions, and respected them.

"You're welcome. Thank you for the orgasm." She turned pink. "Forget I said that. I'm still half-asleep."

No matter how tense the situation, she always made him smile.

"You're only thanking me for one? What about the others?"

"I lost count."

His gaze met hers and the air in the apartment heated with the shared intimacy.

He thought that if he did what he was burning to do it would end in disaster and she wouldn't be thanking him for anything.

She'd be cursing the fact she'd ever met him.

THE STORM HAD now fully passed, the streets were cleared and gradually people were venturing out again, wrapped up against the cold as they prepared for the holiday season. There were gifts to be purchased and wrapped, trees to be decorated, store windows to admire and parties to attend.

Eva concentrated on her work and tried not to think too much about that night with Lucas.

It had been so special it deserved to be thought about, but at the same time thinking about it made her yearn for something that wasn't on offer.

Neither of them spoke about it, but that didn't mean the tension wasn't there. It simmered under the surface, creating tiny ripples in the otherwise smooth atmosphere. Until now she hadn't realized how much could be conveyed by a touch or a glance.

She envied Lucas his self-control.

"I mean, if it was me, I wouldn't be able to resist." She spoke to Paige, while she stirred, whisked and baked. She'd told her friends the truth about what had happened that night, omitting everything Lucas had told her. That wasn't hers to share. "He's the kind of guy who can have chocolate in the house and not eat it. Why wasn't I blessed with ruthless self-control? I'd be thin and successful."

"You were blessed with plenty of other things, and no man would swap your curves for 'thin.'"

"You think I'm fat?" She glanced over her shoulder, trying to see her bottom. "I've been using Lucas's exercise bike every day and lifting weights. I'm looking toned, but not thin. Probably because I haven't mastered self-control."

"Self-control is overrated. So he hasn't mentioned that night? Not once?"

"Apart from the very awkward morning-after-the-night before conversation, no." She sifted more flour into the bowl. "We're ignoring it. On the surface, at least." Underneath? Underneath the tension was rising. The time they spent together was so intense it was becoming harder and harder to behave normally. She'd almost reached the stage where she couldn't remember what normal was.

"Mmm." Paige didn't sound convinced. "Are you sure you're happy to stay there? I wouldn't want you getting serious about him."

Eva pulled a carton of eggs out of the fridge. "I'm not serious."

"I know you. With you, sex is always serious. I don't want you to get hurt."

"It had been a while for me so I guess that makes it different. It wasn't serious." If she said it enough times, she might even start to believe it.

"But you wish it was?"

"I'm not letting myself think like that." She closed the fridge door, thinking that maybe she had more self-control than she thought. She wasn't great at resisting sugar, or lipstick, but she was doing pretty well resisting her feelings for Lucas.

Over the next few days Lucas spent most of his time closeted in his study, only emerging to eat the meals she prepared. She wondered if he was isolating himself because he needed to work or because the intensity of their relationship was starting to get to him, too. There was as much meaning in their silences as there was in the words they exchanged. There were times when she thought she might burst into flames.

And then there were the moments she worried that by being alone in his office he'd retreated back into his own private hell. And she couldn't help wondering whether he was thinking of her at all while he brooded.

As promised, he'd turned over the third bedroom for her to use as an office. He'd moved the desk, giving her a view across the city and the park.

It took all her self-discipline not to spend all day staring out of the window.

She kept her laptop there, and her planner, and checked in regularly with Paige and Frankie. On one evening she joined them for an event in midtown, but other than that almost all her work was conducted on the phone and the internet. Her working day was spent organizing food for events, liaising with venues and clients. The rest of her time was spent in the kitchen.

Christmas had been a time of year she and her grandmother had both treasured and memories were everywhere, in flavors and fragrance, in textures and taste. There were some dishes she hadn't cooked since her grandmother's death, but she cooked them for Lucas and discovered that there was comfort as well as sadness and nostalgia in doing so.

Despite, or perhaps because of, his preoccupation with his book, Lucas was an appreciative audience. He was complimentary about everything she prepared, and seemed genuinely interested in her creative process.

Dinner became the most important meal of the day for her, because it was the only real time they spent together. Breakfast was often eaten standing up, lunch was equally quick and sometimes Lucas simply loaded his plate and took it back to his office.

Dinner was the one meal he lingered over. He always questioned her carefully about what they were having, and then chose a wine he thought would complement the food. She was impressed by his expertise.

"So some of the wines you have are very old and very valuable?"

"Yes."

"And sometimes you buy them at auction?"

"That's right." He poured wine into a glass and handed it to her. "Try it. Tell me what you think."

The first time he'd asked her to do that she'd been embarrassed. She knew nothing about wine, and wasn't about to try to bullshit her way past an expert.

"I like it. That's all I can tell you."

"Why do you like it?"

"Because it tastes good and makes me want to finish the whole bottle." She smiled over the rim of her glass. "Sorry to disappoint you, but I don't get any more technical than that. How did you learn about wine?"

"From my father." He topped off his own glass. "It's his hobby. Growing up, we used to tour vineyards in California, New Zealand and France."

Between his upbringing and his book tours, he was well traveled.

"I've only ever been to Europe once. I spent a month working in a kitchen in Paris." She took another sip of the wine. "You've been everywhere."

"Not everywhere, and even when I travel I don't see much of the places I stay. If it's a book tour then invariably all I see is the airport, the inside of a hotel and a bookstore, before moving on to the next place. Tell me more about Paris. What did you love about it?"

"So many things. The bread, the passion for cooking, the quality of ingredients."

She was flattered by his interest in her. She'd been on dates with men who seemed to want only to talk about themselves. Lucas asked questions and paid attention to the answers.

He was a generous listener and she found herself telling him about her upbringing, and small details about her grandmother that she hadn't shared with anyone else.

"Puffin Island is small, so our house was always full of people. After Gramps died, we didn't have to cook for about six months. There was always a casserole on the doorstep. And Grams loved that. She worried that it was just the two of us and she wanted to make sure there were plenty of people in my life, so she used to cook constantly and invite people over to sample what she'd produced."

They moved away from the subject but a few nights later he raised it again.

"Why did you leave Puffin Island?"

"I went to college." She added a tiny drop of truffle oil to the pasta she was making. "Grams decided it was time for her to make a change, too."

"That was brave of her."

"She was an amazing woman. She always looked forward, not backward, and she never doubted that she could do something. She moved to New York City after living on a rural island in Maine, and she made it her home."

"Having been an English professor she must have enjoyed the access to culture."

"She did. And for the first few years she had a small apartment on the Upper West Side. Being close to Central Park was her way of keeping green space in her life. We used to take picnics to the park. I loved feeding the ducks."

"Did she miss the island?"

"I don't think so." Eva served the pasta and put the plates on the table. "She thought it was marvelous to be able to listen to outdoor concerts in the summer, and to be able to buy any ingredients she wanted and not rely on the one store on the island to have it in stock."

"Did you miss it?"

"No." She sat down opposite him. "I loved the island, but New York City was like paradise for me. The day I discovered Bloomingdale's was the day I knew I was home. That, and the shoe floor of Saks Fifth Avenue. It's big enough to earn its own zip code. There's even an express elevator that takes you straight there."

"Straight to heaven?"

"Something like that."

"Your grandmother sounds like an extraordinary person. It's no wonder you had a special bond."

"She was my everything," Eva said. "My whole world. She was the type of person who tried always to focus on what was right in her life, not what was wrong. If I looked out of the window and said 'it's raining, Grams' she'd say it would be good for the plants, or that we'd be able to go out and have fun splashing in puddles. We were snowed in for half the winter once, like the rest of the island, but she never complained. She said it was the perfect weather to cozy up in the kitchen and cook. She was so—sunny."

"She passed that on to you."

"I used to think so, but now I'm not so sure." She poked at her food. "Since she died, I feel more like a raincloud than sunshine. She was the most important person in the world to me and I don't think I'm adjusting very well to being without her—" She blinked, automatically hauling her feelings back inside. "Sorry. Let's talk about something else."

"Do you want to talk about something else?"

No. She wanted to talk about her grandmother. She wanted to talk about her feelings. "I don't want to moan on about my problems."

"Because that's what your grandmother taught you?" He studied her thoughtfully. "You're allowed to feel down, Eva. And you're allowed to talk about feeling down."

"I think part of me is afraid that if I start, I won't stop. My friends have been so good, listening to me and hugging me when I'm upset, but I know I need to sort myself out."

"You were the one who told me there was no time frame to adjusting to loss."

"I feel as if I'm letting Grams down. I'm trying really hard to be the way she taught me to be, but it's hard."

"Could it ever be anything else? After Sallyanne died I read a lot about the theory of grief, but grief is personal and in practice all you can do is keep going, day after day, and hope it gets better."

"What do you miss most about her?"

"Sallyanne?" He put his fork down. "I don't know. Probably her irreverent sense of humor. What do you miss most about your grandmother?"

"The feeling of being wrapped in love. The sense of security that came from knowing she loved me no matter what. Since I lost her, I feel as if I'm lying in a big cold bed and someone has ripped the covers from me. And then there are the hundreds of small things I miss. Like calling her to tell her my news, and hearing her tell me what's been happening in the assisted living community she was in—the latest funny thing that Tom said, or how Doris left her teeth in a cup and scared the mailman. I used to go to their Christmas party. I miss that." She reached for her wine and gave Lucas an apologetic smile. "Sorry. Self-indulgent rant over."

"Don't apologize. And for the record, I don't think you're self-indulgent. Far from it." He helped himself to more food. "From what you've told me, I think you've been keeping too much of it to yourself. You should talk. It's important."

"You don't talk."

"I write. That's my way of relieving tension."

"You kill characters?"

"That, too." He gave a soft laugh and she laughed, too.

She realized she felt better than she had in ages. "Thank you for listening. It's easy to talk to you, perhaps because you've lost someone, too. You know how it feels. You understand."

It was something else that connected them, another layer of intimacy deepening what they already had.

She'd given up trying not to want him. She wanted him desperately. She wanted him to take her to bed and make love to her the way he had the night of the ball, but no matter how late they talked into the night, no matter how personal the conversation got, he didn't touch her again. And she tried desperately not to touch him.

Once, she'd touched him by accident while handing him a plate and she'd pulled back so sharply the plate had almost landed on the floor. He'd caught it one-handed and the brief flame in his eyes had told her he was not only aware of her struggle, but he was experiencing it, too. But even though the sexual tension simmered hotter than anything she cooked up in his kitchen, he did nothing about it.

And neither did she.

She told herself that he was being sensible, but still there was a dull ache of disappointment that things couldn't be different and a sharp edge of longing. Her nights were disturbed by sweaty, erotic dreams, the images from which she found it hard to erase in the light of day.

She tried to lure her mind away from thoughts of sex. "How is the book going?"

"It's going well, thanks." He poured more wine. "I wrote another ten thousand words today. Enough to make me think this book might actually be finished on time."

"As I'm in it, are you going to let me read it?"

He reached for his glass. "You don't read crime fiction."

"I've never played a starring role before."

"I never let anyone read my work until it's finished."

She felt a stab of disappointment. "All right. But I expect a signed copy."

"Even if there's blood on the cover?"

"I'll wrap it in flowery pink paper."

She served a light *tarte au citron* inspired by the summer she'd spent in Paris, and afterward Lucas returned to his study.

Eva caught up on her emails, updated her social media accounts and made two calls to clients.

On her way up to bed she made herself an herbal tea, and took Lucas one, too.

The door to his study was open, but there was no sign of him.

She put the tea down on his desk, and noticed the words on the screen. He'd obviously stopped in the middle of a chapter.

Curiosity tugged her toward the screen.

She felt a flash of guilt that she was peeping without asking him, and then shrugged it off. She was his inspiration. Surely that entitled her to at least take a look at the character he'd created?

She stared at the screen, intending only to read a few lines.

But then she kept reading. She kept reading even though her mouth was dry and her hands were shaking.

She was so absorbed, she didn't hear Lucas come back into the room.

"Eva?"

His voice cut through her shock and she backed away, stumbling over a stack of books he'd left on the floor.

"It's me." The words jammed in her throat. "You said I was your inspiration—"

"Eva—"

"I'm the murderer. I thought I was a nice, kind character but I'm the murderer? *You made me the murderer?*"

"It's not you. My characters are not real people."

He hesitated. "It's true I took some of your character traits."

"She has blond hair and a DD cup. She's a brilliant cook! You might as well have called her Eva! Everyone is going to know it's based on me and it's h-horrible." She couldn't push the words past the tense ball of anger in her chest. "And the detail—"

"Eva, please—"

"All those questions you asked when we were together. I thought it was because you were interested in me. Because you wanted to get to know me, but you wanted more detail for your book."

"That isn't true." He stepped toward her but she lifted her hand.

"Do *not* come any closer. Do not touch me, Lucas, because right now I'm *so mad.*"

"You're overreacting. At most it's loosely based on you, that's all."

"All?" She stalked forward, her finger outstretched. "I've got news for you, Lucas. I *am* a real person. A real, flesh-and-blood person with emotions and f-feelings. I am *not* one of your characters and we are *not* in one of your novels. This is real life. This is *my* life and you don't get to—" She stabbed him hard in the chest, her breathing shallow and rapid. "You don't get to turn me into a murderer."

"If you'd listen—"

"Don't placate me. You think I'm capable of murder? Well, I've got news for you—" she spat the words out "—since I met you, I just might be. Right now I can think of at least a dozen interesting ways I could kill

you that you've probably never even thought of." With that she turned on her heel and left his office, slamming the door behind her.

She went to her bedroom and slammed that door, too, so upset she couldn't breathe.

He'd made her the murderer.

All this time she'd thought they had something special, that this new intimacy was genuine and deep, and all the time he'd been using what he'd learned about her in his book. He wasn't interested in her because he cared about her, but because he cared about his story.

She'd kidded herself that she was helping him by being here, inspiring him. Instead she'd given him the inspiration to turn her into a bad person.

She paced the floor, so monumentally stressed she had no idea what to do to calm herself. A drink. She needed a drink. It worked for Lucas in times of stress, so why not her?

She stalked downstairs to the kitchen. She ignored the whiskey and instead reached for a bottle of wine from the rack.

Footsteps sounded behind her but she didn't turn.

She didn't want to look at him, let alone talk to him.

How much of it had been real? Those lingering glances, the almost agonizing restraint they'd both shown when they were in the same room—had she imagined all of that?

She'd told him things she hadn't even told her closest friends, and instead of guarding those confidences like treasure, he'd stolen them for profit.

She thumped the wine down on the counter and grabbed a corkscrew.

"Whatever you do don't drop that," he breathed. "It's a bottle of—never mind."

"Great value, is that what you were going to say?"

"There are only eleven bottles left in the world. It's the best."

She gave him a long, hard look and then yanked the cork out of the bottle. "Now there are ten." She poured the wine into a glass and lifted it, challenging him with her eyes. "To murder." She took a sip and closed her eyes briefly. "Mmm. You're right, that is *good*. They say crime doesn't pay, but in your case it obviously pays extremely well. You should have bought the other ten bottles."

He eyed the open bottle. "I did."

She lifted the bottle and topped off her glass, temper simmering. "Where are they?"

"In storage."

"So what's this one doing here?" She took another mouthful. He was watching her with the same degree of caution he might have shown an unexploded bomb.

"I was keeping it for a special occasion."

"Doesn't get much more special than this. It's not every day a girl finds out she's a murderer. It's not exactly the career I had mapped out for myself and I'm not sure my grandmother would be proud, but I believe in celebrating every little thing. I hope I'm good at what I do. Am I?" She drained the glass and thumped it back down on the counter.

He winced. "You shouldn't drink that so fast. You'll get a headache."

"I'll drink it any damn way I like and you can watch me do it."

"This isn't like you."

"Maybe it is. Maybe this is the side of me you haven't seen before. You're the one who is always telling me people have other sides to them. You think because I'm optimistic and like to see the best in people that makes me weak? You thought I wouldn't dare open your superexpensive wine? Think again, Lucas." She sloshed more wine into the glass. "How much is this bottle worth?"

He named a figure that almost made her drop the bottle, but she tightened her grip. "Right. Then I'd better savor every mouthful."

"You're not planning on sharing it?"

"No. You're going to watch me drink it, and that is as close as I am ever going to get to torturing someone. And it's the closest I'm going to get to satisfaction."

His gaze was wary. "What do you mean?"

"I liked you, Lucas." Her hand shook on the bottle. "I *really* liked you. And I thought—never mind what I thought. I was stupid. You can put that in your book if you like. Might as well get the facts down."

"If you're implying that our sleeping together had something to do with my book, then you're a million miles from the truth."

"Really? And yet we haven't had sex since. So either you didn't enjoy it, or you got what you wanted, and—"

"Eva—"

"I don't want to hear it. Truly."

"The book has nothing to do with why we haven't had sex since that night."

"Save it. From now on I'm not saying a single word because that way you can't use what I say for evidence, or characterization, or—" She waved the bottle. "Or other nefarious gains. *Nefarious.* You see? I know words other than *nice* and *fine*. Are you impressed?"

"I think you probably need to stop drinking."

"Don't tell me what I need. Are you suggesting I can't hold my alcohol? Because I'll have you know I could drink you under the table." She swayed and just about managed to stay upright. "Screw you, Lucas. Oh wait, I already did that." Deciding to exit while she could still walk without falling over, she scooped up the wine and stomped up the stairs, slamming the bedroom door behind her.

CHAPTER FOURTEEN

A good friend is cheaper than therapy.

—Frankie

THE FOLLOWING MORNING Lucas was downstairs before Eva was.

She finally emerged, holding tightly to the banister as she walked down the stairs, as if the slightest movement caused her pain. Judging from the look she sent in his direction she didn't seem any more inclined to forgive him than she had the night before.

He took one look at her pale face and opened the drawer where he kept medicines. "Painkiller?" He held out the packet, but she ignored him.

"My head is perfectly fine. I've told you, I can hold my drink."

He knew she was lying but she didn't hang around for a discussion.

She walked away and came back moments later carrying her coat and hat.

"Where are you going?"

"Somewhere I can't be tempted to do you physical harm. I don't want to spend Christmas in jail." She tugged the hat onto her head and fastened her coat. "Go and work. That's what you care about, isn't it?"

"It's freezing and icy out there. You can't go out."

"I can look after myself." She pulled on her gloves. "*Don't* follow me."

She stomped toward the door and slammed it behind her.

Lucas ran his hand over his face and swore softly. Now what?

He returned to his study, hit a button on the keyboard to wake up the screen and once again scanned the section she'd read the night before. At the time he hadn't been able to see why she was so upset, but now he realized that he was so involved in the story and his characters he hadn't been able to read it the way she'd read it.

It was still in draft form of course, which meant that much of it would be edited later and cut or changed, but the way it stood he could see why she'd been upset.

Unfortunately for him, she'd read the passage where his heroine was cooking dinner for her latest victim.

Looking at it objectively, he could see how the words on the screen could have upset her.

Swearing under his breath, Lucas grabbed his own coat and took the elevator down to the ground floor.

Albert was behind the desk. He hadn't even known his name was Albert until Eva had talked about him.

"If you're looking for Eva, she left the building."

One glance at Albert's stony face told him that

Eva's inability to hide her feelings didn't abandon her in moments of stress. "Did you see which direction she went in?"

Albert remained stone-faced. "I wasn't paying attention."

Which meant he knew, but he wasn't telling.

"She's upset," Lucas said. "I want to talk to her."

"Do you know who, or what, upset her?"

"I did." Lucas knew he deserved the look Albert sent him. "Which is why I want to find her."

"So you can upset her some more?"

"So I can try to fix it." And it wasn't until that moment he realized how badly he wanted to fix it. Yes, he was worried about her walking the icy streets on her own, but that wasn't why he'd run out of his apartment.

"Eva is a very sensitive woman. She's special."

"I know."

Albert paused, studying Lucas's face as if looking for something. "She went to the park."

"The park? You're sure? She didn't go shopping? It's freezing out there and they're promising more snow. Why would she go to the park?"

"She told me she was going to spend time with the only type of man who interested her."

Lucas shook his head, confused. "Who?"

Albert gave him a pointed look. "A snowman."

SHE SHOULD HAVE been frozen, but it turned out humiliation was an effective thermal insulator. It heated her from the inside, and scalded her from the outside.

She was a fool. A gullible, trusting fool. And as if that wasn't bad enough she'd gone and spilled her feelings all over him. She could have played it cool and pretended to just be annoyed that he'd made her the murderer in his book, but over the past few days she'd lost the last of her barriers around him. Not only had she started to believe he might be interested in her, she'd actually told him as much.

So now he knew she'd read more into their relationship than was really there. And on top of that her head felt as if a rock band was having a party. She should have taken the painkiller.

"Eva?"

His voice came from behind her and her stomach dropped.

He'd followed her?

The only way to hide how embarrassed she was seemed to be to plant her face in her snowman.

"What are you doing here?"

She scooped more snow up with her gloves, but didn't turn to look at him. How could there be so much heat in her face when it was freezing outside? "You can't work without me there? You need some other intimate detail about me you can use in your book? Because if that's what this is, don't waste your time. You already know everything there is to know about me." *Oh God*, if only that wasn't true. Why couldn't she have applied at least a tiny filter to the information that had poured out of her?

There was a scrunching of snow and his boots came into view.

"I can see you're still angry—"

"You're right, I'm angry and it takes *a lot* to make me angry, in case you haven't worked that out in those sessions where you pretended to be interested in me. When you told me I shouldn't trust people and should look deeper, I didn't realize you were warning me about yourself."

"Come back to the apartment and we can talk about this in the warmth."

"I'm happy here. I'm hoping the weather might cool me down." She stabbed the carrot hard into the snowman's face and then felt Lucas's arm brush against hers as he dropped to his haunches next to her.

"I am interested in you, Eva. And I like you. You weren't wrong about that."

"I suppose your character goes around threatening to fillet men if they don't help her use up her condom by the expiration date."

"Nothing about the night we spent together has gone into the book." He sounded calm and for some reason that made her even angrier.

"I'm sorry you didn't get anything useful from it."

"That night was special, and private, and had nothing to do with research." The carrot fell out of the snowman's nose and Lucas picked it up and pushed it back into the softly packed snow. "You need eyes."

"I have eyes. I don't always use them, that's all."

"I was talking about the snowman."

"Oh." She wished he wasn't so close to her. The jut of his knee brushed against her leg and the width of his shoulders blocked out some of the icy wind. "You need to move. You're blocking my pile of snow."

He shifted enough to give her access and she leaned across and scooped another handful, packing it down against the snowman's rounded body.

"I wasn't trying to make a fool of you. You knew you were the inspiration behind a character."

"You didn't tell me which character."

"Which part of this has upset you most? Discovering you're the inspiration behind my murderer who, by the way, is nothing like you, or the fact that you think all that time we spent talking was just so that I could find information to use in my book?"

"I'm equally upset by both parts."

His breath clouded the freezing air. "How can I fix it?"

"You can't. It's up to me to make sure I don't tell you anything else you can use against me."

"You only read one page, Ev. If you read the whole thing you wouldn't recognize yourself."

"Only my closest friends call me Ev."

"I would have thought what we've shared gave me that right."

The reminder made her cheeks burn. "No, because it wasn't real."

He swore under his breath. "How much more damn real could it get? You know it was real."

"How am I supposed to know?"

"What do your instincts tell you?"

"Thanks to you, I no longer trust my instincts. Turns out I'm a bad judge of character."

He inhaled deeply. "I haven't been to bed with a woman since Sallyanne. I haven't wanted to. That has to tell you something. And it had nothing to do with the book. Read it, and you'll see that you're wrong."

"You don't let anyone read your work before it is finished."

"Normally that's true, but if that's what it takes to convince you that this character is not you, then I'm willing to make an exception. We'll go back right now and you can read every damn word."

She thought about the number of people, including Frankie, who would do anything to be given an early glimpse of his book. "No," she said, "but the fact that you offered means a lot."

"Why don't you want to read it?"

"Because the bit I read is likely to give me bad dreams. I can't imagine what the rest of it would do."

He gave a soft laugh. "Come back to the apartment, Eva."

"I haven't finished building my snowman. And I never walk away from a man until I've finished with him." And she didn't trust herself to go back with Lucas yet. She wasn't quite ready to forgive him.

"Then I'll help you finish him."

LUCAS HADN'T BUILT a snowman since he was a kid living in Upstate New York with his parents. "I'm not even sure I know how to do this." But he was willing to do pretty much anything to fix the problem he'd created.

She rocked back on her heels. "You're telling me you've never built a snowman?"

"Once or twice, but my brother and I were more into destruction than construction. We had plenty of fights involving snow, but normally the only thing we created was mayhem."

"This is the first time you've mentioned your brother." She gathered another heap of snow and patted it into her snowman. "You're not close?"

It was a relief that she was willing to talk about something other than her role in his book.

"We're close enough. But we're both busy. He's a banker."

"I know. Mitzy told me. I met him once and gave him our business card."

It was news to him. "Urban Genie does work for my brother?"

"No. I was going to contact him, but then we had an explosion of work and I didn't need to. But it was kind of your grandmother to give me his card."

"I went to see her."

"You did? When?"

"Before I visited your offices. I tried to get her to give me your home address. She wouldn't."

"So now she knows you weren't in Vermont."

How honest should he be? He weighed up his options and decided he didn't want to risk any more misunderstandings. "She always knew I wasn't in Vermont, Eva."

"But—" She stopped patting the snow and looked at him. "That would mean she lied to me."

"I love my grandmother, but she's not above telling a lie when she thinks it might benefit someone close to her."

"Well—" Eva sat down on the snow with a soft thump. "The crafty—"

"Yes."

"And now I suppose you think that proves that I knew all along."

"I know you didn't. What I think," he said, "is that my grandmother genuinely loves you." And it wasn't hard to see why.

"I love her back."

"My grandmother has two sons, and two grandsons. She has always yearned for female company."

"Your mom?"

"My parents live in Upstate New York in the house where I grew up. They travel a lot. My brother and I are the ones who live closest and neither of us is great at visiting. We should do it more. She thinks you and I would be good for each other."

Eva smacked another lump of snow into her snowman, harder this time. "She was wrong about that."

"Maybe."

"Maybe?"

It was his job to use words to manipulate people's emotions. He knew how to create anticipation, excitement and sheer terror. But he had no idea how to handle this situation. All he knew was that when Eva had walked out, his apartment had once again become dark and soulless. She'd taken the sunshine with her, and he missed it. "You weren't the only one who spilled secrets, Eva. I did, too. What we shared had nothing to do with my book. It had nothing to do with information gathering. It was about intimacy." It was hard for him to admit it, but he knew it was true. There was something about the warmth of her that encouraged confidences.

"Sex, you mean."

"We both had clothes on when we spilled our secrets, and I spilled more than you. There is plenty you could do with that information if you wanted to."

Her eyes grew fierce. "I would never do that."

"I know. And that's my point. I trust you, and I'm asking you to trust me. I'm creating a character, that's all. Does she have some of your adorable traits? Yes. But it's those traits that will make her appealing to the reader."

She was silent for a moment. "You think I have adorable traits? You're not just saying that to stop me knocking you unconscious with the carrot?"

"I'm not just saying that."

"She's a murderer."

"She's human. Characters in books are more believable if they're not black-and-white. The all-good person is boring to read about and the all-bad person makes readers roll their eyes because the truth is there is good and bad in all of us and it's what brings out the good and the bad that makes for interesting reading."

"Are you saying my character used to be a good person?"

"She's a psychopath, but she also shows slight narcissistic tendencies and traces of mixed personality disorder. With a different upbringing and early life experience it's possible she might have turned out differently, but everything that happened to her fed into that side of her personality."

"Poor her."

It was a typical Eva remark and it made him smile. "She's fictional. That's the great thing about writing, you can create the character that interests you. Books are so much more interesting when the characters are complex. There will be elements of her that readers will sympathize with. She had a rough start in life. They will be shocked by what she does, but a tiny part of them will wonder whether those guys deserved it."

"Do you think you'll finish the manuscript in time?"

"I don't know. Are you going to come back with me?

"If it's going well, you don't need me anymore."

"I need you." He'd woken that morning and realized that the freezing fog that infected his brain at this time of year had lifted, burned away by the brightness of Eva's smile and the warmth of her personality. He didn't know what would happen if she left, but he didn't want to sink back into the agonizing darkness. There was something about her that nourished his starved soul. Something that had nothing to do with her abilities in the kitchen.

"You need me for your book."

"I need you." This time he said the words slowly and succinctly, and she stopped building the snowman and gave him a long look. He knew she was deciding whether or not he could be trusted and he had no idea whether he'd passed her test.

He wanted to grab her, cup her rosy cheeks in his hands and kiss her mouth until she could no longer remember her name.

"I need twigs for arms and then I'm done." She stood up and brushed snow from her coat. "Guard our snowman, I'll be back in a minute."

He watched as she picked her way along the snowy path toward the trees.

The park was surprisingly quiet. Although the blizzard had passed, only a few hardy dog-walkers and photographers had ventured out.

He was musing whether he could afford to take the evening off and take Eva out to dinner when he heard her call out his name. There was a note of urgency and panic in her voice that brought him to his feet in an instant.

"Eva?" For a moment all he could see were trees, and then he caught sight of her coat. She was on the ground and there was blood on her hands. His stomach lurched and for a moment he thought she'd hurt herself, but then he saw something move in her arms.

"What the hell is that?"

"A puppy. It was in a bag on the ground. I saw it move." Her voice was thick with tears and anger. "Someone must have dumped him here. He's hurt, Lucas. His legs are tangled up in the bag and he's so cold. Who would do something like this? What do we do?"

Lucas dropped to his haunches next to her, flooded

with relief that the blood wasn't hers. His hands were shaking so badly it took him a minute to formulate his thoughts.

The puppy was gazing up at Eva with huge eyes, as if he knew she was his last hope.

"Hold him still." Lucas tried to slide his fingers between the twisted plastic and the dog's leg. "He's been struggling. His leg is tangled."

"Of course he's been struggling. If someone had left you in a bag in a storm, you'd be struggling, too." She stroked the dog, crooning softly. "Your Uncle Lucas is going to get you out of this."

"Uncle Lucas" had no idea what he was going to do with the dog, but one glance at Eva's expression told him he'd better do *something*, and fast.

"We need to get him to a vet." He already had his phone in his hand but she shook her head.

"I know someone. Can you hold him while I make a call? He's filthy, though. He'll probably ruin your coat."

Lucas looked from Eva's huge eyes to the thin, shivering dog. "Coats can be cleaned."

"Good answer." Carefully, she deposited the freezing, trembling dog into his arms and tugged out her phone. "Fliss? It's Eva. I have a crisis." She outlined what had happened to the person on the other end of the phone and then ended the call. "Fliss says there is a brilliant vet directly across the park. We can take it in turns to carry him."

"He doesn't weigh much. Who is Fliss?"

"She and her sister run The Bark Rangers. They

provide dog-walking all down the East Side of Manhattan. We often use them. And Harriet volunteers at the animal shelter and sometimes fosters."

The name was familiar, but he couldn't think why. "You think she'll foster this one?"

"I don't know. Fliss says she's looking after a litter of puppies at the moment, so maybe not. If she can't, then I'll keep him until we can find him a good home."

Looking at her Lucas knew that she would, no matter what the inconvenience to her.

"Where are you going to keep him?"

"Are you worried about your pristine apartment? Because don't be. I'll take him home to mine."

"My apartment hasn't been pristine since the day you moved in."

"You're talking about the Christmas tree?"

"Your belongings have a habit of straying into every corner. By the way, if you're looking for your scarf, I found it in my study yesterday."

"The green one? I've been looking everywhere for that!" She started taking off her coat and he reached out and stopped her.

"What are you doing?"

"I'm going to wrap my coat around him to give him extra warmth."

"It's not going to help him if you die of hypothermia." Lucas unbuttoned his own coat and tucked the puppy inside. Immediately he felt the chill of its damp body soak through his sweater. "Let's go."

"So now you've ruined your cashmere coat *and*

your cashmere sweater." Eva peered anxiously at the puppy to check he could breathe. "Is this your way of making it up to me?"

"No. I have other ideas for that but we'll talk about those later."

THE VET HAD already been called by Fliss and saw them immediately.

"Dogs can get frostbite, just like humans." He examined the puppy thoroughly and the dog started to whimper. "This guy survived because he was left by the tree, which provided at least some shelter."

"What about the blood?"

"He has a small cut. There was probably something with a sharp edge under the snow. Twig? Stone?" The vet gave him some shots and then glanced up as a young woman burst into the room. Her coat was open and she was wearing a bright red scarf around her neck. Her hair was silver blond and caught back in a ponytail. It was obvious from the vet's relaxed smile that he knew her. "Hi, Harry. How's Fliss? Did she get over the flu? She sounded better on the phone."

"She's good, thanks. Sends her love and wanted me to tell you that Midas is doing really well since his operation. She's bringing him back for a checkup next week. How is this little guy doing?" She smiled briefly at Eva but then turned her attention back to the dog. "Fliss told me about your call so I thought I'd come down and see if I could help. Aren't you a cutie…" She stroked the puppy's ears gently and he instantly stopped yowling and pushed his nose into her hand. "You poor baby. You're safe now. It's lucky Eva found you. What were you doing in the park, Ev?"

"I was building a snowman."

"No, I mean why aren't you in Brooklyn? I assumed you'd be going crazy organizing Christmas events." Harry kept her hand on the puppy's head, reassuring him as the vet finished his examination.

"I'm working around here for a couple of weeks. Cooking, helping with Christmas preparations, that kind of thing. This is Lucas. Lucas, this is Harriet Knight. She is one half of The Bark Rangers."

"The Bark Rangers?" He remembered where he'd heard the name before. "You've helped my grandmother out a few times."

Harry unwrapped her scarf from her neck with her free hand. "We have?"

"Mary Blade."

Harriet's eyes widened. "You're *the* Lucas? Lucas Blade, the crime writer? Fliss is going to be so mad that she didn't come down here with me. She has all your books. She loves your work. She and Frankie are rabid fans." She smiled at the vet. "Probably shouldn't use that phrase here, should I?"

"Lucas Blade?" The vet glanced up briefly, surprise on his face. "I'm a fan, too."

Harriet was still stroking the dog's ears. "If I'd known, I could have bought a book for you to sign. I have no idea what to get Fliss for Christmas. She's impossible to buy for. That would have been perfect."

Lucas caught Eva's gaze. "I'll sign a book for you," he said. "I assume Eva has your address?"

"She does. You'd seriously do that? Thank you. That's so generous." Harriet held the dog while the vet finished his examination. "Well?"

The vet checked the dog's ears. "I don't think he had been in the park for long. A few hours at most, I'd guess."

Harriet smoothed the puppy's head. "I'm going to take you home and give you a lovely warm bed, and tomorrow I'll contact the animal adoption center."

"You'll take him?" Eva looked doubtful. "Fliss said you were already fostering puppies."

"I am, but Fliss is home recovering from the flu so she can help me. And anyone who spent the night out in the park last night deserves some home comforts. I can tell you, too, that this little guy will be rehomed fast. He's adorable."

Lucas watched as Eva stroked the puppy's head. The yearning look in her eyes tugged at something deep inside him.

After all the conversations they'd shared, he knew that the death of her grandmother had left a deep void in her life. She was looking for a way to fill it. She wanted love because she thought love was something beautiful and simple.

He knew better. Love was messy and complicated and full of pain. It had sharp edges and a dark side and he wanted nothing to do with it ever again. Which was why he hadn't touched her since that first night. He knew now that she was vulnerable and lonely.

It would be too easy for her to fall for him, and he wasn't going to do that to her.

He didn't allow himself to think about the risk that *he* might fall for *her*.

He wondered if she was going to suggest keeping the puppy, but instead she smiled at Harriet.

"Thank you for coming, and for taking him."

"Thank you for all the business you've put our way. We've had our best year ever. We've had to take on more dog-walkers. We're covering the entire East Side now."

"Paige told me."

Lucas noticed that Eva was shivering. "You're cold, Eva. You need a hot shower."

Harriet looked concerned. "You *do* look cold. Go. I'll finish up here."

Lucas settled the bill and bundled Eva into a cab.

She put up a feeble resistance. "I might still be angry with you."

He almost smiled at the "might." "You're not sure?" Luckily for him, she wasn't a woman who could be angry with anyone, or anything, for long.

"You came after me, instead of locking yourself in your study. You prioritized a wet, wriggling puppy over expensive cashmere. That won you points. As did building a snowman."

"While you're working out whether you're still mad or not, I'll warm you up." He pulled her against him. "You're shivering as badly as that puppy."

"We could have walked. Your apartment is only steps away."

"Enough steps for you to get hypothermia."

"Can I ask you something? If going to bed with me had nothing to do with the book, why did you do it?"

It was a question he'd asked himself. "Because my self-control isn't as impressive as I thought it was."

"Your self-control has been just fine since."

"I've been working on it, for both our sakes. Your teeth are chattering." He rubbed his hands over her arms. "Tell me how you met Harriet."

"You're changing the subject?"

"Yes. I don't care what we talk about as long as it's not sex."

"Because you do, in fact, want to have sex with me again." She peeped up at him. "That's interesting."

"Eva—"

"Harry and Fliss are twins, and their brother is a friend of Matt's. When Daniel found out that we'd lost our jobs and were setting up on our own, he thought we might want to offer dog-walking as part of our concierge services. To begin with we had no business, but it has grown, and they've grown with us. You'd be surprised how many people in Manhattan own dogs. Fliss is the business brain, but Harry has a special gift with animals. Thank you for offering to sign a book. It was good of you to do that for her."

"I didn't do it for her. I did it for you. I'm trying to get back into your good books, remember? So far it's cost me near-frostbite and a cashmere coat."

"Why do you want to be in my good books?"

"Because if you walk out on me I can't write, and I don't get to eat delicious food." He wasn't ready to consider that it might be more than that. He felt the softness of her hair brush against his chin. She smelled of sunshine and summer fruits. "I thought you were going to ask if you could keep that puppy."

"I almost did, but my practical side took over. There are days when I hate my practical side." She sounded despondent and he eased her away from him so that he could see her expression.

"Did you want him that much?"

"A dog loves you unconditionally. And now you're going to tell me that's my fairy-tale view and that the puppy would probably savage me when it grows up."

He leaned forward to pay the cabdriver. "I think any dog living with you would be lucky."

And any man.

They rode the elevator to the top floor and he kept his arms wrapped around her. He told himself he was holding her because he wanted to warm her up, but he knew he was lying to himself. He was holding her because it felt good and he was in no hurry to let her go.

She leaned her head against his chest. "I'm still mad at you for making me a murderer."

"You don't sound mad."

"What? This is my angry voice."

"I think your angry voice might need work. Or you could just stop being angry." He wondered if she'd ever been able to be mad with anyone for more than five minutes. "If it helps, I'll be groveling for days."

"What form does groveling take?"

"Whatever works. If you want a favor, now would be the perfect time to ask. You want to sacrifice another bottle of my ridiculously expensive wine? No problem."

There was a pause and then she looked up at him. "Sex," she said simply. "I want you to take me to bed and give me another orgasm."

CHAPTER FIFTEEN

Laughter is good for the abs.

—Eva

EVA FELT THE sudden loosening of his grip and for a moment she regretted speaking. She should have stayed silent and let it happen. Because it *would* have happened, she was sure about that. There had been something in his touch that wasn't all about warming her.

"I'll give you anything else, but not that." His voice was rough, his powerful body taut with restraint.

"Why?"

"You know why. We want different things."

"I want sex. What do you want?"

He cursed under his breath. "We are coming at this from a different place."

"As long as we're coming, it doesn't matter."

He didn't laugh. "You're a dreamy romantic!"

"You're worried I'll fall in love, but I won't. Take a close look at me." She lifted her face to his. "Do you see stars in my eyes? Do I look dreamy? Am I gazing at you as if you're a gold-plated unicorn? No. And that's because you're not looking at a woman in love, Lucas, you're looking at a woman who wants sex. Are you in or out?"

A smile touched his mouth. "Are you talking figuratively or literally?"

"Both, I hope."

His smile faded and he grazed her cheek with his fingers. "Feelings aren't that easy to control."

"So now you're saying you're irresistible? That's arrogant."

"I'm saying you're vulnerable. And I don't take advantage of vulnerable women."

"I'm not vulnerable. I'm open. It's not the same thing. I'm not scared of feelings, Lucas. That's the difference between us. Feelings are part of life. Feelings are how we know we're alive."

He stared into her eyes for a long moment and when the elevator doors finally opened he took her hand and led her to his apartment. "You need a hot shower to warm you up."

"Are you taking one with me?" She slid her hand under his shirt and he clamped his hand over hers.

"Eva—"

"I'm taking your advice about that shower. I just hope you'll join me." She walked toward the stairs, unraveling her scarf as she walked. She dropped it on the floor, and then unbuttoned her coat, glancing at him in invitation. "I'm still shivering. I might die of hypothermia if you don't warm me up fast."

"So keep your coat on." He spoke through his teeth and she smiled and shrugged it off, draping it over the back of a chair.

"I need to get out of these wet things." She pulled off her sweater and heard the sharp intake of his breath. "It's the Dance of the Seven Veils, thermal edition."

Hoping that his need for her was stronger than his willpower, she walked toward the bedroom she'd been using.

She wanted him, and now she knew he wanted her, too, she was tired of holding back.

He followed her, but paused in the doorway, his hand on the doorjamb. His knuckles were white, as if he was preventing himself from taking those final steps into the room. "This is a bad idea."

"Good sex is never a bad idea." Her wet clothes stuck to her skin and her fingers were so cold she could no longer feel the tips, but somehow she managed to undress and walk toward the shower. She took her time, knowing he was watching her.

She wanted him, and she'd made it clear she wanted him. That was enough. She wasn't going to beg.

She hit the jets with her numb fingers and closed her eyes, gasping with relief as the heat of the water warmed her freezing skin. Through the steady raindrops of water she heard his voice.

"We both know this isn't just sex, Eva."

His voice melted over her, rich and soothing, layered with a strength that relaxed the tension in her muscles. Her body responded to those deep tones and she kept her eyes closed, knowing that they always gave everything away in the few seconds before her mouth opened and did the rest.

"Do we?" She turned and let the water drench her hair and flow over her skin. "How many orgasms make a relationship?"

"I don't know. You're shivering. You're still cold?"

"I'm not cold." It had nothing to do with that, but she couldn't begin to explain how she was feeling. She watched as he undressed and stepped into the shower unit, and then melted as she felt his hands stroke over her skin and the solid muscle of his thighs brush against hers. She held her breath, savoring the steamy, intimate contact of his skin against hers. She'd forgotten how good it felt to be touched, and she wasn't sure it had ever felt as good as this. She told herself it was because she'd been starved of physical intimacy, but she knew it went deeper than that.

He eased her back against the wall so that the water ceased to drench her and instead thundered over his shoulders and down his back.

His hand was in her hair, infinitely gentle, sliding through the dripping strands, smoothing the droplets of water away from her face. He kissed her eyelids, then her cheek and finally, when excitement was a tight coil in her stomach, he kissed her mouth.

"Eva." He breathed her name against her lips and she closed her eyes, sinking slowly into the deep, warm pool of desire that threatened to drown her.

She felt his mouth find a path from her jaw to her neck and from there to her shoulder. Anticipation was sharp and exciting, and when his lips closed over the tip of her breast she gasped and dug her fingers into the hard muscle of his shoulders.

"Now." A single word, but infused with all the urgency of a command.

She half expected him to argue but instead he closed his hands over her bottom and lifted her, trapping her between the heat of his body and the cool tiles of the shower unit. The water thundered down, turning the atmosphere steamy and humid. Or maybe it was the chemistry between them that was responsible for the torrid, sweltering heat. All she knew was that she was no longer cold, and the parts of her that had been numb had thawed. Now she felt with every part of herself. Her skin, her lips, her fingertips. She pressed her mouth to his, feeling the dampness of his skin. His hair was sleek against his head, droplets of water clinging to his thick lashes and she felt him against her, brutally aroused.

Keeping his gaze locked with hers, he adjusted his hold on her and then entered her with a slow, deliberate thrust. Her muscles clamped around him and she dropped her head to his shoulder, welcoming the invasion, feeling his fingers gripping her bottom as he surged deep.

It was unbearably erotic, the restrained urgency, the heated intimacy. She wanted to stay like this forever, joined, connected, *one*.

She felt dizzy and breathless, and shockingly aroused. She tried to say something, tried to tell him how she was feeling but the only sound that emerged from her lips was a moan. Instead she showed him, sliding her hands over his shoulders, and down, lingering on the swell of his biceps, feeling the flex and ripple of muscle as he held her weight and drove deep. He kept up the slow relentless rhythm, thrusting deep, his mouth fused with hers, until pleasure crashed down on both of them.

MOONLIGHT PLAYED ACROSS dark shadows and Lucas heard the soft sound of Eva's breathing as she slept against him, curled into him like a kitten seeking refuge. He'd promised himself he wouldn't do this again, that what had happened after the ball was a onetime thing. And here he was, naked and wrapped around Eva.

He wondered what it was about her that smashed through his self-control.

When he was with her, need overwhelmed caution.

It was a type of infatuation. A sexual infatuation that clouded his thinking. Or maybe it was just that he hadn't allowed himself to get this close to anyone in a long time.

Whatever it was, it certainly wasn't love.

His body might be well and truly seduced, but his heart was untouched by anything they'd shared. Frozen? Damaged? He didn't know.

Some of his tension must have communicated itself to her because she snuggled into him and yawned. Her limbs tangled intimately with his. "You're quiet. Tell me what you're thinking."

He was thinking that she was a woman who looked for, and expected, happy-ever-afters and nothing they shared could end that way. He knew nothing about happy-ever-afters. All he knew was that she wanted love, and he didn't.

"I'm not thinking anything."

"You are. You're wondering what this means and where it leads."

"It doesn't lead anywhere, Eva."

"Because you never want to fall in love again." There was a long silence. "You think you're such an expert on love, but what if you're not?"

"You're saying I didn't love my wife?"

"No, I'm not saying that." Her voice was soft in the darkness. "I'm saying that there are as many different ways to love as there are people in the world. No two relationships can ever be the same. If they were, then there would only ever have been one love story written."

"You're telling me that Romeo didn't feel the same way about Juliet as Heathcliff did about Cathy?"

"Why must you always pick doomed relationships as examples? I'm saying that love is as different as the people who feel it. You could say that bread is just flour and water, but with a few subtle tweaks you can produce something different each time. Love doesn't have to be a tragedy. It can be happy." She hesitated. "Don't you believe in second chances?"

"Failing in a marriage isn't like failing an exam. You don't get to do it all over again and aim for a better grade. At least, not in my case."

"Is that how you see it? As failure?"

"There was something fundamental that was missing in our relationship. Something I failed to give her."

"Maybe no one could have given her what she needed. Maybe what she needed was something only she could find." She paused. "You've decided you don't ever want to love again, but what if there is a different type of love out there for you? One that lifts you, instead of crushes you? You don't want to miss that. Life is too short and precious to be lived without love, Lucas."

Did she really believe that?

Hearing her words cemented his belief that this was a giant mistake. "How have you made it this far in life without being thoroughly disillusioned?"

"You're assuming you're right and I'm wrong, but what if I'm not the one who's wrong?"

"I've been in love, Eva. I know what love is."

"You know what love was for you last time, but you don't know what love could be. Next time it could be different. Just think about it."

He didn't know whether her view on the world was inspiring or terrifying.

"What I think," he said, "is that you're living in fairy-tale land again."

"My friends call it Planet Eva. But it's nice here." Her voice was soft and breathy. "Maybe you should join me, even if it's only for a minibreak."

Despite all the warnings in his head, she made him laugh and he lowered his mouth to hers and pressed her back against the bed. She was luscious and succulent, like her food. "Maybe I will."

"There's only one rule. No baggage on Planet Eva. We travel light here. Hand luggage only."

EVA SLEPT THROUGH the alarm twice and woke grumpy and flustered.

She found Lucas in his bathroom, shaving. A towel was knotted round his waist.

"It's *late*. Why didn't you wake me?"

"Because you're terrible in the mornings, and even worse when you're tired. And you had reason to be tired. You had an active night."

"You were there, too, remember?"

His eyes met hers in the mirror. "I remember."

She backed away but he snaked out a hand and closed his fingers round her wrist. "Where are you going?"

"To make breakfast."

"Not today. I'm taking you out. There's a place around the corner. French bistro. You'll love it." He released her and turned back to the mirror.

"But your book—"

"I've finished a first draft. I need some space away from it before I tackle it again."

"You've finished it?" She was thrilled for him. "How many words?"

"A hundred thousand. And a first draft doesn't mean it's finished."

"A hundred thousand?" Eva felt weak. "If I write a hundred words for my blog I think I'm doing well. Do you usually write that fast when you get going?"

"No."

"But this time you were desperate."

"This time I was inspired."

Even though she'd given herself a firm talking-to about not reading more into their relationship than there was, his words warmed her insides. "Because I'm the perfect murderess."

The smile spread across his face, slow and sexy. "You're the perfect something. I haven't worked out what yet."

"Unless you want me to remove that towel and do bad things to you, I should probably get dressed."

"That sounds like a good idea. I can't have sex again until I've replenished some of the ten million calories we used up last night."

It was another hour before they finally left the apartment and headed out.

The French Bistro on Lexington Avenue was cozy and personal and Eva was charmed.

"It's like being back in Paris. How did I not know about this place?"

"You live in Brooklyn."

It was obvious Lucas was a frequent visitor. The café was packed, but they were shown to a little table by the window.

Eva shrugged off her coat and slid into her seat. "I had a text from Harry. She's keeping the puppy for another few days, but she's been in touch with the animal adoption center and they're confident they won't have any trouble finding a loving home for him."

"That's good."

It was good. So why did she feel a tug of disappointment?

Reminding herself that she didn't have time to care for a dog, Eva glanced down at the menu in front of her but Lucas picked it up and handed it back to the waiter.

Without consulting her he ordered for both of them and Eva raised her eyebrows.

"Are you developing controlling tendencies?"

"You've been deciding what we eat for the past couple of weeks. It's my turn. And I eat here all the time. I know what's good." He sat back in his chair. "You wanted that puppy, didn't you?"

"No." She said it firmly. "I don't have time. We're really busy building up the business."

He gave her a long, steady look but didn't pursue it. "Do you have any work events between now and Christmas?"

"A couple, but nothing I need to attend in person. I'm using a company called Delicious Eats, and they're great."

"What about the Christmas party at the assisted living community? Are you going to go?"

Eva wondered why he was asking her that question. "Why would I?"

"You said that you missed seeing the people there. They probably miss you, too. Why not go?"

It was an option that hadn't occurred to her. "I don't know. I thought about going to visit a couple of times after Grams died, but it was so hard—" She tested the idea and felt a flutter of mixed emotions.

"I'm worried that going somewhere so full of memories will be painful."

"Or they might make you feel connected. I'm sure the staff and residents there have memories of their own. They might appreciate sharing them with someone who knew her and loved her."

The waiter appeared, delivering hot coffee, plates of eggs Florentine and French toast.

Eva stared at her food without seeing it, thinking about Tom and all her grandmother's friends. "I've neglected them. I should have gone and visited but—"

"It feels daunting. So take someone with you for moral support."

"There isn't anyone. Paige and Frankie are so busy I couldn't possibly ask them. Matt is working on a project out in Long Island so he's away a lot and Jake—well, Jake is great, but not the sort of guy I'd want to cry on."

"I'll come with you. And you've already cried on me so we've covered that one."

His offer took her by surprise. "You'd do that?"

"You've helped me by being here. If I can help you, then I'd like to."

She was touched, and part of her wondered why he'd make such a generous offer. "You'd be mobbed. One of my grandmother's closest friends is a fan of yours."

"I appreciate fans. Without them, I wouldn't have a job. The only part that makes me uneasy is when women send me their underwear."

"That happens?"

"More than you'd think." He told her a few stories about various incidents at book signings and she listened, amused and intrigued.

"I had no idea being an author could be so exciting. You should get danger money. But Tom is ninety, so I don't think you'd be in any physical danger from him."

"Eat." He gestured to her plate. "And think about it."

She thought about it as they ate, and afterward as they strolled down Fifth Avenue to the Rockefeller Center to admire the Christmas tree.

"I used to come here with Grams." She leaned against him, watching the skaters glide around the ice rink in a blur of color, wrapped up against the crisp, cold air. Skyscrapers sparkled behind them, dazzling in the winter sunshine. "Sometimes I'd skate and she'd watch. I wish she was here now. I miss talking to her."

"What would you talk about?"

"I'd ask her advice. Sometimes when I'm not sure what to do about something, I close my eyes and try to imagine what she'd say. Does that sound crazy?"

"No." He slid his fingers under her chin and lifted her face to his. "What advice do you need? What would you ask her if she were here?"

She'd ask her grandmother what she should do about Lucas.

"Nothing specific." She forced a smile. "I'm freezing. We should get back to the apartment so you can work. Thanks for breakfast."

CHAPTER SIXTEEN

Love is a journey. Carry a map.

—Paige

LUCAS GAVE UP trying to stay away from her. Partly because his willpower was weaker than a single strand of thread, and partly because Eva wasn't someone who valued emotional distance or personal space. She was like the puppy they'd rescued. Affectionate, trusting and tactile.

He went back to work, and for the next few days submerged himself in his fictional world and his characters. They occupied his mind to such an extent that the real world faded to nothing. He knew beyond a shadow of a doubt that this was the best book he'd written to date. Now, finally, he almost had something he was excited to show to the world.

Beyond the windows of his study the sun shone, touching the snow-covered trees with dazzling flecks of silver, as if someone had decorated the park in glitter especially for the festive season. People rushed about in the streets, keen to finish Christmas shopping. Lucas saw none of it. He wrote and rewrote, editing ruthlessly, tightening the story, deepening the characters, polishing the prose. Night merged with day and he worked such long stretches that occasionally when he glanced up and saw that it was dark again he realized he'd missed almost all of the daylight hours.

If it hadn't been for Eva, he would have starved or died of dehydration, but she appeared by his side at regular intervals, bearing nutritious treats that barely required him to remove his hands from the keyboard. Tiny bite-size quiches made with crisp buttery pastry and garlic-infused slivers of exotic mushrooms, crostini with roasted peppers and goat cheese, a light-as-air mousse made from smoked salmon and cream. Each piece was a feast of melting flavor, designed to be eaten in one mouthful, but without a compromise on taste and quality. Sampling her food, he had no trouble understanding how Urban Genie's success had grown so rapidly. Eva had an innate sense of what food would perfectly complement the occasion, whether that occasion was a glamorous wedding, or an author who didn't have time to look up from his manuscript.

Apart from those moments where she brought him food and drink, she was careful not to disturb him, although occasionally he heard her on the phone talking to Paige and Frankie, or singing in the kitchen as she cooked.

They always ate dinner together, but afterward he often worked late into the night. It was during one of his late-night work sessions that he heard her screams.

He was out of his chair in an instant, heart pounding, his tension magnified by the fact that he'd been reading over a scary scene.

He pushed open the bedroom door. The bedside light was on and he saw Eva sitting up in bed, her hair soft and tangled, her eyes wide.

"Eva? What the hell is wrong?" He looked around the room, expecting to see masked raiders, but instead there was just Eva, shivering. "What happened?"

For a moment she didn't answer and then she pulled the covers up under her chin. "Can you put the light on?"

"The light is on."

"I mean the main light. I want more light." Her teeth were chattering and he flicked on all the lights in the room and strode to the bed.

"What happened?"

She looked white and shaken. "Bad dream."

"You had a nightmare?" He settled on the bed next to her and pulled her into the curve of his arms. "What about?"

"I was in the kitchen, and I was cooking for a bunch of people, and— On second thought, I don't want to talk about it."

He glanced at the nightstand. "You read one of my books?"

"I thought it was the polite thing to do. Big mistake. You're good at what you do, but what you do isn't for me. Don't be offended."

Far from being offended, he was touched. "I can't believe you read my book."

"I wanted to know more about your writing. Now I wish I didn't."

Smiling, he tightened his grip on her. "It's fiction, sweetheart."

"I know, but it's also scarily real. I don't mind books about zombies and aliens because I don't bump into many of those in Bloomingdale's, but the guy in your book was charming and I don't know if I would have spotted that he was a killer."

"You have excellent radar, remember? You would have detected that something wasn't right."

"I might not. I'm not programmed to be suspicious."

"I love that about you." He wished he hadn't used the word *love*, but she didn't seem to notice.

She rubbed her fingers over her brow. "I'm seriously spooked. Don't you spook yourself when you write it?"

"Sometimes, that's when I know that what I'm writing is good."

"Do you have to write with the lights on?"

He smiled. "No. I prefer to be in the dark. Scarier that way."

"Do you ever read happy fiction where the characters are still alive at the end?"

"Not often."

She shivered and glanced toward her phone. "What time is it?"

"Three in the morning. I was writing. I didn't realize it was so late."

"Sorry I disturbed you. You'd better go back to work."

"I was thinking it was time to go to bed." He stood up, stripped off his clothes and slid under the covers with her, drawing her into his arms again.

"Can we leave the light on?"

"Are you serious?"

"Yes. If there's a serial killer in the room, I want to see him."

TWO DAYS LATER Eva walked into his office and put a parcel down on his desk. "Merry Christmas."

"You bought me a gift? That's sweet of you, but you shouldn't have. There's nothing I need."

"That's a matter of opinion. Open it."

He turned back to the package and slid his finger under the paper, releasing the tape. "It's a book."

"Not just any book."

The paper fell away and he picked up the book and turned it over. "*Pride and Prejudice*." He looked up at her. "You bought me Jane Austen?"

"You need to discover another side of reading. Relationships don't all end in death and misery. The story is emotionally complex and, most important, it has a happy ending. I'm trying to show you that not all fiction has to end with all the characters sliced into tiny pieces, or with broken hearts. There are other options."

He put the book down. "Eva—" His tone was patient. "I write about crime."

"I know! Your book gave me screaming nightmares." She was still embarrassed about that, but had decided there was no point in pretending to be someone she wasn't. She didn't want to be scared in her reading. "Thanks to you, I'm never going to be able to sleep with the light off again and I'm probably not going to be able to take a cab anywhere."

"It's crime fiction. People die."

"But why can't they just be injured and then cured by a kind, caring doctor?"

He looked amused. "Because then the book wouldn't be about a serial killer."

"He could meet someone kind and fall in love—"

"Eva," he interrupted her gently. "Don't read what I write. Then it won't upset you."

"But maybe if you wrote happier fiction, you might not have such dark, twisted thoughts about love. You could start with a short story where no one dies." She looked at him hopefully and he sat back in his chair and shook his head.

"So if this is a Christmas gift, I guess I need to give some thought to yours."

"There's nothing I need."

"You haven't written a letter to Santa?"

"I wrote my letter to Santa months ago. I asked for sex—from a hot guy, not from Santa—and he delivered. And there is no point in me writing again because since I wrote my last letter I've been a bad, bad girl." She leaned forward and kissed him. "What does Santa do to very bad girls?"

"I don't know, but I can tell you what I do with very bad girls." He stood up and pulled her against him.

She curled her fingers into his shirt, determined to say what had been on her mind all day. "Lucas?"

"What?"

"I've been thinking about what you said."

His mouth hovered close to hers. "What did I say?"

"That I should go to the assisted living community and that you'd come with me. Did you mean it?"

He eased away. "Of course I meant it."

"Sometimes people say things they don't mean. And this is a pretty big deal. You'd be giving up a whole afternoon and I know you're busy and it's important you get your book done."

"This is more important." He threaded his fingers through hers. "You'd like to go?"

"Yes, although part of me is scared I'll make a fool of myself. I haven't been back there since I lost Grams. What if I start howling?"

"Then I'll sing loudly to cover the noise. Christmas carols."

"You hate festive music." She smiled, wondering how he always managed to make her feel better. "Be serious."

"I am being serious." He squeezed her hand. "No one is going to judge you, Ev. If you cry, you cry. I hope you don't because I don't like seeing you upset, but no one will blame you. And if it feels like too much and you need to leave, then we'll make some excuse. Leave it with me. You're talking to the guy who is an expert at avoiding social events."

"But you're willing to do this for me." She stared

down at their linked hands, suddenly choked by emotion. "Why?"

"Because I'm hoping you'll be grateful and have sex with me."

"Not an answer."

"Because I know how hard it is." He lifted her hand to his lips. "And because I care about you."

"You'll end up signing books."

"I can live with that."

CHAPTER SEVENTEEN

Love your life, it's the only one you have.

—Eva

ANNIE COOPER HAD been in charge of the assisted living community since she'd left her job at one of the city's busiest hospitals. Lucas had no problem imagining her running a department with brisk, kindly efficiency.

She embraced Eva warmly. "We missed you, honey."

"I missed you all, too. How is your son?"

It was typical, Lucas thought, that the first words Eva spoke were asking after someone else. She was always more concerned about others than she was about herself.

"He's doing well, thank you for asking. And from what I hear, you've been busy, too. I read about Urban Genie."

"I should have visited sooner—"

"You had other priorities, and that's as it should be. Such an exciting time for you. We all watch your YouTube videos. We particularly love your date, almond and oat bars. Your Grams would have been so proud to see you doing so well." Annie shook hands with Lucas. "Eva told me you'd be joining us, Mr. Blade. Everyone is excited. It's not every day we have a famous author visit. I hope you can cope with rabid fans. We have all your books in our library. Would you mind signing a few?"

"I'll sign anything you'd like me to sign." Lucas was watching Eva. On the journey, she'd been unusually quiet, her normal friendly chatter reduced to monosyllabic responses.

Annie smiled. "That would be wonderful, and I know a few residents are bringing their personal copies for you to sign, too. Maybe you could do a reading?"

The question woke Eva from her trance. "I'm not sure that's a good idea." She looked alarmed. "No dripping blood or sharpened knives."

"Oh, the suspense is the best part." Annie led them down the sunny corridor. "Lucas's book was our book club choice a few months back and we were all impressed that he'd hidden the killer's identity so well. What a twist. Every one of us was fooled, and Tom normally guesses before anyone. Do you read his books, Eva?"

"Just the once. I've been in therapy since. I'm a coward." Eva's normally cheerful smile seemed a little forced and Lucas moved closer to her.

Being here proved she was anything but a coward.

Annie opened a door. "Everyone is at Chair Yoga at the moment, but they'll be finished soon. I thought we could set up tea in the Garden Room." She led the way into a spacious room overlooking gardens that led down to the Hudson River. Large windows ensured it was flooded with natural light.

"This was my grandmother's favorite room." Eva stared out of the window and Lucas wondered if he'd done the wrong thing by suggesting she come here. He was aware that he could easily be accused of hypocrisy. What had he done to reach out to people since Sallyanne's death? Nothing. On the other hand the circumstances were different. The gulf between people's image of what had happened and the truth was so great he had no idea how to bridge it. It had made communication with people who had known them as a couple false and pointless. Their condolences had grated over his raw feelings like sandpaper on flesh, another factor that had contributed to his self-imposed isolation each time the anniversary of her death came around.

Annie moved a couple of the chairs closer to the window. "Our chef has made turkey sliders."

"And I made cakes." Eva seemed to rouse herself as she reached for the bags she and Lucas had carried from the cab.

"Then I'll round up the troops while you're getting everything ready."

Lucas took the bags from Eva and carried them to the table. "Are you all right?"

"I'm good."

If she hadn't been living in his apartment for weeks, a situation that had given him insight into her every mood, he might have been fooled. As it was, he knew she was lying but there wasn't much he could do about it while they were surrounded by people.

He cursed himself for suggesting this visit. "We could make our excuses and leave."

"That would be rude. Can you help me arrange the cakes?"

She'd made cupcakes and each one was a work of art, individually decorated with meticulous attention to detail.

He studied the intricate pattern on one of them. "Did you study art at school?"

"No. The only thing I create with paints is a disastrous mess." She arranged the cakes on a plate. "Cooking is the only thing I'm good at."

"I think you're good at a lot of things." He handed her another plate. "You're running a successful business in New York City. Do you know how many startups go belly-up in this city?"

"I don't want to know. Of course frightening people is your special skill so that's probably your intention."

"I would never want to frighten you."

She turned her head and her gaze met his.

"Lucas—"

"You can do this, honey." He spoke softly, for her alone, and she gave him a grateful look.

"Those cakes look delicious." Annie joined them and there was no opportunity for further conversation because the residents started arriving and soon Eva was surrounded, swallowed up by the community of people who had been her grandmother's friends. Her

warmth and kindness drew people to her and he noticed that she took time to talk to everyone, including new residents she hadn't met before.

The afternoon passed quickly and at some point
attention turned from Eva to him, and he duly signed
a stack of books and answered what felt like a million questions.

He met Tom, who seemed to be hanging on his
every word. "My wife loved your books, too. We
used to talk about them together. Talking about books
was one of the things I missed most after she died.
Conversation with a feisty woman is the best mental
stimulation, don't you think? I miss that."

Eva slipped into the chair next to him. "You should
get married again, Tom."

Tom gave her a wicked smile. "Are you proposing?
Because in my day that was the man's role."

"You're behind the times. These days we women
go after what we want. I'd marry you tomorrow, but
I'd drive you crazy because I'm untidy and terrible
in the mornings." She leaned across and kissed his
cheek and he gave her hand a squeeze.

"Sixty years ago you wouldn't have stood a chance.
I'm a man who recognizes gold when he sees it. Some
man with sense is going to snap you up fast." He
glanced up and Lucas was left with the uncomfortable feeling that some part of that remark had been
directed at him.

Had Tom guessed they were involved in some
way?

Reminding himself that Tom interfering in Eva's

life was no different than his grandmother interfering in his, he said nothing.

"How long were you married?"

"The first time, twenty years."

"The first time?"

Tom shrugged. "What can I say? I enjoy being married. Martha and I met on our first day at school. I pulled the ribbon out of her ponytail and she hit me with her book bag. I knew from that moment she was the only woman for me. When she died, and it was natural causes, so don't start spinning one of your stories, I thought that was it. I didn't think a man could get lucky twice in a lifetime but I did. I met Alison at a book group meeting. I noticed her because she was the only one who didn't like the book we were reading and she wasn't afraid to stand up and say so. I asked her to marry me a week later because when you know you're in love, there's no point in waiting. I know Martha would have liked her."

Eva's eyes misted. "That's a lovely story, Tom."

Tom squeezed her hand. "Your grandmother would be so happy if she could see you now. Running your own company and in love with a handsome young man."

"I'm not in love, Tom. Who said I was in love?" Eva's cheeks turned the color of cherry blossoms. "Who would I be in love with?"

Tom's gaze shifted to Lucas who decided that this visit definitely hadn't been one of his better ideas.

It was like a visit to his grandmother multiplied a thousand times.

"I saw you and Lucas talking, over by the cakes."

"He was helping me. We're friends."

"Good. Friendship is the most important part of any relationship. You can be setting fire to the sheets, but if there isn't a bond of friendship you have nothing."

Eva sent Lucas a mortified glance and he decided he'd better intervene before Tom found someone to marry them on the spot.

"Eva is working for me right now. That's all it is."

Tom gave Lucas a long look that said he didn't believe a word of it. "Some people don't believe you can fall in love more than once. I did it twice. I'm living proof that it's possible."

Lucas was spared the need to respond because at that moment the chef and two of the kitchen staff walked into the room with trays of turkey sliders. Eva sprang to her feet and went to supervise.

Before Lucas could follow her, Tom leaned forward.

"That girl," he said, "is special."

Lucas wasn't about to argue with that, even though agreeing was bound to get him into deeper trouble. "She is."

Tom eased out of his chair. "It's easy to develop attachments when you're lonely. Easy to misinterpret feelings."

"That's true, but although Eva is a romantic, she's actually pretty levelheaded and sensible about relationships."

Tom gave him a long look. "I was talking about

you." He walked over to join the rest of the residents who were helping themselves to the sliders.

Lucas stared across the room at Eva. What did Tom mean? He wasn't the one who was lonely, she was. Damn it, he'd been perfectly happy holed up alone in his penthouse until she'd come along.

He signed two more books for residents who were hovering and then joined everyone else to eat the sliders and cakes.

After they'd eaten, Eva was persuaded to sing while Tom accompanied her on the piano.

By the time they arrived back at his apartment building, it was dark.

"I'm sorry about that. Talk about awkward." Eva was wrapped up in her scarf, her voice muffled. "Tom was embarrassing."

"He's protective of you. He wants you to be happy, that's all." And being with him wouldn't make her happy, he was sure of that. Not in the long-term. Tom's words had proved a sharp reminder that Eva wasn't a woman to be satisfied with a brief, superficial relationship. Everything about her went deep. Her feelings, her hopes and her expectations.

He thought she was wrong about a lot of things, including her ridiculously fairy-tale views on love and marriage, but he didn't want to be the one to prove that to her. It would be like catching a butterfly and breaking its wings. Over the past few weeks he'd grown to admire her steadfast optimism. He didn't want to find out what it would take to break that.

And it didn't make any difference to him that Tom

had been married twice. It wouldn't have mattered to him if Tom had been married six times.

He'd done it once, and that was it. As far as he was concerned, having your heart ripped out once in a lifetime was more than enough. But right now, Eva was the one who was vulnerable, not him. He guarded himself so carefully he was bulletproof.

"My grandmother and Tom were great friends. It was generous of you to play billiards with him." Eva waited while he unlocked the door of his apartment. "And to let him win."

"I didn't let him win. He thrashed me." He didn't add that he'd been paying more attention to her than to the game. He watched as she walked into the kitchen and flicked on the lights. Something was different about her. She'd lost her usual bounce. "Interesting guy. Did you set up that conversation about falling in love twice in a lifetime?"

"No." Turning her back to him, she poured herself a glass of water. "I haven't seen him since Grams died and you were the one who offered to come with me." She lowered the glass. "What he said wasn't exactly revolutionary, Lucas. It isn't part of a conspiracy. He believes in love, that's all. And of course he would, because he's experienced it twice. When something has happened to us, we don't have any trouble believing in it."

"I never said I didn't believe in it. Just that I didn't want it again. But Tom does." He wondered why she wasn't looking at him. "My guess is he'd make you his third wife given half a chance."

"Maybe that's the answer. I should marry Tom."
She took a swallow of water and put the glass down.
But she still didn't look at him.

"What's wrong?" It bothered him that there was
something she wasn't sharing.

"Nothing. Are you hungry?"

"No. I ate enough carbohydrates at the party to
insulate me for a month in Alaska." He followed her
into the kitchen and closed his hand over her shoulder. "I want to know what's going on in your head."

Instead of relaxing and sliding her arms around
him, she stayed rigid in his arms. "I miss her, that's
all." Her hair brushed against his chin and he lifted
his hand and stroked her back gently.

"Do you wish you hadn't gone today?"

"No." She eased away from him, but she still didn't
look at him.

"Did someone say something that upset you?"
There had been plenty of occasions when he hadn't
been by her side when that could have happened.

"No. They were all lovely. I promised Annie I'd
go back soon. But now I have some work to do and
I'm sure you do too after giving up a whole afternoon
for me." She grabbed her purse and her phone and
made for the stairs.

He stared after her in frustration. She wasn't someone who hid her feelings well, so to see her trying so
hard to do so made him uneasy.

"Eva—"

She paused at the top of the stairs. "Thanks for
coming with me today. I enjoyed talking to them,

and talking about Grams was good, too. It helped. I thought it would make me miss her more, but it didn't. It made me feel better."

He frowned. If she was feeling better, why was she looking so thoroughly miserable?

Eva locked the bathroom door and sat down on the edge of the bath.

She was in love with Lucas.

Tom had seen it right away, so why hadn't she?

She'd assumed falling in love would feel like a long, slow slide into a comfortable warm pool. She hadn't anticipated the suddenness, more of a plummet than a slide, that ended in a breathless plunge into water that felt shockingly deep. Everything felt out of her control. It left her breathless and unbalanced. Terrified and exhilarated and yet at the same time she had no doubt it was real, that what she was feeling was something deep and permanent that wasn't going to be erased by time.

Because she'd known him for only a few weeks, and because she didn't *want* to fall for him. It wasn't wise or sensible. He wasn't interested in another serious relationship. She'd seen how uncomfortable Lucas had been when Tom had mentioned that he'd been in love twice.

Not that she wasn't capable of having a relationship just for fun, she was. But Lucas—

She swallowed hard, remembering the reassuring warmth of his presence when she'd walked into the Garden Room. She remembered the way he'd held her when she cried, the way he'd stayed by her side at the ball, fiercely protective. The way he'd listened to her chatter and laughed at her observations. The way he savored her food.

He was everything she'd ever wanted, and so much more.

She gave a groan and covered her face with her hands.

Now what?

She dug in her purse for her phone, her hand shaking. "Paige? I think I might be in trouble."

"You're pregnant?"

"Why does 'trouble' always have to mean pregnant?"

"I don't know. It just came out. Tell me what's wrong. You've dropped red wine on his white sofa? You deleted his book by accident?"

"I'm in love with him. And if you say 'I told you so,' I'm hanging up."

Paige didn't say that. "Is there any chance he might feel the same way?"

"No chance."

"Are you sure?"

Eva thought about his determination never to fall in love again. "I'm sure. It's definitely not on his bucket list."

Her chest ached. Her brain ached.

Lucas was right. Love wasn't a fairy tale. It was messy and painful.

"Does he know how you feel?"

"Not yet. But I'm not exactly good at hiding my feelings, as you know. I'm not sure what I should do."

There was a pause. "You can end the job if you want to. Make an excuse that we're busy and we need you."

"No. If I do a job, then I see it through. This job is worth a lot to us." But that wasn't the whole reason. She wanted him to finish his book. She knew how important that was to him, and if her being here helped him do that then she'd stay. "I'm already in love, so staying isn't going to make that part any worse. The only thing that worries me is that he'll find out."

"Would that be such a bad thing?"

"It would be pretty awkward. Damn." She slumped on the side of the bath.

She'd wanted to love deeply, and now she did.

What she hadn't wanted was to fall in love with a man who wasn't interested in risking his heart a second time.

That was the ultimate twist.

That, she thought, was her idea of a horror story.

CHAPTER EIGHTEEN

Less is more, unless it's love or chocolate.

—Eva

IF SHE WAS sensible, she probably would have tried to distance herself.

She believed it was possible to fall in love more than once, but what if it never happened? What if this was the only experience of real love she was going to have in her lifetime? In case it was, she wanted to make the most of it. But every moment they spent together was tinged with poignancy, sharpened with an edge of sadness, because she knew it was going to end.

Now that he had a completed draft, some of the urgency left him and he reduced his crazy work sessions where he sometimes didn't seem to come up for air.

He surprised her by taking her to the Metropolitan Opera House to see *The Nutcracker*, and she held his hand all the way through it, tears blurring her vision as she watched the snowflakes and the Sugar Plum Fairy and remembered all the times her grandmother had taken her when she was young.

Lucas leaned closer. "I can imagine you in a tiny pink tutu and tights. I bet you were cute."

"I was cute, but a little clumsy. I was the only Sugar Plum Fairy who fell over her own feet. I didn't know you liked the ballet, too."

"I don't."

"Then why are we here?"

"Because I know you do."

She was deeply touched, not just that he'd done that for her but because he'd listened and stored the information when she'd told him she'd done this with her grandmother.

"For an arrogant cynic, you can be pretty thoughtful. And as your reward I'm going to dress up and dance for you later."

His gaze dropped to her mouth. "I'd prefer it if you undressed and danced for me."

He didn't mind that she was untidy, or that she was terrible in the mornings. She didn't mind that he locked himself away for long periods in his study.

Once he came out with a thunderous look on his face and she froze, wondering what had happened.

"You have writer's block?"

"Have you been in my study?"

"Yes. You weren't there but I left a plate of cookies and an herbal tea on your desk."

"You changed my manuscript."

"Excuse me?" Eva opened her eyes wide, trying to look innocent. "I don't know what you're talking about, I'm sure."

"You are a truly terrible liar. You can't have two FBI agents hugging."

"Why not? What's wrong with supporting your colleagues at work? I happen to think it makes them more human. They witnessed something horrible."

"Eva, I'm writing a horror story."

"Well, now it's a little less horrific. You're welcome."

He ran his hand over the back of his neck and looked at her in exasperation. "Eva—"

"What? I read a few pages and those two clearly have chemistry. I thought maybe they could get together and fall in love. What is wrong with trying to put something happy in your book?"

"You've killed the tension."

"I have?" As someone who wasn't good with tension, it sounded like praise. "Good."

"It's not good, Eva. *It's not good.*"

"That's a matter of opinion."

"You want me to write happy thrillers?"

"It could be a whole new genre. It might be a big hit."

"My career would be over."

"Don't be dramatic."

The banter continued, and they regularly argued over their taste in music, books and movies.

She forced him to sit through *While You Were Sleeping*, and in return she watched *Rear Window*, although she had her hands over her eyes for most of the movie and insisted on sleeping with the light on afterward.

He wrapped up a night-light and gave it to her as an early Christmas gift.

"I don't need a night-light."

"You always sleep with the light on."

"Only since I met you."

When she told him she was going to do the last of her Christmas shopping, he offered to go with her.

"You can help me choose something special for my grandmother," he said. It was the only reason he gave when she probed as to why he'd want to brave the crowds.

The blizzard had passed, leaving behind snowy streets and a perfect blue sky. The sky and sunshine made it seem like they might have been in the Mediterranean had it not been for the biting wind and bitter cold.

Eva snuggled deep into her coat and slipped her hand into his.

He closed his fingers around hers and they walked down Fifth Avenue together, past glittering shop windows illuminated by twinkling fairy lights, each telling a different story. They strolled across to Rockefeller Center to admire the towering Christmas tree and then wandered down to Bryant Park and browsed the shops that were set up for the holiday period.

Eva lingered, examining jewelry, artisan goods and local foods. She sent Lucas an apologetic glance. "Are you bored? Shopping with me is probably a whole new definition of horror for you."

He took her bags from her. "I'm not good at Christmas shopping. If you can help me with that, then I'll owe you a debt I can never repay."

"You already owe me. Because of me, you won't miss your deadline. I'm a walking miracle. How did your writing go this morning?"

"It went well. I'm on my final read. I'll be sending it to my agent and my editor tomorrow. Thanks to you. And you're right. You are a miracle."

"Maybe we should forget shopping. I could take you home and perform a few more miracles." He slid his arm around her shoulders and she snuggled closer, wishing that being with him wasn't quite so easy. "But we can't leave until we've found the perfect present for Mitzy." She turned back to the stall and Lucas released her reluctantly.

"I have no idea what the perfect present looks like."

"That's why you have me."

It was several hours later when they arrived back at the apartment. After dropping their packages in the hallway they made straight for the bedroom.

Their mouths fused, the fact that both of them knew they were coming to the end of their time together adding a touch of desperation to every encounter.

Eva knew there was little time left. A few more days and she might never see him again. A few more days, and after that he would never know how she really felt.

The words were in her head as he made love to her slowly, stretching out the moment until she was almost screaming with need. Time and time again he drove her right to the edge, and held her there, hovering in a state of breathless desperation. And she knew that there never was going to be a right moment to say what she wanted to say, so she might as well just say it because if this was going to end and she hadn't told him how she felt, she'd always regret it.

"I love you." She whispered the words into his neck and felt him go still. "I love you, Lucas."

He brought his mouth down on hers, silencing her. His fingers tightened in her hair and his measured thrusts deepened and became more urgent. But he didn't stop kissing her, as if he was afraid that if he did she might say those words again.

She didn't, but she showed him with the arch of her body and the gentle stroke of her hand.

She felt him shudder and drive deeper still, the erotic force of each thrust sending her into the most intense orgasm of her life. She cried out and felt him shudder above her as he reached his own peak, and still he held her and kissed her until she was dizzy with it.

Afterward she lay still, weakened by pleasure, pinned by his weight and the unimaginable intimacy of being with Lucas.

She wanted it to last forever.

He was her first love, and she so badly wanted him to be her last, but if this was all they could ever have then she'd take it.

THE FOLLOWING MORNING she sensed the change in him.

The warmth, the humor, the closeness, were gone. Instead his reaction to her was almost…polite.

She watched him, bemused, her insides plummeting like an elevator with mechanical failure. "Lucas?"

"This thing between us has moved into an area I never wanted it to go."

She hadn't expected him to be quite so direct, or say those words quite yet.

She'd been hoping for more time, even though she knew there was no more time to be had.

She wanted him to stop talking. She didn't want to hear what he was about to say because she knew it signaled the end.

"You mean because I told you I love you? I freaked you out."

"We've known each other for a month, that's all."

"And it's been the best month of my life. It isn't the length of a relationship that matters, Lucas, it's the depth. Don't you ever wonder why some people are together for years without ever getting married, and then one of them meets someone and that's it. They're married within a month."

His face was expressionless. "Are you proposing?"

"No! I'm saying we've spent more time together in the past month that most people do in six months of dating. And I love you. I refuse to lie about that." She saw the tension stamped in his handsome features.

"This can't happen, Eva."

"You're saying I don't matter to you."

"You matter to me. But you want the fairy tale. I could never give you that."

"Oh, Lucas." She felt a rush of sadness and mixed in with the sadness was frustration that he still didn't get it. "The fairy tale isn't Prince Charming or magical unicorns. It's love. What I want is to love someone, and for them to love me back. For me, that's the fairy tale."

"Love isn't what you think it is."

"It isn't what *you* think it is. Love isn't a curse, Lucas, it's a gift." She took a breath and then a risk. Why not? At this point she had nothing more to lose. "I'm offering you that gift. All of my heart, forever."

His face was chalk white. "Eva—"

"I love you, and I know it's been fast and maybe it's crazy to say those words after such a short time, but I know this is real and good. *We're* good. You make me happy. With you I've never once felt as if I had to put on an act, or hide how I was feeling. It may have been a short relationship, but it was the most honest, real relationship I've ever had." She tried to explain. "Sometimes when you date someone, it takes ages to see who they really are. That didn't happen with us. You cared how I was feeling. It was only when I was with you that I realized how exhausting it is pretending to be okay all the time, when really you don't feel okay at all. And that's not a reflection on my friends, it's a reflection on me. I was the one putting pressure on myself to always be happy and positive. With you, I didn't feel I had to do that. Thanks to you, I feel better than I have for over a year. And I've talked and talked and now it's your turn."

He wore a hunted look and the hand he dragged through his hair was unsteady. "I don't know what to say."

Disappointment thudded through her. "There were a few things I was hoping you'd say, and that wasn't one of them."

He pressed his fingers to the bridge of his nose and then let his hand drop. "You say I make you happy, but for how long? How long would that last? What happens when you wake up one morning and discover I don't make you happy any longer? I don't want to be the one who kills your optimism or your illusions. I don't want that responsibility."

"So don't kill them. Tell me you love me, too, and we'll spend the rest of our lives making each other happy."

"You really think it's that simple?"

"I think it can be if you let it."

"I disagree."

Her heart felt as if someone had crushed it.

Summoning the last of her strength, she straightened her shoulders. "I never thought you were a coward."

"I tell you I'm protecting you, and you call me a coward?"

"We both know that the person you're protecting is yourself. I know you loved Sallyanne. I know you grieved, and are still grieving, and I know it was complicated and messy. I understand why you'd want to protect yourself but you don't need to, Lucas, because what we have is precious and I would never damage it."

"But I might."

"No." She softened her voice because she understood what was going on in his head. "You wouldn't do that, and deep down I think you know it, but you're too scared to admit it." Forcing her leaden legs to cross the room, she walked away from him toward the stairs.

"Where are you going?"

"To pack."

"You're walking out?" His voice was raw. "You're leaving?"

Only if you don't stop me.

"What is there to stay for, Lucas? The job is finished. I've done what you paid me to do. There's only one other reason to stay and you don't want that." She was halfway up the stairs when his voice stopped her again.

"Wait!"

Hope flickered inside her like a candle that had wavered in the wind but hadn't quite been extinguished. She turned slowly, her heart racing.

"What?"

"Stay a little longer."

"And then what?" When he didn't answer, she started up the stairs again, weary to the bone. "There are a lot of things in this life I'm prepared to fight for. My friends, my job, my future, but I won't fight for your heart, Lucas. If you can't give it willingly, then I don't want it."

CHAPTER NINETEEN

Treat life like a workout. Stay flexible.
—Frankie

MISERABLE, EVA WALKED along Fifth Avenue and felt another flutter of snow.

She tilted her face to the sky and closed her eyes.

On impulse she walked into St. Patrick's Cathedral, an oasis of calm and peace in the busiest part of New York.

Her grandmother had brought her here many times, but it was the first time she'd been inside since her death.

Remembering was painful and she slid into one of the pews and sat quietly, admiring the stunning architecture and the stained-glass windows.

The choir was singing, their clear voices filling the soaring space.

A lump formed in her throat, so huge it prevented her from swallowing.

She'd been so sure he loved her, but he hadn't actually said as much, had he? Maybe she'd been wrong. Maybe she'd let her hopes and dreams cloud reality.

She thought of all the things she'd learned since she'd been with him.

"You weren't right about everything, Grams," she murmured. "It's good to be the sunshine, but sometimes it's all right to be the rain, too. A good, balanced life needs both."

Lucas had taught her that.

He was the first person she'd been totally open and honest with and that, as much as the sex, was what she was going to miss most.

She'd always thought the worst thing would be never to fall in love, but she'd discovered that far, far worse than that was falling in love with someone who didn't want your love.

"Merry Christmas, Grams," she whispered. "I miss you."

She sat for a while longer, lit a candle for her grandmother and trudged home, through snowy streets and a crowded subway, jostled by families overloaded with packages and excited about Christmas.

Paige was at a function with Jake, while Frankie and Matt were traveling back from a job in Connecticut, which meant she'd have the apartment to herself.

Alone. But this time it wasn't her solitude that was at the front of her mind, it was his.

Lucas.

She unlocked the door of her apartment, dropped her bags by the door and flopped onto the sofa without bothering to take off her coat.

What was he doing now that he'd finished his

book? He no longer had an excuse to hide himself away. Who would he share his thoughts and secrets with? Would he go through the rest of his life without revealing the truth about his dead wife to anyone but her just to protect Sallyanne's family?

"So ARE YOU joining us for Christmas? Your brother will be here. Goodness knows it's hard enough to get the two of you in a room at the same time. Lucas, are you listening to me? Why are you staring out of the window?"

Lucas turned and tried to give his grandmother his full attention. The only thing in his head was those few breathless moments when Eva had told him she loved him. How had that happened? He'd put up barriers, and she'd breached them. "Sorry. What did you say?"

"I said that I'm marrying a twenty-one-year-old opera singer and moving to Vienna."

"That's good to know." He thought of the night Eva had cried. *Was she crying now?* Guilt tore at him.

She'd walked out. Eva had walked out. She'd said she loved him. She'd exposed her heart and offered him everything.

And then left.

He breathed deeply, acknowledging the truth. She'd left because he'd given her no reason to stay. And why would he? Love couldn't be that easy, could it? It couldn't be as simple and uncomplicated as Eva made it seem.

"Lucas?" His grandmother's voice was gentle. "It's

always delightful to see you, of course, but why come here if you didn't want to engage in conversation? Are you going to tell me what's troubling you, or are you just going to stand there staring out of my window?"

"Nothing's wrong. I brought you a Christmas gift." He handed her a neatly wrapped parcel. "You can open it now if you like. You don't have to wait until tomorrow."

His grandmother took it and placed it on the side table. "Unless your gift is the news that you proposed to Eva, it can wait until tomorrow."

"Proposed?" Lucas tensed. "That isn't going to happen."

"Because you're a stubborn fool?"

"Because I'm not in love." Even as he said it, he knew the words felt wrong, like putting on a coat that didn't fit.

His grandmother watched him thoughtfully. "Would you like a slice of cake?"

That was it? One minute she was talking about love and the next she was talking about cake? "You've been baking?"

"Eva did the baking."

"She was here?"

"Why do you look surprised? My relationship with her preceded yours, Lucas."

"How did she seem? Was she upset?" He wasn't sure what he wanted the answer to be. If she was upset then it meant *he'd* upset her, but if she wasn't then it meant she didn't care. That she hadn't meant those things she'd said to him.

Love couldn't be that simple.

His grandmother reached for her glasses and slid them onto her nose. "Did you give her reason to be upset?"

A thousand reasons, but he was damned if he was going to tell his grandmother the intimate details of his life, no matter how much chocolate cake she'd fed him as a child. "It's a difficult time for her. She lost her grandmother last year."

"I know. We've talked about it often, but we both know that isn't why she's upset now."

Lucas felt as if he was on the witness stand. "Did she—"

"Talk about your relationship? Not much. She didn't have to. Everything she feels shows on her face. Eva is delightfully uncomplicated. The way she spoke about you told me everything I need to know. It's a shame her feelings aren't reciprocated." She removed her glasses and polished them carefully. "Is that what's wrong? You're feeling guilty? Because you shouldn't. No man should ever feel guilty for not loving a woman. It isn't something that can be switched on and off at will. Right now Eva is upset, but she's a special girl and she'll find someone else soon enough."

Someone else?

It was a possibility that hadn't occurred to him. "What do you mean?" His mouth was so dry he could barely force the words out and his heart pumped, as if it was punching him for being a fool.

"You don't really think a girl like Eva will be on

her own for long, do you? She has the most generous heart and sweetest nature of anyone I've met. Some very lucky man will get wise to that soon and snap her up. I wouldn't be surprised if she's one of those people who get married instantly, with no waiting. She knows what she wants and she trusts her own feelings. And she has courage. So really, you don't need to worry. And as you don't love her, you'll probably be relieved when she falls in love with someone else." She eyed him closely. "You look a little pale all of a sudden. Have you been working through the night again? Such an unhealthy habit. Now that the book is done, you should take some time off."

Peanut nudged his ankle and Lucas stooped to pick him up, thinking of the night he and Eva had rescued the puppy in the park.

His grandmother was right. A woman like that would move on. She wouldn't spend many nights crying over him. She'd pick herself up.

Loving him was a wound, but it wouldn't be fatal. She wouldn't let it be fatal.

The thought of her with someone else made him want to punch a hole through something.

What if it was someone who didn't understand how sensitive she was? Someone who took advantage of that generous nature or was clumsy with those dreams of hers?

His grandmother was holding out a slice of cake, an elaborate confection of light sponge cake, whipped cream and fresh strawberries. It made him think of creamy skin and ruby lips. Of softness and silk and the smell of Eva's shampoo.

To be polite, he cut into it and forked up a mouthful, but discovered he had no appetite.

He put it down, china clattering on the table. "Damn it, Gran, Eva's head is full of dreams. She sees the world as this bright, sunny place."

His grandmother rescued the fork before it could fall onto the floor. "I see her as a woman who makes the best of things and knows what she wants. There's nothing wrong with having dreams, Lucas, especially if you have the courage to follow them. She does."

I love you.

Eva had that courage. She'd exposed her feelings without hesitation, even though she'd had no guarantee that those feelings were returned.

"I can't be what she wants me to be."

His grandmother took another sip of her tea. "Are you sure you're thinking about Eva, and not Sally-anne?"

He stared at her, instinctively defensive. "What do you mean?"

"Sallyanne was a complicated woman, and what you shared made you believe that all relationships are complicated. She had issues, but none of her issues were linked with you. You can't fix everything and you can't make a person what you want them to be."

His heart was pounding. He hadn't talked about this with his family. Ever. "After she died, I kept thinking there must have been something I should have done differently."

"And you tortured yourself with that." She nodded, her gaze sympathetic. "There were so many times when I wished you'd talk about it. It killed me to see you holding all that hurt inside."

"I didn't want to destroy the image the world had of her. Despite everything, I loved her."

"And she loved you, even though she had no idea how to handle that love."

"In the end, I didn't know what she wanted from me."

His grandmother smiled and put her cup down. "I think what Sallyanne wanted, and what she would want if she was here now, was for you to be happy. Maybe sometimes life, and love, really is as simple as that."

"TELL US EVERYTHING." Paige poured wine into three glasses and Eva sank down onto the sofa.

Matt and Jake were playing poker with a couple of friends, including the twins' brother Daniel, so Paige, Frankie and Eva had the apartment to themselves.

"I'm in love with him." She didn't see any point in lying about it, or prevaricating. Her insides were churned up and she was never any good at hiding her feelings.

Paige picked up her glass. "And?"

"And nothing. That's it."

"He doesn't feel the same way?"

Eva stared into the ruby-red liquid in her glass, remembering the night she'd opened one of his most valuable bottles of wine. "I don't know. I think it's possible he does, but he just doesn't want to feel that way so he is never going to admit it. I love him. I think he loves me. It should be simple."

"I am going to kill him." Frankie thumped her glass on the table and reached for the bottle. "I don't have your sweet nature, so I will have no problem finding him and removing his bones one by one."

Eva shuddered. "The two of you would have gotten along so well. Why are you so angry?"

"I'm not angry."

"I haven't seen you this dangerous since Roxy's ex showed up here and you almost broke his arm. What have I done to upset you?"

"Nothing. You haven't done anything. It's him." Frankie simmered for a moment and then stuck her hand out. "Give me your phone."

"Why?"

"Just give it to me."

"Not until you tell me why you want it."

"Someone needs to tell him he's an asshole and given that you're too nice, it's going to have to be me." Frankie snapped her fingers. "Give."

"No way. What is *wrong* with you? This is my pain, not yours."

"Wrong. When you hurt, I hurt, and I hate hurting. Crap." Frankie sank onto the chair next to her. "Of all of us, you're the one whose relationship should have run smoothly. You should have danced into the sunset with your dream man on matching unicorns."

Eva smiled through her tears. "I've never seen a unicorn dance."

Frankie spread her hands. "And I've never seen a unicorn at all, so that proves my point."

"Can we get back to reality?" Paige tactfully took charge. "Frankie, Eva is right, this is her problem."

"You're saying I can't break his neck? Jake and I could fillet him."

"That isn't how we do things." Paige topped off Eva's glass.

"You can't force someone to love you," Eva said. "That isn't how it works."

"Which proves what I've always known, that falling in love is a pile of crap." Frankie drained her glass. "Fill it up, Paige. I want to make a toast."

"Are you sure you haven't had enough?"

"I haven't even started." She pushed her glass across the table and waited while Paige filled it. "Okay, lift your glasses. First we're drinking to our business success. What a ride. To Urban Genie." She lifted her glass high, and Paige and Eva did the same.

"Urban Genie."

They all drank and then Frankie lifted her hand. "I'm just getting started. To us, for managing not to kill each other despite having different styles."

Eva looked doubtful. "You wanted to kill me?"

"Raise your glass, damn it."

Eva dutifully raised her glass.

"To friendship," Frankie continued. "Because true friendship transcends differences. I'd rather read a thriller, you'd rather read a romance. It's okay. I forgive you for having weird taste."

Eva raised her eyebrows. "Thanks."

"To forever friendship." Frankie stuck her glass in the air and Paige grinned.

"I think this had better be our last toast or you'll have a headache in the morning and it's Christmas."

"One more." Frankie reached for the bottle and topped off their glasses. "To having each other's backs, no matter what." She looked at Eva and her gaze softened. "To sisterhood."

Eva felt her throat thicken. "To sisterhood."

Paige lifted her glass. "Sisterhood."

The door opened and Matt and Jake walked in, arguing about whether Jake had cheated or not.

"Just because you lost doesn't mean I cheated." Jake kicked the door shut. "You need to learn to be a better loser."

"I'd be fine about losing if I'd actually lost, but I beat you and—" Matt broke off, staring at Eva's face. "What happened? What's wrong?"

His concern warmed her. "It's nothing."

"You don't cry over nothing."

"She cries over romantic movies." Jake hung up his jacket. "Technically speaking, that's nothing."

Frankie rolled her eyes. "Shut up, Jake. Not everyone is as insensitive as you."

"I'm not insensitive. I've cried over movies in a 'get me out of here' kind of way. And since when did you turn into Miss Sensitive?"

Matt ignored them both. "Eva?"

"Nothing's wrong. Frankie said something nice, that's all." She wasn't going to mope and she wasn't going to moan. Lucas didn't want love. There was nothing she could do about that. Nothing except move on.

It was Jake's turn to raise his eyebrows. "Our Frankie? That doesn't sound like her."

Frankie gave him a look. "If you weren't going to marry my friend, I'd fillet you."

"In a fight, I'd win. You may have a black belt in karate but I fight dirty."

"Enough! It's Christmas. No one argues at Christmas, and no one fights." Paige glanced toward the door. "Where is Daniel?"

"He's gone home. It's family time. Even Daniel takes time off from seducing women at Christmas."

Eva sat, soaking up the healing warmth and banter. *Forever friendship*, she thought. Not just with Frankie and Paige, but with Jake and Matt. She no longer felt as if she was alone on a desert island. She felt cocooned, connected, surrounded, *loved*.

"I have a toast," she said, reaching for her glass. "To family. You can be born into one, or you can adopt one, but either way it's the best thing. Thank you for being mine."

There was a moment's silence.

Jake spoke first. "Carry on like that and you'll make even me cry." He removed Paige's glass from her fingers and raised it high in the air. "To family. Can't live with them, can't live without them."

"To family," Eva said.

"Family," chorused Frankie and Matt.

"Steal my wine again," Paige said pleasantly, "and you'll soon find out how to live without them."

CHAPTER TWENTY

Happy-ever-afters are like people. Each is unique.

—Eva

ROMANO'S WAS CROWDED with people and Eva dragged her misery to the kitchen to help Jake's mother, Maria. They'd decided on a set menu to make it easier to cater for large numbers and as Eva had helped design it, she didn't need briefing. Maria had suggested she sit down and enjoy the meal with her friends, but in any case, Eva was grateful for anything that took her mind off Lucas.

If it hadn't been Christmas she would happily have spent the day in bed with her head under the covers.

If her grandmother had been alive, she would have gone to her and told her everything and Grams would have managed to make her feel better, and stronger, about everything.

As it was, she had to do it on her own. She felt bone weary and perilously close to tears.

It was going to be another Christmas where she had to struggle to make it through the day without breaking down.

What was Lucas doing? Was he on his own or had he at least joined his grandmother?

"How are you doing, honey?" Maria's cheeks were flushed from the heat of the oven and the fact that she'd been rushing around the kitchen for several hours already.

"Doing great." Eva caught Maria's eye. "Okay, not so great. Part of me, the stupid dreamy part, thought Lucas cared. I really believed that."

"Perhaps he did."

"Not enough." Eva picked up a bulb of garlic. "And who falls in love after a month? That's crazy, right?"

"Is it?"

"Paige and Jake have known each other forever, and so have Frankie and Matt."

"There's more than one way to fall in love, honey, and it sounds as if you and Lucas had a connection."

"We did." Listless, Eva stared at the garlic in her hand. "I told him things. He told me things. I guess I thought—" She broke off. "Never mind. I'll get over him."

"Don't cry. It's important that you don't have red eyes today."

"I know, it's Christmas and I mustn't ruin anyone's day."

"It's your day I'm thinking of." Maria took the garlic from her. "I know you. You're going to want to look your best. Go and put some lipstick on."

"Why?" Eva was bemused. "I don't think a side of beef and a tray of roast potatoes is going to care if I'm

wearing lipstick." Everyone around her seemed excited and energized. It made her struggle even harder.

"You'll be glad you've done it." Maria leaned in
and gave her a big hug. "Your grandmother would be
so, so proud of you, honey. And now we need to get
the beef out of the oven or it will be charred."

Eva didn't think her grandmother would be proud
to see her dripping around the kitchen like a raincloud, but she said nothing and focused on the cooking. For her, working in the kitchen was a type of
therapy. She sliced, chopped and sautéed with her
mind on automatic.

Maria's kitchen was a well-oiled machine, and she
slotted in easily and found the routine soothing. She
didn't have to think too much.

"Ev?" Frankie appeared in the doorway and exchanged knowing looks with Maria. "Can you come
out here? We have something for you."

"Can it wait? I'm serving lunch for eighty and I
have beef—and pie." She was proud that she sounded
strong, even though she didn't feel it. She removed
a tray of sizzling potatoes from the oven. "I thought
we were doing presents later."

"This present isn't something you can wrap."
Frankie's voice sounded strange. Somewhere between
smug and excited. "You're going to be pleased."

"There's nothing I really want."

"Will you get out here and stop arguing?" Frankie
glared at her. "I am no good at this cloak-and-
dagger stuff."

"But I have to make a red wine reduction."

"I'll do it. If I take the red wine and drink half of it, that reduces it, right?" Frankie gave her a push. "I will be Maria's right hand."

"And I'll take those." Maria took the potatoes from her and gestured toward the door with her head. "Go."

Eva was about to ask what was going on, when Paige strode into the kitchen.

"Wait. Don't move." She was carrying Eva's purse and she opened it and delved inside for makeup. "Hold still."

"I truly have no idea what's happening. You all think I look like crap? First Maria says I need to wear lipstick, then—"

"Stop talking. I can't do your makeup while your face is moving." Paige gave her a mini makeover, transforming her with an expert flick of a brush and a sweep of lipstick. "There. You look amazing." She snapped her fingers and Jake appeared with Eva's coat.

She took it, confused. "I wish someone would tell me what's going on."

"It's a surprise," Paige said and then smiled. "Merry Christmas to the best friend any girl could have."

"Hey, *I'm* the best friend any girl could have." Frankie brushed flecks of flour from Eva's dress. "You go, girl. Your carriage awaits."

"My carriage? Have you been drinking? Because you've all lost it." Wondering what they had planned, Eva let them bundle her from the kitchen and into the restaurant.

For a wild, crazy moment, she'd actually wondered if Lucas might be there. If he might be the surprise they were talking about, but there was no sign of him and the strength of her disappointment shocked her.

She briefly caught a glimpse of Matt smiling at her from the doorway of the restaurant and Roxy looking dreamy-eyed with little Mia bouncing in her arms.

They all looked so pleased, she didn't want to hurt their feelings so she smiled back and tried not to think about Lucas.

Whatever it was they had planned, she'd look pleased. She could manage that, surely?

"Call us later." Paige hurried her through the door and Eva gasped as the icy cold hit her face.

"Holy crap, it's cold." There was a yellow cab waiting with the engine running and standing by the open door was—

"Albert?" Eva stared at him, bemused, and Frankie pushed her forward.

"It's more of a cab than a carriage, but this is New York City. At least it's yellow. If you drink a bottle of wine you could kid yourself it's a pumpkin. Here you go, Albert. Signed, sealed and delivered just as we promised. The rest is up to you. Don't let her argue with you."

Albert hugged Eva and then whisked her into the warm cab.

"Let us know how it goes," Paige said in the second before Albert closed the door and the cabdriver pulled away.

"How what goes?" Eva shifted in her seat so that

she could look at Albert. "What's going on? Why didn't you come in and stay for lunch?"

"I'll be coming back for lunch after I've done my part."

"What is your part?"

"First, I'm supposed to give you this." He handed her a silver package tied with ribbon and she looked at it, confused.

"I have *no* idea what's going on." She looked at the gift tag and recognized Lucas's writing.

You gave me a book, and now I'm returning the favor.

"This is a Christmas gift from Lucas?" She looked at Albert, but he simply smiled and looked out of the window.

"Don't you love New York in the snow?"

"He bought me a book?" She ripped open the packaging and a slim volume fell onto her lap. On the cover was a simple illustration of a couple walking hand in hand.

She flipped it open and again saw Lucas's bold scrawl on the flyleaf.

I hope you enjoy this story.

She started to read, and didn't look up once until the cab came to a halt on Fifth Avenue.

"Eva?"

Pleased for an excuse to stop reading, she closed the book, slightly dazed. "Tiffany's? What are we doing here, Albert? They don't open on Christmas Day."

"It seems they're willing to make an exception for a special person. Go on in. They're expecting you."

"I don't know what you—" The door opened and she stared at the man standing there. "Lucas?"

She forgot about the book in her hand. She forgot about everything. Her knees weakened, her heart thudded and she knew it would be a long time until she was over him, if she ever was. What did he want? It was one thing being brave in front of her friends, but quite another to keep up an act in front of him.

He was wearing his long black coat and judging from the dark shadows under his eyes, he hadn't slept in the few days since she'd left.

She stumbled out of the cab, and then turned to Albert. "Aren't you getting out here, too?"

"No. I've done my part. The rest is up to you." He raised his hand to Lucas and then slid back into the cab. "I'm going back to my Christmas lunch. Maria is saving my place at the table."

"You've met Maria? You're leaving me on my own?"

"Maria and I have spoken a few times over the past week, and you're not on your own, honey. Someone like you will never find herself alone. Merry Christmas, Eva." He pulled the door shut and she stood on the sidewalk clutching her book and shivering as the cab vanished in the direction of Brooklyn.

What now?

"Eva?" Lucas's voice came from behind her. "Will you come inside before we all freeze?"

"All?" She turned slowly, emotionally exhausted. "I don't know what's going on."

"If you come inside, you'll find out."

Still clutching the book, she picked her way across the sidewalk and then gasped as he caught her in his arms.

"Oh! A hug." She didn't dare think it was anything more. She didn't dare wonder why they were standing in the doorway of her favorite jewelry store.

"Did you like my gift?"

"What gift?"

"The book."

She bit her lip, wondering how honest to be. He'd given her a gift, and she should thank him. On the other hand… "Honestly? I haven't finished it yet, but what I read freaked me out a little. You know I'm not good with scary things," she said quickly, "so don't be offended."

"Scary?" He sounded astounded. "It wasn't scary, it was a love story."

"A love story?" She stared at him, bemused, and then at the book in her hand. "But—he blindfolds her and takes her into this dark room and then locks all the doors—I was terrified he was going to murder her. I stopped reading."

"He blindfolds her so that nothing could spoil the surprise."

"The surprise of being locked in a dark room?"

"The room is a jewelry store. It was *supposed* to be romantic." He spoke through his teeth. "If you'd carried on reading, you would have seen him propose."

"How? With a knife to her throat?" And suddenly she was laughing, laughing so hard she could hardly speak. "It was like something out of a horror film, and—" She broke off, an awful suspicion forming in her head. "Lucas, are you—did *you* write this? There was no author name on the cover."

"Yes. I wrote it for you." He raked his fingers through his hair, his voice raw and emotional. "You wanted me to write something where everyone lived happily ever after."

"I would have been happy with a story where everyone lived. That would have been a good start."

"I wrote you a love story. It was the hardest thing I've ever written. I thought I'd done a good job. There was a diamond ring and—" He swallowed. "Shit. I messed it up. I got it wrong, didn't I?"

He'd tried to write her a love story.

He'd written it for her.

There was so much she wanted to say, but her heart was too full. "Oh, Lucas—"

"You hated it. I *did* mess it up."

Emotion clogged her throat. "I think you should stick with writing what you write best. Horror."

"I wanted you to love it."

"I love that you wrote it for me. I really love that."

"I can't believe I screwed it up. Let's hope I get it right when it counts." He muttered the words under his breath and she frowned.

"What are you talking about? When what counts?"

Instead of answering, he pulled her through the doorway into the store and she blinked, dazzled by the lights. There were two other people in the store, a man and a woman, both of them smiling as they kept a discreet distance.

"What am I doing here, Lucas? What's going on? It seems everyone is in on some great plan except me. And what does Albert have to do with it?"

"When I told him my plan, he wanted to help. As did your friends, my grandmother and Maria. Frankie threatened to neutralize me if I hurt you. I don't know how you could ever have thought you were alone in the world. You have a ring of protection around you that the president would envy."

"But—"

"Eva, I've got a lot to say so just this once you're going to let me talk without interrupting me."

"I will, but—"

He covered her lips with his fingers, a gleam in his eyes. "Forget the blindfold, I'm going to gag you if you don't stop talking. I'm trying to get this right, and you're distracting me."

"I'm silent." She kept her mouth clamped shut, but her heart was racing along with her mind. What was it he wanted to say?

"I'm going to get straight to the important part and leave the backstory until later. A great number of people love you, sweetheart." He stroked her cheek with his thumb. "And I'm one of them."

She hardly dared breathe. "You love me?"

"Yes, and I should probably be using flowery words—hell, words are my job, but right now I'm so damn scared of using the wrong ones it's safer to keep it simple. I love you."

"But you didn't want to fall in love again. You think love is complicated and exhausting."

"Someone wise told me that there are as many ways to love as there are people on the planet. Turned out she was right." He slid his hand behind her head and lowered his mouth to hers. "There's so much I want to say to you, but these good people have already given up part of their Christmas Day for me, so let's not keep them waiting."

"Waiting for what? I don't even know what we're doing here." Her head was spinning. He loved her?

The smile was back in his eyes. "What does your infallible radar tell you?"

They were in a jewelry store. *The* iconic New York jewelry store. But she didn't dare jump to conclusions. "I think my radar might be jammed. I live on Planet Eva, remember?"

"Your radar is perfect."

"You don't know that. You don't know what I'm thinking."

"I know how your mind works."

"I'm predictable."

"You're adorable. I love you, sweetheart, and we're here because when a guy knows he's in love, there's no point in waiting. Tom taught me that. And Gran. She reminded me that she and Gramps got married after four weeks."

"That was different. There was a war. Everything had to happen fast."

"They were married for sixty years, and Gramps put a ring on her finger after two weeks. I've waited a little longer than that."

Her head was spinning. "A ring? You want to buy me a ring?"

"You should have finished the story. Then you would have known how it ended."

"If I'd finished your story I have a feeling I might have ended up in therapy."

"Let's forget the story." Smiling, he lowered his head and kissed her gently again. "I'm hoping you'll let me join you on Planet Eva. I'm traveling with hand luggage only, and I think I know the rules of the place."

Her heart swelled in her chest.

This was happening. It was really happening.

Lucas. Her Lucas.

Tears jammed in her throat. "Are you sure? Only a certain type of person can survive on Planet Eva."

"A lucky person." He reached out his hand and the man discreetly handed over a small box. "I know this is fast, and we can wait as long as you like, but I want you to marry me, Ev." He lifted the ring from the box, slid it onto her finger and kept hold of her hand.

She stared down at the ring on her finger and her heart ached. "You want us to get married?"

"Yes. I love you, and I can tell you exactly how much when we're back in my apartment, but right now so that these poor people can get back to their families, just tell me yes or no."

"Yes. Of course, yes." It was such a simple answer.

"You know I love you. I already told you that and I haven't changed my mind. Nothing would make me change my mind."

"I was banking on it." Without letting go of her hand, he thanked the two grinning staff members and led her to the door.

"Er—are we stealing this ring? Because I'm not in a hurry to meet your friends in the NYPD again. They weren't very smiley."

"It's all handled."

"You handled it? That's impressive. If I'd said no, would they have given you a refund?"

"I knew you wouldn't say no. You're not the sort of person who falls in and out of love."

They strolled along Fifth Avenue, their feet crunching on the fresh snow, holding each other tightly. She felt the weight of the ring on her finger and the firm grip of his fingers on hers.

"How much did you have to pay them to open the store on Christmas Day?"

"It cost me less than that bottle of wine you drank."

She blushed, remembering. "It gave me *such* a headache."

"That tends to happen when you inhale the entire bottle without pausing to swallow."

"Do you forgive me?"

"Do you forgive *me*?" He stopped and turned her to face him, everything he felt showing in his eyes.

"Forgive you for what?"

"For turning my back on what you offered so generously." He stroked her hair back from her face with gentle hands. "When you told me you loved me—I was terrified. Terrified of hurting you, terrified of being hurt myself—"

"I understand." The cold slid under her coat but she didn't notice.

"I'd been living in the dark for three years and then you showed up, with your full wattage smile and your sunbeam personality, and you shone a light on all the dark corners of my life. My whole life changed that night. You changed it. You made me want to be in love again. Damn it, you could make me believe in fairy tales." He took her face in his powerful hands and lowered his mouth to hers.

She kissed him, her arms locked around his neck. "You're going to make me cry."

"I thought you were a dreamer. I thought what you wanted didn't exist, and I carried on thinking that right up until the moment you walked away from me. That was the point when I realized I wanted to be part of your dreams. I want to share my life with you, all of it, the good, the bad, the terrifying and the exciting. I love you, Eva." He whispered the words against her lips. "You are the kindest, sweetest, strongest person I've ever met and I can't believe you're mine."

Her heart was so full she could hardly speak. "I love you, too. So much."

Snow started to fall, dusting her hair and her coat like confetti and he brushed it away and took her hand. "Let's get inside."

They arrived at his apartment and she paused as she looked around the now-familiar space, so happy she could hardly breathe. "I should call my friends and tell them."

"They know. How else do you think I managed to persuade them to help me? They refused to put you in a cab and send you uptown until I assured them I was going to give you the happy-ever-after you deserve. They're very protective."

"So they knew before I did?" Without letting go of the book in her hand, Eva toed off her boots and shrugged off her coat.

"Not the detail. Just that I love you. And Frankie made some pretty gruesome threats that I most definitely intend to use in a book at some point. That girl has a warped mind."

"You have a lot in common." She closed her fingers around the lapels of his coat. "I thought you loved me, but you were so determined to push me away—"

"My relationship with Sallyanne was volatile and unpredictable. Sometimes it was exhilarating, but mostly it was exhausting. I assumed that was the way love was, and then I met you and you taught me something different." He brushed the backs of his fingers over the soft curve of her cheek. "You taught me that love didn't have to feel like a battle, or like finding your way through a maze in the dark."

"I know you loved her, Lucas. I would never want you to pretend that you didn't."

"I did love her, but what you and I share is different, I won't lie about that. So different that to begin with I didn't even recognize it. I thought love was this dark, complicated thing and then you came into my life with your sunshine and optimism. I didn't know love could be that simple and easy. You wanted a dream and I thought there was no way I could live up to that dream. I couldn't stand the thought of another relationship crumbling around me. But then I realized what it would mean not to have you in my life. If you'll have me, I promise to spend every day for the rest of my life living up to your dreams."

Her eyes filled. "Dreams aren't real, and I want what's real. I want you. The real you. Not better, or different. I can't believe you wrote a book where the characters live." She was still clutching the book and he gently removed it from her grip.

"We should get rid of this. It needs some serious editing."

"No." She took it back from him. "I want to keep it, just as it is. It's the best gift ever, and it's all mine."

"You haven't read the ending."

"Do they both live?"

He gave a slow smile. "Yes."

"That's all I need to know, although I hope their happy-ever-after includes plenty of hot sex. And about the part when he blindfolds her—" She narrowed her eyes. "Maybe we could move that scene to the bedroom."

His eyes gleamed. "That's not a bad idea. Turns out you're a pretty good editor."

"I think so." She stood on tiptoe and wrapped her arms around his neck. "Of course it's important to try these things, to see if they work in real life. What do you think?"

"I think that sounds like the perfect ending to me." And he scooped her into his arms and carried her up the stairs.

* * * * *

Thank you

I write uplifting contemporary fiction where generally speaking no one dies on the page. Getting into the mind of my hero Lucas, who writes horror/crime, wasn't easy for me and I want to thank author Graeme Cameron, who was generous with his time giving me insight into the mind of a crime writer. Graeme, your book *Normal* kept me awake all night and definitely contributed to a rise in my electricity bill because I had to sleep with the lights on. Lee Child described the book as "hypnotic and chilling," and it's a testament to your skill as a writer that you kept me reading despite the fact that "chilling" isn't usually the first thing I look for in a story. You even managed to add quirky humor to a serial killer.

This year I was proud to be invited to be part of the Get In Character campaign run by the charity CLIC Sargent, who raise money to support children and young people with cancer. My thanks to Ann Cooper, who generously bid to name a character in this book. "Annie Cooper" is a nurse, and a warm, wonderful person just like you. I hope you like her!

Also a big thank you to Laura Coutts, who bid for signed books from me as part of the same auction. Your generosity is much appreciated.

As ever, thank you to all my wonderful readers for choosing my books, and for all your kind messages.

Sarah
xx

One Man. One Woman. Two dogs.

Meet Molly and Daniel.

They both think they know everything there
is to know about relationships.
They're both wrong.

Turn the page for a sneak peek of
Sarah Morgan's fabulous new book,
NEW YORK, ACTUALLY.
Available soon!

HE SMILED AT HER. "If you're not interested, why have we spent so much time chatting?"

"Our dogs are best friends."

"So if I didn't have a dog you wouldn't be interested?"

"You *do* have a dog, so that question doesn't arise. And you shouldn't say things like that in front of Brutus. You don't want him to feel insecure."

There was a pause. "Just so we're clear—when I buy a woman dinner I *don't* invite Brutus."

The conversation was light, but she was conscious that underneath the banter was a seam of delicious tension. She was trying to work out how to respond when it started to rain—a light patter that chilled her skin.

Daniel cursed softly and grabbed the cups. "Time to shelter."

"Why? It's only a few spots. Don't be a wimp."

"Are you calling me a wimp?"

"Yes, but don't worry. It's good to know you have a weakness."

The rain grew heavier and huge drops thundered down, soaking everything they touched.

"You're right. We should shelter."

She scooped up her tea and ran, her feet splashing through newly formed puddles, the rain soaking through the thin fabric of her shirt and flattening her hair to her head.

Valentine barked, excited and fired up by this new urgency, and Brutus followed. The two dogs were side by side as they made for the shelter of the trees.

She dived through the long, pendulous branches of a weeping willow, feeling the leaves brush her face and her arms. She knew Daniel was behind her. She could hear the heavy thud of his running shoes on the ground and awareness chased across her skin, the feeling so intense it was like pressure. He could catch her easily. And when he did...

She stopped under the tree, unsettled by the explicit nature of her own thoughts. It had been a while since she'd been interested enough to risk getting involved with someone. The last three years had been spent focusing on rebuilding her life, and sex hadn't been part of that.

She turned in time to catch the gleam in his eyes, and gasped as he backed her against the thick trunk of the tree.

She told herself it was the sprinting that had made her chest tight and her breathing rapid, but she knew she was lying to herself. It was him. This man with the wicked eyes and the slow, dangerous smile. This man who made her feel a million things she never usually felt, all of which terrified her.

Did he know? If so he was a sadist, because he gave her no breathing room, no space in which to gather herself. Instead he stopped right in front of her—so close she was forced to take a step back or touch him.

She felt the rough bark of the tree press against her back and knew there were no more steps back to take. From here it was stand still or move forward.

"What are you doing?"

"I'm keeping you dry. Protecting you from the rain." He grinned. 'Showing you my weakness.'

But this close she saw nothing but strength. There was strength in the arms that caged her, in the dip and swell of muscle, in the width of the powerful shoulders that blocked her view of the world. There was strength in the lines of his cheekbones and in his jaw, shaded by stubble.

Her gaze met his and his eyes made her think of long summer days filled with blue skies and endless possibilities.

"I don't mind the rain."

His mouth hovered dangerously close to hers. "I forgot you were British. We probably have a different relationship with rain."

"Rain and I are intimately acquainted."

"I never thought I'd envy the rain."

He lifted his hand and stroked her damp hair back from her face. She felt the tips of his fingers brush across her skin, lingering, and knew this wasn't about clearing her vision of damp hair and rainwater.

It was about exploration. Possession.

It had been so long since she'd been touched like this and she was super-sensitive, her imagination and her senses keenly aware of every touch.

> *Dear Aggie,*
>
> *There's this guy I find impossibly sexy, and when I'm with him I forget everything. He doesn't want a relationship, so I know that anything we share will be short-term. I'm worried he'll break my heart. But if I walk away I'm afraid I may be losing something special.*
>
> *What should I do?*
> *Yours,*
> *Light-headed.*

The rain was coming down harder now, but only the occasional drip managed to squeeze its way through the cascading branches of the weeping willow. They were sheltered in their own private glade, protected by the tangled labyrinth of green and gold.

She'd thought there would be plenty of people seeking shelter, but it seemed everyone else had chosen to leave the park. They were alone—or at least it felt that way—trapped by the weather and cocooned by nature. It was as if someone had drawn curtains around them, concealing them from the world.

She was aware of the muted thud of raindrops as they pounded the canopy of the trees, of the rustle of leaves and the whisper of the breeze through the branches. And she was aware of the beat of her heart and the uneven note of his breathing.

She raised her hand and brushed a raindrop from his jaw, feeling the roughness of stubble under her fingers.

Dear Light-headed,

None of us can predict the course of a relationship. All we can do is go into it with an open heart and trust our instincts.

It's hard not to worry about being hurt, but when we insulate ourselves from hurt we also risk insulating ourselves from the very thing we are seeking. Love. Instead, have confidence in your ability to handle whatever comes. You can fly, but first you have to trust your wings.

As he lowered his head she rose on tiptoe and lifted her mouth to his, meeting him halfway. Or that was what she told herself. Truthfully, from the moment his mouth met hers there was no doubt who was in control.

He cupped her face in his hands, kissing her with slow, leisurely purpose. There was something aggressive about the way he held her prisoner, but something infinitely gentle about the coaxing pressure of his mouth on hers.

With each brush of his mouth and each stroke of his tongue he stoked the heat until she was shaking and dizzy with desire. The pleasure was disorienting—a low drag in her belly, a shimmer of electricity across her sensitized skin.

Her fingers speared the soft silk of his hair as she tried to pull him closer.

Reason and logic were drowned by the rising tide of arousal. She was unable even to pose a question—which was a good thing, because she wouldn't have been able to speak. All she could do was feel.

The world around them vanished, until there was only the erotic touch of his mouth and the soft patter of rain on the leaves.

She melted under the dizzying strokes of his tongue, swaying against him, and felt his hand stroke down her back and linger on the base of her spine, pressing her close. That touch confirmed everything she already knew about his body. That it was hard and strong, conditioned and athletic. The unyielding pressure of his muscles suggested he did more to keep himself fit than just chase a dog around the park.

She didn't know how she'd got there, but somehow she was trapped between the sturdy tree and the power of his frame.

And still he kissed her.

He left her nowhere to hide—exploring, demanding, discovering, until she was a trembling mass of nerve-endings. He showed no signs of stopping, and her brain wasn't functioning well enough to come up with a single reason why *she* should be the one to stop doing something that felt so good.

His hand moved to her breast, his thumb stroking over the tip. The delicious friction made her shudder, and she moaned and pressed closer. She felt his fingers at the hem of her tee shirt, and then the warmth of his hand settling on bare skin.

It was like being on fire. The excitement was burning over her skin and settling low in her belly.

This is why people do crazy things, she thought. *Because denying sexual attraction this intense feels like going against human nature.*

She had no idea how far they would have gone, but at that moment Valentine barked.

Daniel eased back with obvious reluctance. "Maybe we should take this indoors."

Indoors?

The word seeped through the clouds of desire fogging her brain and finally settled into her consciousness.

Indoors. Because currently they were *outdoors.* In public.

She wrenched herself out of his arms, winced as she grazed her arm on the bark of the tree.

"Hey, slow down." Daniel's gaze was still fixed on her mouth. "Good job you picked a weeping willow, otherwise we would have just put on a public display."

Hearing those words was like being plunged headfirst into a bucket of cold water.

Panic swarmed up her skin. What had she been *thinking*? She was careful never, *ever* to put herself in a position where her professional credibility could be questioned. And yet here she was—kissing in the park like a teenager, in full view of anyone who happened to be passing.

All it took was a single photograph. A Facebook post. A tweet. Before you knew it your life was trending—every single private thing about yourself uncovered and laid out for the malicious delectation of a public thirsty for another public shaming.

She took several deep breaths, reminding herself that even if someone had seen them no one would have connected her with *Aggie*. She'd created that persona for exactly this reason. For protection. An extra layer of defense to add to the other layers.

And that was the scariest thing of all. Since she'd arrived in New York no one had breached a single layer of her defenses. No one.

Until now.

"Come home with me." He spoke the words against her mouth. "We'll get out of these wet things and take a shower together. You *know* it's going to be good."

Yes, she knew. Which was why she was backing away.

Fire like that inevitably ended up with someone being burned.

How had this gone from a fun flirtation in the park to something so real?

But she knew the answer to that. The moment he'd started kissing her she'd forgotten everything.

Even now she was tempted to ignore the sensible voice in her head and go with him.

"No."

She pulled away from him so suddenly that he had to plant his hand against the tree to steady himself.

She empathized. From the moment he'd kissed

her she'd lost faith in the ability of her knees to support her.

If Valentine had been a few inches taller she would have climbed on his back and ridden him home.

She bent and grabbed his collar, clipping on the lead quickly.

"Molly, wait—"

Daniel's voice had thickened. He sounded almost drugged—as if he'd just indulged in a serious binge on an illegal substance.

She knew that feeling too. Only in her case *he* was the illegal substance.

She really liked him, and with that extra connection came the risk of heartbreak.

She wasn't going near *that* again.

Copyright ©2016 by Sarah Morgan

USA TODAY bestselling author

SARAH MORGAN

introduces *From Manhattan with Love*, a sparkling new trilogy about three best friends embracing life—and love—in New York.

Cool, calm and competent, events planner Paige Walker loves a challenge. After a childhood spent in and out of hospitals, she's now determined to prove herself— and where better to take the world by storm than Manhattan? But when Paige loses the job she loves, she must face her biggest challenge of all—going it alone.

Except launching her own events company is nothing compared to hiding her outrageous crush on Jake Romano—her brother's best friend, New York's most in-demand date and the only man to break her heart. When Jake offers Paige's fledgling company a big chance, their still-sizzling chemistry starts giving her sleepless nights. But can she convince the man who trusts no one to take a chance on forever?

Pick up your copy today!

Be sure to connect with us at:
Harlequin.com/Newsletters
Facebook.com/HarlequinBooks
Twitter.com/HQNBooks

www.HQNBooks.com

PHSAM91

USA TODAY bestselling author

SARAH MORGAN

brings you the second installment in
***From Manhattan with Love,* an irresistible trilogy
about three best friends taking chances and
finding love in the city that never sleeps.**

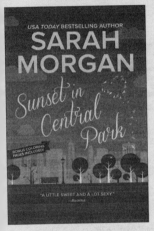

*In the chaos of New York, true love
can be hard to find, even when
it's been right under your nose all
along…*

Love has never been a priority
for garden designer Frankie Cole.
After witnessing the fallout of
her parents' divorce, she's seen
the devastation an overload of
emotion can cause. The only man
she feels comfortable with is her
friend Matt—but that's strictly
platonic. If only she found it easier
to ignore the way he makes her
heart race…

Matt Walker has loved Frankie for
years but, sensing how fragile she is beneath her feisty exterior, has
always played it cool. But then he uncovers new depths to the girl
he's known forever and doesn't want to wait a moment longer. He
knows Frankie has secrets and has buried them deep, but can Matt
persuade her to trust him with her heart and kiss him under the
Manhattan sunset?

Pick up your copy today!

www.SarahMorgan.com

www.HQNBooks.com

PHSAM923

REQUEST YOUR FREE BOOKS!

2 FREE NOVELS
FROM THE ROMANCE COLLECTION, PLUS 2 FREE GIFTS!

YES! Please send me 2 FREE novels from the Romance Collection and my 2 FREE gifts (gifts are worth about $10). After receiving them, if I don't wish to receive any more books, I can return the shipping statement marked "cancel." If I don't cancel, I will receive 4 brand-new novels every month and be billed just $6.49 per book in the U.S. or $6.99 per book in Canada. That's a savings of at least 18% off the cover price. It's quite a bargain! Shipping and handling is just 50¢ per book in the U.S. and 75¢ per book in Canada.* I understand that accepting the 2 free books and gifts places me under no obligation to buy anything. I can always return a shipment and cancel at any time. Even if I never buy another book, the two free books and gifts are mine to keep forever.

194/394 MDN GH4D

Name	(PLEASE PRINT)	

Address	Apt. #

City	State/Prov.	Zip/Postal Code

Signature (if under 18, a parent or guardian must sign)

Mail to the **Reader Service**:
IN U.S.A.: P.O. Box 1867, Buffalo, NY 14240-1867
IN CANADA: P.O. Box 609, Fort Erie, Ontario L2A 5X3

Want to try 2 free books from another line?
Call 1-800-873-8635 or visit www.ReaderService.com.

*Terms and prices subject to change without notice. Prices do not include applicable taxes. Sales tax applicable in N.Y. Canadian residents will be charged applicable taxes. Offer not valid in Quebec. This offer is limited to one order per household. Not valid for current subscribers to the Romance Collection or the Romance/Suspense Collection. All orders subject to credit approval. Credit or debit balances in a customer's account(s) may be offset by any other outstanding balance owed by or to the customer. Please allow 4 to 6 weeks for delivery. Offer available while quantities last.

Your Privacy—The Reader Service is committed to protecting your privacy. Our Privacy Policy is available online at www.ReaderService.com or upon request from the Reader Service.

We make a portion of our mailing list available to reputable third parties that offer products we believe may interest you. If you prefer that we not exchange your name with third parties, or if you wish to clarify or modify your communication preferences, please visit us at www.ReaderService.com/consumerchoice or write to us at Reader Service Preference Service, P.O. Box 9062, Buffalo, NY 14240-9062. Include your complete name and address.

ROM15R

Turn your love of reading into rewards you'll love with

Harlequin My Rewards

**Join for FREE today at
www.HarlequinMyRewards.com**

Earn **FREE BOOKS** of your choice.

Experience **EXCLUSIVE OFFERS** and contests.

Enjoy **BOOK RECOMMENDATIONS**
selected just for you.

PLUS! Sign up now
and get **500** points
right away!

Earn
FREE
REWARDS
HarlequinMyRewards.com
Join
Today!

MYR16R

SARAH MORGAN

78934	MIRACLE ON 5TH AVENUE	___ $7.99 U.S.	___ $9.99 CAN.
78923	SUNSET IN CENTRAL PARK	___ $7.99 U.S.	___ $9.99 CAN.
78915	SLEEPLESS IN MANHATTAN	___ $7.99 U.S.	___ $9.99 CAN.

(limited quantities available)

TOTAL AMOUNT $ _____
POSTAGE & HANDLING $ _____
($1.00 FOR 1 BOOK, 50¢ for each additional)
APPLICABLE TAXES* $ _____
TOTAL PAYABLE $ _____

(check or money order—please do not send cash)

To order, complete this form and send it, along with a check or money order for the total above, payable to HQN Books, to: **In the U.S.:** 3010 Walden Avenue, P.O. Box 9077, Buffalo, NY 14269-9077; **In Canada:** P.O. Box 636, Fort Erie, Ontario, L2A 5X3.

Name: _____
Address: _____ City: _____
State/Prov.: _____ Zip/Postal Code: _____
Account Number (if applicable): _____
075 CSAS

*New York residents remit applicable sales taxes.
*Canadian residents remit applicable GST and provincial taxes.

HQN™

www.HQNBooks.com

PHSAM1216BL